The DISINHERITED CHILDREN

A STUDY OF THE NEW LEFT AND THE GENERATION GAP

Christopher Bone

Schenkman Publishing Company
Halsted Press Division
John Wiley & Sons
New York, London, Sydney, Toronto

Copyright © 1977
Schenkman Publishing Company, Inc.
3 Mount Auburn Place
Cambridge, Massachusetts 02138

Distributed solely by Halsted Press, a Division of
John Wiley & Sons, Inc., New York, New York

Library of Congress Cataloging in Publication Data

Bone, Christopher.
  The disinherited children

  1. Radicalism — United States. 2. Youth — United
States — Political activity. 3. United States — Popular culture. I. Title.
HN90.R3B57   322.4'4   74-19086
ISBN 0-470-08770-6
ISBN 0-470-08771-4 (pbk.)

This book is dedicated to
Tyler Fleeson, John Hagman, Robert Hallauer,
Linda Brown, the entire Grear family, and
oppressed people everywhere.

Contents

Preface

At five o'clock in the morning on December the 29th, 1968, in a New York City hotel room, I awoke from a sound sleep and said the following sentence to the gray polluted dawn: "If you don't do it, nobody will." At that time I resolved that I would write what I considered to be what was really happening to my generation and to the United States. Unfortunately, I was unable to start the story because I was still finishing a Ph.D. degree at the University of Chicago. After that I was obliged to begin teaching at Washington State University, so I could not really begin serious writing until 1970. The summer of 1970 I spent in San Francisco hammering out the initial chapters of this book.

I have been presumptuous enough to write this work because I do not believe the true story was ever told and that no satisfactory analysis has yet been made. You, the reader, may think me mistaken and arrogant. Nevertheless, I will run that risk. Some of my ex-colleagues were opposed to my taking on this task. However, most of my students, my parents, and members of the Movement were encouraging. Indeed, without their assistance, this book could never have been written.

I wish to acknowledge with extreme gratitude the help and cooperation I received from Mr. Bob Dylan, Mr. Paul Kantner and other members of the Jefferson Starship, and Mr. Huey P. Newton, and Professor Joseph Huthmacher. I also wish to acknowledge that this book was in part made possible by a grant from the Graduate School of Washington State University.

Christopher Bone
Chicago, New York, Seattle,
San Francisco, London, Pullman

Introduction

There's something happening here,
What it is ain't exactly clear.
There's a man with a gun over there
    tellin' me I got to beware.
I think it's time we
        STOP
children what's that sound
Ev'rybody look what's goin' down*

On April 17, 1965, approximately 20,000 people gathered in Washington, D. C. for what was to become the first demonstration of large proportions against American military involvement in Vietnam. The participants ranged from hippies to Senator Ernest Gruening. The audience listened to speeches by history professor Staughton Lynd, journalist I. F. Stone, organizer Bob Moses of the Student Nonviolent Coordinating Committee (SNCC) and President Paul Potter of the Students for a Democratic Society (SDS). Loudspeakers carried the voice of Joan Baez singing Bob Dylan's cynical elegy of war, "With God on Our Side." Nearly everyone cheered with a bitter determination. It was the largest assemblage of America's alienated young people that Washington D. C. had witnessed since the 1930's. And it was recognized officially in the press as the birth of "A New Left."

But the New Left was not really born as a political protest movement over the war in Vietnam. The press had mistakenly attributed a political nature to a widespread youth rebellion which was just then going political. For the

*"For What It's Worth," words and music by Stephen Stills. ©1967 by Cotillion Music, Ten East Music, and Springaloo Toones. Used by permission of Atlantic Recording Corporation.

April 17 demonstration brought together for the first time the two most important forms of youth protest. These two forms, the hippie dropouts and the committed politicoes of SDS and SNCC, were merging to create an élan which appeared in politics and society throughout the 1960's and continues to make its presence felt in the 1970's. The Washington, D. C. demonstration brought together the heirs of the Beatniks and the intellectual followers of radical sociologist C. Wright Mills. Yet there was no suggestion by the participants that a political movement or party be formed as a vehicle of power. It was quite by accident that the April 17 demonstration set the style and that its veterans offered the leadership for the subsequent antiwar marches, sit-ins, be-ins, love-ins, campus occupations, the Democratic National Convention of 1968, and the Woodstock Festival of Life in 1969.

In actuality, what the press described as a "New Left" in April 1965 was only distantly related to what sociologist C. Wright Mills meant when he coined the term in 1960. And it would be inaccurate to credit him with founding the New Left, or to envision the New Left as solely an American phenomenon. For it was in France that there first arose an organized New Left which gained international recognition and really wielded some political as well as cultural influence. Founded by Claude Bourdet shortly after the Soviet Union suppressed the Hungarian Revolution in 1956, it declared itself to be the Nouvelle gauche. In December of 1957 La Nouvelle gauche combined with two other rebel socialist and communist groups, Jeune république and Mouvement de liberation du peuple. What eventually emerged was the Parti socialiste unifié in April 1960. This became *the* political party for New Left intellectuals, artists, and dissident, revisionist Marxists in France. It gained wide publicity in September 1960 when it sponsored the "Manifesto of 121," a "Declaration of the Right of Refusing to Serve in the Algerian War." Signers included philosopher and resistance leader Jean-Paul Sartre, Florence Malraux, daughter of famed writer André Malraux, actresses Simone Signoret and Daniele Delorme, novelist Françoise Sagan, and the founder of Dadaism, Tristan Tzara. The French New Left and later the American New Left also claimed the brilliant black Marxist writer, Frantz Fanon, who actively supported the Algerian Revolution against France. Fanon, initially impressed by Sartre, became a hero to the Left with the publication of his *Les Damnés de la terre* (1961) and was virtually canonized by the American New Left, especially American blacks, after his book was published in English as *The Wretched of the Earth* (1965). Fanon's contentions that the real international struggle was not so much between capitalism and socialism as between rich and poor and that it would be the poor, the lumpenproletariat, who led revolutions, and that these revolutions would come in Third World countries, has had a profound influence on the thinking of Stokely Carmichael, Eldridge Cleaver, Bobby Seale, and Huey Newton.

Similarly, the New Left in England predated Mills' usage of the term in America. And it was born of much the same revisionist Marxist spirit that characterized it in France. Indeed, in 1959 English academics founded a journal entitled *New Left Review* to supplant the *Left Review* of the 1930's. The former was sponsored by contributors to the *New Reasoner* and the *Left Review*, who, disillusioned with Soviet Communism following the Hungarian Revolution, sought to establish a forum which would be true to what they considered the spirit of the democratic left. This of course opened a wide rift between them and the Communist Party of Great Britain, but served to attract many young artists and writers. It also facilitated a less doctrinaire methodology on the part of those British academics who wished to be considered Marxist or at least Left, but did not subscribe to the Soviet Union's rigid definition of Marxist methodology ("socialist realism"). There resulted the important contributions of Professor Raymond Williams, *Culture and Society, 1780-1950* (1958) and *The Long Revolution* (1961) as well as those of ex-Communist E. P. Thompson, *William Morris: Romantic Revolutionary* (1955) and *The Making of the English Working Class* (1963). The English New Left was active in the Campaign for Nuclear Disarmament (Ban the Bomb) and led demonstrations against NATO, against American policy in South America, and later against the American presence in Southeast Asia.

In the United States, the New Left descended from a journal entitled *Studies on the Left*, founded by historian William Appleman Williams of the University of Wisconsin.[1] The journal soon became less academic than envisioned, took contributions from graduate students, and identified itself with the Freedom Rides taking place in the Civil Rights movement in the South. Nevertheless, the fundamental intention of *Studies on the Left* was to facilitate a "radicalism of disclosure." That is, it was to expose the philosophical and structural problems in American democracy and capitalism and thereby somehow to facilitate correction.

It soon became apparent that such exposure did *not* inculcate correction. At that point, C. Wright Mills wrote his famous "Letter to the New Left," which was published in the September-October issue (1960) of the *New Left Review*. He criticized the intellectuals for their ineffectiveness, pointed out the practical irrelevance of their knowledge, and declared the working class defunct as an agency of revolutionary change. Mills then suggested that a New Left composed of intellectuals and students take it upon itself to be the conscious instigator of change. This was to be done by careful analysis of how the structure of liberal institutions hindered the implementation of meaningful improvement. While he did not mention which institutions he meant, such analysis has since been applied to the military-industrial complex, governmental and business administrative bureaucracy, the Highway

Trust Fund and congressional delegation of powers to agencies.[2] The under-lying assumption was still that alteration of the structures of these insti-tutions would facilitate change. Almost immediately his letter was reprinted in *Studies on the Left* and reissued as a pamphlet by SDS in 1961.

Among the younger followers of Mills there was considerable enthusiasm about the germination of an American "New Left" in the early sixties.[3] There were many reasons for this enthusiasm. Sociologist Richard Flacks, it seems to me, has offered the most tenable. By 1960 there was a substantial professional intelligentsia in their middle years whose optimism, engendered by the New Deal and the triumph of World War II, was beginning to fade. Their confidence that the services of the New Deal would humanize and democratize America was diminishing. Also their personal upward mobility, already achieved at great sacrifice, had hit an impasse with the recession of 1958-60.

Still, most of them passed on to their children the faith that humane values could best be implemented and indeed would be implemented by raising well-educated families dedicated to the ideal of social, economic, and political egalitarianism. Furthermore, as Flacks suggests, because of the economic security in their families and of their secure social position, the normal incentives of the culture—status and income—were of relatively minor importance. Hence, it was fashionable for parents to teach their children to feel that such incentives ought to be disdained. Ironically for those growing up in the late 1950's and early 1960's, "Their own parents' ambivalence toward the occupational structure . . . would make them aspire to construct their lives outside conventional career lines, would make them deeply critical of compromise, corruption and unfreedom inherent in the occupations of their fathers."[4]

Historically this was not a new situation. It resembled the situation which the generation of the 1920's faced in Germany and England. But there was at least one salient difference. In the 1960's if one were well-educated and privi-leged, there was not a dearth of jobs as had been the case in the interwar period. On the contrary, there was a virtual guarantee of a job—as a profes-sional. But the careers seemed to offer no chance to assist in social amelioration or to achieve personal fulfillment. This was the case primarily because there was no consensus of national purpose, and there were no collective aims such as had been offered by the New Deal and the Second World War to the generations of the thirties and forties. For example, Franklin Roosevelt could say for the generation of the thirties: "To some generations much is given. Of other generations much is expected. This gene-ration of Americans has a rendezvous with destiny." But the famous rock group, Jefferson Airplane, now renamed Jefferson Starship, could only say for the generation of the Sixties that:

> One generation got old
> One generation got soul
> This generation got no destination to hold.[5]

Indeed, one had the impression that the values of one's parents, values appropriate to a world of material scarcity, did not fit a world of two cars in the carport, a swimming pool, and a cleaning lady. Thus, by the 1960's, the American capitalist values of scarcity, frugality, postponement of sensuous gratification, careful career planning, and guarding of one's personal reputation seemed empty, no longer generative. Many growing up in this privileged atmosphere, despite their material inheritance, felt spiritually disinherited. The nature of the disinheritance few if any really understood. But later this feeling of estrangement became recognized as a major ingredient of the "generation gap."

It was out of this cultural estrangement that the radical impulse of the 1960's was created—or created itself—in this country. It began as a cultural malaise and turned political in the Civil Rights movement. For the Civil Rights movement offered the generations of the 1950's and 1960's something like what the New Deal offered men like Rex Tugwell, Arthur Goldberg, or Lyndon Johnson and their generation: politics as a vocation. Politics seemed to offer a meaningful, acceptable role in society. And this became (temporarily at least) a panacea for the cultural deracination of the 1950's and 1960's. One had the feeling that the sixties were pregnant with promise, that they would have crucial national and world-wide ramifications and that one wanted to be part of the sixties in a collective political sense. There was something ineffable in the air which made politics seem honorable, necessary, and the best way of bridging the generation gap.

Now, at this distance in time, we know more about the nature of the postwar generation and we know more about its chief political manifestation, the New Left. We understand that there is a generational discontinuity. And it seems to have been caused primarily by the drastically different environments in which the pre-World War II generations and the post-World War II generation came to maturity. Since 1945, events and conditions have radically altered men's relations to one another, to the natural world, and, more importantly, to how one perceives the world. The postwar generation is a pioneer generation, living in totally new conditions. Its young persons grew up and are growing up in a scientific milieu abounding with discoveries of vast, often unforeseen applications and implications (two-thirds of all scientific knowledge has been formulated since 1945). Among these scientific accomplishments are: the harnessing (for good and for ill) of atomic energy, the invention of the computer, the isolation of a virus which may be the key to human life, the almost total exploration of this planet, the beginning of the exploration of the moon and solar system, manned spacecraft orbiting the earth and the moon, a rapid growth in population combined with accelerated urbanization and destruction of the natural world, instant communication by satellite and television, transportation by supersonic aircraft, the overcoming of scarcity in America, Sweden, Switzerland, and many Arab nations, and the emergence of poverty (faulty distribution) as the chief economic problem.

It is imperative to realize that all these changes were consummated during the formative years of a single generation. Today, because of television, young people in the advanced industrial countries experience most of the world visually and aurally at the same time (simultaneously). More important, they have never known any other mode of experiencing the world. Hence, they share a kind of experience that none of their elders had. And the younger generations can never, despite the effort of contemporary historians, experience the realities of the 1920's, 1930's, and 1940's. They can never feel the sense of accomplishment at having incorporated the most rapid social and technological changes ever known—changes in the sources of power, the means of communication, the limits of the explorable universe. Nor can they know the agony, fear, and grim hopelessness of living during a world-wide economic depression for which there was no known solution. And they do not feel the pride associated with having overcome both the Depression and the horrible possibility of the whole of Europe succumbing to Fascist and Nazi totalitarianism. Rather, the experiential world of the 1920's, 1930's, and 1940's seems to many of the young, especially in the newly awakened groups like blacks, Chicanos, Native Americans, and women, to be a colossal unintelligible failure apparently perpetrated by an older generation which now has the power to destroy the entire planet.

Anthropologist Margaret Mead is correct when she says that "this break between generations is wholly new: it is planetary and universal." [6] It is obvious that today's youth have grown up in a world their elders never knew. But what is so frustrating for young people is that few of their elders admit that they had no idea of what this postwar world would be like. And now that it is here, those who probably best know it and grew up in it are almost never allowed to contribute to its direction. Indeed it seems that their voices, whether raised over war, imperialism, racism, sexism, poverty, education, ecology, or defense, are studiously unheard. It is understandable, therefore, that the generation gap has hostile aspects which manifest themselves both culturally and politically. Young people rebelled in the sixties and still rebel against the controls to which they are subjected—against the educational systems, the apprenticeship systems, the career ladders which have been created for them by previous generations.

Because they must wait so long for positions of leadership, many in the postwar generation feel disinherited (thus the title of this book). But the practical, visible, matter-of-fact disinheritance does not compare in magnitude to a spiritual disinheritance which torments the modern young. For despite all their dissent and prolonged dialogue with the Establishment, young people have been unable to communicate just what is troubling them and why. Prisons, high schools, colleges, and universities have been assigned by society the task of understanding youth and transmitting their sensibility to the Establishment, which presumably would then institute reforms incorporating some of what youth wants. But thousands of young people simply retort, to use the phrase of Jerry Rubin, that these institutions serve as the Establishment's "deluxe toilet training" for misfits. Institutions which are supposed to be the forum for creativity and dissent seem to them irrelevant and ineffectual.

These institutions *are* irrelevant because implicit in their functioning and implicit in the thinking of older generations is the assumption that there still is general agreement about the good, the true, and the beautiful. Hence psychology and advertising operate on the premise that human nature with its needs, modes of perception, and feeling, is essentially constant and therefore can be manipulated, satisfied, or at least mollified. Such beliefs are utterly incompatible with the findings of many eminent contemporary historians, anthropologists, and sociologists. Radically different life environments make radically different people. The generation of the thirties, which grew up with scarcity, great industrial expansion, and attack by three world powers, cannot be expected to perceive the world like the generation of the sixties or seventies. Until the inflation and energy shortage of 1973-1976, most of this generation experienced abundance, a post-industrial technocracy, and a lengthy war of massive American intervention in Asia. Or, expressed in a non-generational way: a seldom employed, disenfranchised Chicano with a fifth-grade education does not look at the world as does a white, Harvard-trained, bank president. Productive dialogue between these two persons or between the prewar and postwar generations implies a common framework of experience and a common language. Because of the substantial environmental differences, no such common ground exists.

In addition, the postwar generation is spiritually disenfranchised because the experiential *symbols* which make social intercourse possible and which society assumes to be effective are, in fact, almost meaningless to postwar children and youth. Thus, communication between generations is increasingly tenuous. Communication before World War II was intellectually indirect: the printed or spoken word assembled in a linear order. The experiential landscape was symbolized by levers, pylons, the assembly line, the bulldozer, the blast furnace—characteristics of the developing industrial base of a mechanized civilization. Communication for the postwar generation is direct: television, highly graphic underground newspapers, and electronic rock music bring discontinuous experience. (There were no television sets in 1930; by 1964, 92 percent of American households had at least one television.) The experiential landscape of the 1960's and 1970's is symbolized by the computer, the huge rock 'n' roll amplifier, the laser beam, the transistor, the atom bomb, the spaceship—characteristics of a post-industrial, totally technological world. So, as I suggest in later chapters, the generation gap, the disinheritance of youth, is in some measure attributable to the simultaneous presence of two modes of communication: discursive (word symbols) and non-discursive (immediate auditory, visual, and tactile experience).

The prewar era was experienced by its historical participants using exclusively a discursive system of communication: words. The postwar era is being experienced by historical participants who are increasingly using a nondiscursive mode of communication: sensate impression. Thus, persons coming to maturity in the sixties and seventies are doubly disinherited. Not only does the material environment experienced during maturation differ radically from that of previous generations, so also the means of understanding and communicating reality differs. Thus, these children found and may well continue to find themselves in a world from which they feel irremediably alienated. And mama and papa often awake to find that they are unable to comfort their children, for the very means they utilize to assist their children seem only to alienate them further, e.g., a nanny, a car, and an expensive education.

From the foregoing, it should be clear that the author takes as a premise the existence of a generation gap. In this book I seek to illuminate the nature of the gap by examining its *political as well as its cultural manifestations, instead of divorcing the two.* There are many studies of the political manifestation (generally histories and analyses of the New Left). There are also studies of the cultural manifestation (generally exposés of various aspects of the counterculture). And most studies usually acknowledge that the New Left and counterculture are parts of a larger phenomenon, a peculiar development in the consciousness of postwar youth. But what is necessary for an adequate grasp of the postwar generations is a single, unified, schematic approach which makes sense both of the New Left and the counterculture. More importantly, such an approach would have to connect these two broad manifestations of generational revolt in such a way that we can understand what they mean in the 1970's. I believe that this can be done, and it is the intention of this book to offer just such an integrated approach. But my approach is not linear and utilizes several different forms. Accordingly, the book is divided into three parts, *each of which has a different structure.* The first part is a brief history of the important political aspects of the generation gap, loosely subsumed under the rubric of the New Left. The second part sets forth what the young radicals on the left believe to be bothering them. The third part attempts to suggest the significance of the New Left and the counterculture in the larger philosophical and historical context of American and Western Civilization in the twentieth century.

Notes to Introduction

1. *Studies on the Left* is now defunct, but some of its contributors write for *Socialist Revolution,* published in San Francisco.

2. Mills himself had supplied a methodological model with his controversial book, *The Power Elite* (1956).

3. Mills died while on a European tour in 1961, thus leaving a great vacuum in the academic leadership of the American New Left.

4. Richard Flacks, "Young Intelligentsia in Revolt," *Transaction* (June, 1970), p. 49.

5. *Volunteers,* words by Marty Balin, music by Marty Balin and Paul Kantner, © 1969, Icebag Corporation. All rights reserved. Used by permission.

6. Margaret Mead, *Culture and Commitment* (New York, 1970), p. 64.

Part 1

The Origins and Growth of a New Left

Introduction to Part 1

Isn't this . . . something of what we are trying to mean by the phrase, "The New Left?" Let the old men ask sourly, "Out of Apathy—into what?" The Age of Complacency is ending. Let the old women complain wisely about "the end of ideology." We are beginning to move again.*

What is the New Left? Why did it originate? Why did it gain such notoriety in the 1960's? What does it mean? To paraphrase the now defunct rock group, Buffalo Springfield, What *is* "happening here," and why "ain't it exactly clear?" In Part I of this book I hope the answers to these questions will emerge. The approach is basically historical, covering the period from 1960 through 1976. Because the New Left grew so rapidly and became so diffuse, I am able only to select what seems to me to have been the most influential events, organizations, and people contributing to the development of the New Left. In this sense, this brief descriptive history in Part I is necessarily incomplete and is neither intended to be thoroughly analytical nor deeply academic. Since the author was present and involved in some of the events herein recorded, he believes he is justified in describing them without necessarily having to present "all sides" or to footnote every detail.

It is virtually impossible to fit the New Left into a tidy history with neat, clearly defined chapters—either chronologically or topically. Therefore, I have tried to proceed both chronologically *and* topically. The origins and early development of the New Left are rather easily recounted. Its spectacular expansion beginning in 1965 is more difficult to narrate. The very complexity

*C. Wright Mills, *Letter to the New Left*

of the story serves to illustrate the Buffalo Springfield's statement that what is happening "ain't exactly clear." For the development of the New Left in the late sixties and its change in leadership in the early seventies cannot be satisfactorily understood using the traditional linear approach to history. To find or delineate a *pattern* of development, a line of direction with specific milestones or guides to its validity is in my opinion probably a fruitless endeavor. Consequently, the chapter headings are meant to be suggestive rather than definitive. Chapter One is designed to examine the nature and activities of the most important early student left organizations, SNCC and SDS. The second chapter explores the influence of the Vietnam War upon the New Left. Chapter Three sketches the contours of the burgeoning student left. Chapter Four looks at the political and philosophical development of a powerful black radicalism. And Chapter Five describes the large "peace" coalition created in 1971 and speculates on the political future of the New Left both within the Establishment and within such underground groups as the Symbionese Liberation Army, the Weatherpeople, and the George Jackson Brigade. These chapters and this first part are designed to be understood in their totality. What emerges should be a distinct impression of what the New Left is and the changes it has been through.

I

The Civil Rights Movement:
SNCC and SDS

We have waited for more than 340 years for our constitutional and
God-given rights. The nations of Asia and Africa are moving with jetlike
speed toward gaining political independence, but we still creep at horse-
and-buggy pace toward gaining a cup of coffee at a lunch counter. Perhaps it is easy for those who have never felt the stinging darts of segregation to say, "Wait." But when you have seen vicious mobs lynch your
mothers and fathers at will and drown your sisters and brothers at
whim; when you have seen hate-filled policemen curse, kick and even
kill your black brothers and sisters; when you see the vast majority of
your twenty million Negro brothers smothering in an airtight cage of
poverty in the midst of an affluent society; when you suddenly find
your tongue twisted and your speech stammering as you seek to explain
to your six-year-old daughter why she can't go to the public amusement
park that has just been advertised on television, and see tears welling up
in her eyes when she is told that Funtown is closed to colored children,
and see ominous clouds of inferiority beginning to form in her little
mental sky, and see her beginning to distort her personality by developing an unconscious bitterness toward white people; when you have to
concoct an answer for a five-year-old son who is asking: "Daddy, why
do white people treat colored people so mean?"; when you take a cross-
country drive and find it necessary to sleep night after night in the
uncomfortable corners of your automobile because no motel will
accept you; when you are humiliated day in and day out by nagging
signs reading "white" and "colored"; when your first name becomes
"nigger," your middle name becomes "boy" (however old you are) and
your last name becomes "John," and your wife and mother are never
given the respected title "Mrs."; when you are harried by day and
haunted by night by the fact that you are a Negro, living constantly at
tiptoe stance, never quite knowing what to expect next, and are

plagued with inner fears and outer resentments; when you are forever fighting a degenerating sense of "nobodiness"—then you will understand why we find it difficult to wait.*

On January 31, 1960, in Greensboro, North Carolina, four black college students from North Carolina A & T College sat down at the exclusively white counter of the Woolworth's department store cafeteria. Only a few feet separated the white counter from the Negro counter. The blacks were told they could not be served. While they were not revolutionaries, they vowed to continue their sit-in tactics. In a matter of days, sit-ins took place in other cities in North Carolina. The press in the East later picked up the story and northern students supported the movement, as did Martin Luther King's Southern Christian Leadership Conference (SCLC). By the end of 1960, at least 50,000 people had demonstrated in 100 cities, resulting in over 3,600 arrests. An older, essentially northern group, the Congress of Racial Equality (CORE), sponsored "freedom rides" in southern cities during the spring and summer of 1961 (CORE had experimented with this tactic as early as 1947). These placed Negroes at the front and middle of buses alongside of whites instead of at the rear, where they had been "officially" seated since the beginning of this century. The movement to desegregate public facilities spread in the South and arrests soared to nearly 5,000 by the end of 1961.

Desegregation, while ostensibly the objective of the early Civil Rights movement, was only a surface expression of a larger phenomenon: a new interest by young people in politics. The Civil Rights movement was not new in its goals: integration, equality, and justice for blacks. It was new in its style: sit-ins, bus boycotts (modeled after the daring Montgomery bus boycott of 1955-56 led by Martin Luther King, Jr.), and the freedom rides. It was new in that it aroused strong feelings in millions of people after a decade of apathy and complacent conformity symbolized by the amiable blandness of President Eisenhower.

Certainly the election in 1960 of a young President, John Kennedy, helped to spur the Civil Rights movement. For throughout his campaign, he had stressed the need for political participation by young people. Kennedy held up a vision of social idealism and dedication to civil liberties. But what occurred in 1960 was a recrudescence of politics itself, a demand for participation in decisions by the people most affected: the blacks and the first postwar generation of young, affluent, white Americans. Accordingly, young blacks formed the Student Nonviolent Coordinating Committee, and young whites formed the Students for a Democratic Society.

*Excerpt from pp. 83-84, "Letter from Birmingham Jail"—April 16, 1963, in Martin Luther King, Jr., *Why We Can't Wait* (New York, 1963). By Permission of Harper & Row, Publishers, Inc.

The Student Nonviolent Coordinating Committee

In April 1960, "with $800 of Southern Christian Leadership Conference money, the prestige of Martin Luther King, Jr., the organizing wisdom of Ella Baker, and the enthusiasm of the rare young people who were leading the new student movement, the Student Nonviolent Coordinating Committee was born." [1] The SNCC was originally conceived as an organization to coordinate the groups which had participated in the sit-ins after the Greensboro incident. It worked with and received money from SCLC but increasingly became the nucleus to which younger activists gravitated. Its approach was less juridical than SCLC and CORE. Instead it used physical confrontation and political organization to register black voters and to pressure politicians to accede to black demands. It espoused no ideology, offered no unified program, maintained no fixed bureaucracy or leadership hierarchy, and altered its structure to fit whatever project it sponsored. Accordingly, its staff and membership varied greatly. To my knowledge it started with two staff members in 1960 and once reached a peak of about 150 in the summer of 1964. Its membership (there were no "official" members) was never more than 400, although in 1976 it still maintained offices in Atlanta and New York.

Yet SNCC became a powerful organization in the South—partly because of the prestige of its ally, SCLC, but especially because of the sheer guts of its leaders and members. The SNCC volunteers lived and worked with the people, usually in rural areas. They badgered fear-ridden blacks to go to courthouses and county stores, to stand up for each other, and to face down white authorities. Its volunteers allowed themselves to be publicly beaten and abused, but they remained defiant. Dashingly handsome and fiercely courageous young men like Bob "Moses" Parris, Julian Bond, and Stokely Carmichael (all barely 20 years old in 1960) brought a pride and daring resoluteness to blacks in such white citadels as Lowndes County, Alabama and Amite County, Mississippi. It is almost impossible to overestimate the pride and courage these volunteers engendered in the early years of the Civil Rights movement.

While SNCC was not ideological in orientation, it had an operational philosophy: nonviolence. Its chief tenet was that without resorting to violence and thereby opening itself to attack, a group of protestors could confront a community with a legitimate request for change and, through persistence, be granted that change. Obviously the success of such confrontation depended primarily upon the existence of a basic goodness or humanity within the southern white community and secondarily upon the sympathy and assistance of white America in general. The SNCC leaders, influenced by Dr. Martin Luther King, Jr., believed that southern whites had at least some respect for blacks as human beings and that the conscience of the nation and the government would restrain southern racists from violent and illegal acts against civil rights workers. The philosophy was set down in the constitution of SNCC: "... Through nonviolence, courage displaces fear; love transforms hate. Acceptance dissipates prejudice; hope ends despair. Peace dominates war; faith reconciles doubt. Mutual regard cancels enmity. Justice for all overcomes injustice. The redemptive community supersedes systems of gross social immorality."[2]

Soon after its inception, SNCC turned its words into action. Sit-ins were initiated to desegregate the South. It was assumed that desegregation implied "integration." That is, the ending of racial segregation in public institutions was presumed to mean that blacks and whites would have equal access to the same institutions, that they would be integrated within the institutions. However, southern whites seemed unalterably opposed to such a form of desegregation. The barrier presented by the southern white power structure remained stable. In an effort to influence the power structure, SNCC initiated voter registration drives, hoping that blacks would be able to elect sympathetic leaders or, at least, to shake the confidence of southern officials. But the threat of black voting strength only further incensed southerners. Civil rights workers were murdered and beaten, blacks were arrested for unlawful assembly. Some blacks who attempted to register lost their jobs. Others were dispossessed of their land (easily done to a tenant farmer as well as a freeholder). Those arrested were frequently abused while imprisoned.

There was an evident lack of concern for civil rights workers by the federal government even though mistreatment often took place on federal property. Pleas for protection were submitted to the president and the Justice Department. The federal government moved slowly and did little to protect black activists from illegal arrests, beatings, and constant harassment by local authorities. And it should be pointed out that in general the white citizens confronted by SNCC workers did not abuse them; the authorities did.

By 1963 SNCC was becoming disenchanted with the Kennedy administration's civil rights policies. The situation worsened with the administration's efforts to blunt the effectiveness of the civil rights march on Washington, D. C. scheduled for August, 1963. The Kennedy administration granted money to the civil rights organizations through the Civil Rights Leadership Conference, which had gone to Kennedy for support of the march. The money was channeled through the CIA and the Taconic Foundation (to which the Kennedy family contributed). As part of the bargain, the Civil Rights Leadership Conference was to see that there would be no violence, no sit-ins, and no inflammatory statements. By August, all groups except SNCC agreed to toe the line. A few hours before the march,

Bayard Rustin, coordinator of the march, pressured John Lewis, chairman of SNCC, to change his speech. The most important change was to be from "In good conscience, we cannot support the Administration's Civil Rights Bill," to "True, we support the Administration's Civil Rights Bill, but this bill will not protect young children and old women from police dogs and fire hoses." This caused disillusionment in SNCC, because Lewis was told that if he did not make the changes, the Kennedy Administration "suspected" that Walter Reuther and other speakers and cosponsors would drop out.[3]

Nevertheless, cooperation between Civil Rights organizations—including SNCC—and the government (then under President Johnson), continued. This lasted only until the Democratic National Convention at Atlantic City, New Jersey, in August of 1964. For at the convention, the Civil Rights movement and the government clashed again. At issue was the seating of the Mississippi Freedom Democratic Party (MFDP), which had been inspired by SNCC and supported by COFO—Council of Federated Organizations—which included SNCC, NAACP, CORE, and SCLC.

The MFDP was the outgrowth of nearly two years of voter registration and freedom school work. It was the climax of the summer 1964 voter drive, led by organizer Bob Moses of SNCC, and the freedom schools, led by historian Staughton Lynd. The Summer Project attracted 800 students from many northern universities; two white civil rights workers and one black man lost their lives in the effort. A full delegation from MFDP was sent to Atlantic City to demand seats. When it became clear that a floor fight might ensue, Hubert Humphrey, Walter Reuther, Martin Luther King, Jr., Bayard Rustin, and Roy Wilkins all appeared before the MFDP delegation and urged compromise. They asked the delegation to accept two token (at large) seats in exchange for a promise of an integrated delegation in 1968. Bob Moses and James Foreman of SNCC urged a stand on principle. The delegation refused to accept a compromise, and SNCC left the COFO. Humphrey got the vice-presidential nomination and labor went solidly Democratic. In the eyes of SDS and SNCC, this meant it was time for the militants in the Civil Rights movement to withdraw from the liberal coalition which was intended to be the backbone of the Johnson Administration.

The Atlantic City convention was a humiliation for the New Left and the Civil Rights movement, but SNCC did not accept its rebuff as final. It challenged the seating of the Mississippi congressional delegation in January, 1965. In September, the House of Representatives finally decided it could not bar the regular Mississippi Democratic Party delegation. Only 149 congressmen voted to accept the MFDP challenge. Civil rights activist and comedian Dick Gregory has, I think captured (albeit a shade exaggerated) the initial religious and altruistic élan of SCLC and SNCC before this political humiliation. "We marched down the street and got shot at because we were black. And for some reason we felt ashamed because we were aggravating the situation to make the white folk shoot black folk. To get rid of some of the shame, we went to the police station and prayed for the sheriff." [4] Within the SNCC ranks, all such generosity of feeling toward whites and toward white-controlled political reform ended in 1965.

The radicalization of SNCC was confirmed on May 16, 1966, in Atlanta, Georgia, with the election of new leaders. The fiery militant, Stokely Carmichael, defeated the more patient and philosophical John Lewis for the chairmanship. Mrs. Ruby Smith Robinson replaced James Foreman, who had resigned as executive secretary. Also, the members determined to deemphasize the role of whites in civil rights activity in the South. On May 17, Carmichael's distrust for the two major political parties was publicized in the *New York Times* as was his leading role in organizing the prototype of the Black Panther Party in Lowndes County, Alabama. It was decided that the coexistence of whites and blacks in the organization created a distracting situation within the committee, making it difficult for blacks to function effectively.

Stokely Carmichael radically changed the philosophy of SNCC, especially regarding nonviolence. Carmichael's attitude toward nonviolence came in a press release on May 21, 1966, in which he indicated that he did not advocate violence, but neither did he advocate turning the other cheek. The new SNCC policy was one of self-defense. Another aspect of the philosophical change was the new goal of "black power." Black power, the committee argued, was nothing more than an extension of the idea of voter registration. The new SNCC leadership contended that the only way any significant advances could be made would be through establishing black economic and political power. This meant than SNCC as an organization would have to move for such power by eliminating white members from staff positions. To put it baldly, white people were no longer wanted in the decision-making body of the black organization. These new goals and tactics were explained by Gloria Larry, a field secretary of SNCC, at a seminar in New York on June 5, 1966. Miss Larry stated that the committee had not been motivated by a desire to become more radical or racist, but had adopted their policies to cope with the reality of American political life.

These developments also brought splits between SNCC, the Southern Christian Leadership Conference, and the National Association for the Advancement of Colored People. These two organizations, expecially SCLC and its leader, Dr. Martin Luther King, Jr., seemed to misunderstand the concept of black power, and they insisted upon strictly maintaining their previous policies of direct nonviolence. Initially Dr. King dismissed black power as not being a "significant trend." As time passed, however, King publicly acknowledged the reason blacks were moving away from nonviolence by placing the responsibility for black militance upon the white power structure's inability to facilitate meaningful improvements for blacks. On October 14, 1966, Dr. King went even further and stated in the *New York Times* that, in fact, "the black power slogan has been exploited by the decision-makers to justify resistance to change."

Carmichael, for his part, became more vocal in his insistence on black power and the necessity of self-defense. The new slogan of SNCC became "Move over, or we'll move over you." The nonviolent Civil Rights movement of the sixties was disintegrating. In January 1967, Carmichael did not seek reelection, and H. Rap Brown became chairman of SNCC. But even before Carmichael's resignation, it was obvious that the unity of the Civil Rights movement was ending. American radicalism, including black radicalism, was moving into a new phase, a phase which would link civil rights to the antiwar movement.

Students for a Democratic Society

The other major organization stimulated by the Civil Rights movement was SDS. It was founded by Al Haber in 1960 at a New York convention sponsored by the League for Industrial Democracy (LID). The latter was founded in New York by Jack London and Upton Sinclair in 1905, and served as an educational and coordinating center for the democratic left. Like SNCC, SDS was originally nonviolent and committed to working within the system. It sought a broad coalition of students, liberals, labor, religious, and civil rights groups. Although primarily a student organization, membership was initially available to anyone. While it had no program of social reform, it did have a philosophy which underlay its motto: "One man, One Soul." This did not mean unbridled anarchy, but that the group should not for any reason violate a person's conscience. The individual was entitled to do as his inner world dictated; he should not be compelled to do what might seem pragmatic or prudent for the interests of the group. Such an ethic distinguished SDS's philosophy from Marxism as practiced by the Communist Party, where one is asked to do what is necessary and to assume that it is right. This was one of the reasons SDS called itself a "New Left" group, carefully differentiating itself from the older Marxist Left. In the philosophy of SDS, to do what was necessary was unrelated to doing what was right. Politics was the servant of the individual, not vice versa.

It was not long, however, before the youthful founders of SDS came to realize that LID intended them to be essentially a labor and socialist (old Left) organization. Resistance to the control exercised by LID culminated in the separation of SDS from its parent organization in 1962. Consequently,

SDS dates its official origin from its *Port Huron Statement* (PHS) drafted by Tom Hayden, the child of an Irish-American family from Detroit. The PHS was submitted to the SDS convention (June 11-15, 1962) at the Franklin Roosevelt Labor Center, Port Huron, Michigan, by Hayden after he had returned from a year in the South as field secretary for SDS.

The PHS is generally considered the first manifesto of an organized New Left in this country. It is sixty pages in length and still represents one of the best political treatises coming from the generation of the 1960's. Among the key concepts it emphasizes are the "generation gap," "participatory democracy," and the "university as a revolutionary cadre." We are guided by "the sense that we may be the last generation in the experiment with living. . . . In a participatory democracy . . . the decision-making of basic social consequence would be carried on by public groupings; . . . A new left must consist of younger people matured in the postwar world. The university is an obvious beginning point." [5]

In 1963 SDS set up national headquarters in the heart of the black ghetto in South Chicago, 63rd Street and Woodlawn Avenue. From a dingy, poorly lit, almost barren floor, its youthful, well-educated leaders, Tom Hayden, Carl Oglesby, Richard Flacks, Todd Gitlin, and Paul Booth, appeared and disappeared, laboriously mapping out projects to assist community development and civil rights for the poor. The SDS concentrated on the North. Programs were initiated to assist the poor (especially blacks in the northern cities) and to organize politically and economically (since 1940, 1.6 million blacks had moved to the northern cities from the South). For two years (1963-65) SDS coordinated the Economic Research Action Project (ERAP). The ERAP had affiliates in New Haven, Cleveland, Newark, Baltimore, Oakland, and Boston. The two most successful programs were in Chicago and Newark. The former, entitled Jobs or Income Now (JOIN), was run directly from SDS headquarters and enlisted the assistance of numerous community and civil rights organizations such as the Woodlawn organization, the West Side organization, and the Southern Christian Leadership Conference. The latter, Newark Community Union Project (NCUP), was led by Tom Hayden from 1965-67 and served as a model for other community organizations sponsored by SDS. Indeed, so successful was Hayden that when the Newark riot occurred in 1967, he was summoned by Governor Richard Hughes of New Jersey at 4:00 A.M. Hayden's advice that the national Guard be withdrawn was taken, and within forty-eight hours the riot ceased, although at least twenty-six persons died.

While SDS did have a national headquarters until 1969 and an official weekly publication, *New Left Notes,* its orientation was always decentralized. Its purpose was to coordinate New Left activities, including civil rights, student activism, political participation, and labor organization. It never pretended to offer an ideology or a national program of either reform or revolution. Consequently, its operational incoherence baffled the government, the public, and the press. Since anyone could become a member, its yearly national meetings attracted groups ranging from the Progressive Labor Party (a youth-oriented vehicle of the Communist Party of the United States) to representatives from women's liberation and, later, the Black Panther Party. Often its national conventions were tumultuous, characterized by spirited debates, and generally inconclusive. Hence issues and policies came more and more to be delineated by the National Council of SDS, which usually met twice a year.

Although SDS had a membership far larger than SNCC, it never had the discipline or singularity of purpose that SNCC had in the early 1960's. Its most difficult problem was divesting itself of the traditional left from which it separated in 1962. Chronically racked by disputes over the nature of the working class, its revolutionary potential and liability, and how to form a student-worker revolutionary vanguard, by 1965 SDS was on the verge of demise.

What saved SDS in 1965 was much the same as what saved SNCC in 1966: new and more militant leadership. Just as John Lewis's nonviolent leadership of SNCC was supplanted by the militant black power leadership of Stokely Carmichael, so the sincere idealism of Todd Gitlin and Carl Oglesby began to give way to the hardened realism of Tom Hayden, organizer of the Newark Community Union Project. For the roseate balloon launched by President Kennedy in 1960 finally burst in 1965. The young president had been assassinated slightly more than a year earlier and the war in Vietnam had been drastically escalated in violation of President Johnson's campaign pledge. Liberal professors Glaser, Lipset, and Feuer had joined the opposition to the Berkeley Free Speech Movement. Julian Bond of SNCC had twice been denied his seat in the Georgia State Legislature. Malcolm X was assassinated, James Meredith gunned down, and the riot in the Watts area of Los Angeles had resulted in thirty-four deaths; most of those killed were black. Despite the 1964 Voting Rights Bill and the 1965 Civil Rights Bill, few radicals in the North or the South saw much improvement. Indeed, rights workers continued to be harassed and murdered. Mrs. Viola Liuzzo was murdered while transporting blacks to march with Martin Luther King, Jr. in Selma, Alabama, on March 25, 1965. The assassin, though identified by two witnesses, was never convicted. The idealism which had inspired SNCC and SDS soured when it became evident that no beneficent federal or local authorities would assist either of the groups to help victimized Americans. Their general reaction was in tune with the cynical tone of Stokely Carmichael's comments at Berkeley in October 1966: "I maintain that every Civil Rights bill in this country was passed for white people, not for black people."

But the leadership of SDS, while now more militant, was unable by itself to rejuvenate the organization. Ironically, the rejuvenation came (unintentionally) from the United States Department of Justice, the Senate Internal Security Subcommittee, and the American press. They mistakenly attributed the organization of the large antiwar marches of October 15–16, 1965, to SDS. In fact, the marches, which brought out over 80,000 people in many cities, were primarily organized by the Berkeley-based Mobilization Committee to End the War in Vietnam. This was the group which Jerry Rubin came to lead. But SDS was suddenly given nationwide publicity and depicted as the vanguard leadership of a national movement of young people to end the war in Vietnam.

Although the SDS leadership now saw the possibility of organizing around the war, they refused to organize nationally around a single issue. But Hayden was quick to see the potential of recruiting on college campuses and that the draft, the military, and the war were particularly relevant to one large group of people: students. Students for a Democratic Society formulated a strategy of "student power" and linked it to the presence of the draft and the military on campuses. Gradually SDS came to see (December 1966) what SNCC had seen earlier (January 1966): that the war in Vietnam, with all its racist, imperialistic, economic, and generational implications, was the issue around which a unified New Left could organize.

Notes to Chapter 1

1. Howard Zinn, *SNCC, The New Abolitionists* (New York, 1965), p. 33.

2. Staughton Lynd, ed., *Nonviolence in America: A Documentary History* (New York, 1966), pp. 398-99.

3. For accounts of this controversial episode in the history of the MFDP, see Stokely Carmichael and Charles Hamilton, *Black Power* (New York, 1967), pp. 86-98, and David Dellinger, "From Atlantic City to Chicago," in *The Conspiracy*, eds. Peter and Deborah Babcox and Bob Abel (New York, 1969), pp. 108-10.

4. Gregory made this observation at a meeting in London in 1968. Never one to end on a gloomy note, he concluded by saying something to the effect that the real failure of the early Civil Rights movement was attributable to blacks themselves; they desegregated the washrooms first and thereby "ruined the greatest thing the blacks had going for them—the myth of the giant cock." Quoted in Richard Neville, *Play Power* (New York, 1970), p. 25.

5. Quoted and excerpted from Massimo Teodori, ed., *The New Left: A Documentary History* (New York, 1970), pp. 163-72.

II

The War in Southeast Asia: From Protest to Resistance

Since barbarism has its pleasures it naturally has its apologists. There are panegyrists of war who say that without a periodical bleeding a race decays and loses its manhood. Experience is directly opposed to this shameless assertion. It is war that wastes a nation's wealth, chokes its industries, kills its flower, narrows its sympathies, condemns it to be governed by adventurers, and leaves the puny, deformed, and unmanly to breed the next generation. . . . To call war the soil of courage and virtue is like calling debauchery the soil of love.*

It is widely believed that the New Left was essentially a young people's rebellion against conscription and American involvement in the war in Vietnam. Many journalists and political analysts had argued that the New Left would disintegrate when the war in Southeast Asia was no longer a public issue. The author has sought elsewhere to refute this interpretation, and the activities of the Symbionese Liberation Army and the George Jackson Brigade would seem to indicate considerable life within the New Left—albeit highly clandestine.[1] Like any dissenting movement, the New Left is not contained by political events or establishment tactics. It is usually propelled by them. Nevertheless, it is true that the New Left, both black and white, gained publicity and achieved a wide following because of its criticism of American policy in Southeast Asia, especially Vietnam. Indeed, the repeated demonstrations and dialogues initiated by the New Left concerning the war in Vietnam were instrumental in persuading the American public that the war was a mistake. It took three years before the public accepted this point of view. In August 1965, a Gallup Poll asked the following question of the American public: "In view of the developments since Americans entered the

*George Santayana, *The Life of Reason*. Reprinted by permission of Charles Scribner's Sons.

fighting in Vietnam, do you think the United States made a mistake sending troops to fight in Vietnam?" Twenty-four percent replied yes, 61 percent replied no, and 15 percent had no opinion. In answer to the same question posed in August 1968, 53 percent responded yes, 35 percent responded no, and 12 percent had no opinion.[2]

Although most groups which can be called "New Left" became involved in antiwar activity, the story of the development of the New Left around the war issue is quite complicated and often ambiguous. Suffice it to say that what began as a movement to oblige America to live up to its promise of "liberty, equality, freedom and justice for all," pioneered by young people in SNCC and SDS, spread in 1966 and 1967 to become an enormous youth protest over the presence of American armed forces defending a government in Saigon which was involved in a Vietnamese civil war and which would by 1973 be fighting in Cambodia and Laos. It is not the intention of the author to argue either the position of the New Left or the American governmental administrations. Rather, it is his intention to present simply and briefly the metamorphosis of the Civil Rights movement into an antiwar movement which became, at least symbolically, the binding force of the New Left in the late sixties and early seventies.

While SDS did not organize either the April or the October antiwar demonstrations of 1965, it supported them. In fact, at the April march on Washington (two months after the U.S. began bombing North Vietnam), SDS president Paul Potter spoke. So successful was the October 1965 march that SDS joined with the National Committee for a Sane Nuclear Policy (SANE) to organize an antiwar march in Washington, D.C. in November 1965. Carl Oglesby, then president of SDS, delivered a now famous speech indicting corporate capitalism and criticizing the inaction of liberals regarding monopoly capitalism and the war. But at that time SDS as a national organization had not passed any resolution condemning the war or urging direct action against it. SDS was willing to go only so far as to recommend conscientious objection. Indeed, they had not yet formulated a precise strategy regarding the war, which was considered a less important issue than community and working-class organization.

SNCC seriously considered the war as an issue earlier than did SDS. This was primarily because of the McComb Leaflet. The leaflet was a statement by a group of blacks in McComb, Mississippi, offering five reasons why black men should not fight for America in Vietnam. It was sent out in July 1965 after the death in Vietnam of a black soldier, John D. Shaw. "No one has a right to ask us to risk our lives and kill other Colored People in Santo Domingo and Vietnam so that the White American can get richer." The leaflet was reprinted in the state newsletter of the Mississippi Freedom Democratic Party and widely circulated by the Mississippi Student Union, a

SNCC affiliate. By August 1965 every civil rights organization was under pressure to take a stand on the war. But NAACP, CORE, and even SNCC refused to make a public stand against the war. The general consensus was that to infuse civil rights with the issue of the war would damage the Civil Rights movement.

Suddenly, in January 1966, SNCC broke ranks and issued a statement condemning the war in Southeast Asia and demanding that participation in the Civil Rights movement be an alternative to military service. When Stokely Carmichael became chairman in May 1966, SNCC turned militantly against the war and conscription. Daily demonstrations against the draft were begun in the Atlanta induction center in August 1966. By the end of the month twelve blacks were arrested and were held fifty-eight days without bond. All but one of them were convicted of interfering with the administration of the Selective Service Act. One demonstrator, John Wilson, was sentenced to three years on a Georgia chain gang. He later became the chairman of the National Black Anti-War Draft Union. In October 1966, Carmichael publicly announced he would go to jail before going in the armed forces; SNCC looked to SDS for support.

After considerable acrimonious debate, SDS made its position public. At the meeting of its National Council in Berkeley (December 1966), SDS passed the following resolution: "(1) SDS reaffirms its opposition to the United States government's immoral, illegal, and genocidal war against the Vietnamese people in their struggle for self-determination. (2) SDS reaffirms its opposition to conscription in any form. . . . (5) SDS believes that a sense of urgency must be developed that will move people to leave the campus and organize a movement to resist the draft and the war, with its base in poor, working-class, and middle-class communities. (6) SDS therefore encourages all young men to resist the draft."

The SDS resolution was made public in the report of SDS national secretary Greg Calvert. Entitled "From Protest to Resistance," the report stipulated that under no circumstances would members allow themselves to be arrested and that local chapters should facilitate resistance by demonstrations at inductions, draft boards, recruiting stations, and circulate *We Won't Go* petitions. The SDS partisans now began wearing buttons with the single word "Resist" on them. The effect of this was almost immediate. At Michigan State University, forty-two draft-eligible men and twenty female supporters signed a *We Won't Go* statement. On February 3, 1967, seventy-five signed a statement at the University of Chicago. They were followed by students at the University of Wisconsin and Queens College. Of the Chicago signatories, six went on to found CADRE—Chicago Area Draft Resisters.

While SNCC and SDS publicly advocated resistance to Selective Service and condemned the war in Vietnam, it was not until the spring of 1967 that the largest and most powerful of the civil rights organizations cast its lot with the fate of Vietnam as a political issue. On April 4, 1967, one year before he was assassinated, Dr. Martin Luther King, Jr. wed himself and SCLC to the antiwar position. In an address delivered at Riverside Church in New York City the powerful civil rights leader asked that "all who find the American course in Vietnam a dishonorable and unjust one," take the path of "conscientious objection." This, of course, did not pledge SCLC to draft resistance or to the abolition of the draft system. But it linked the righteous moral indignation which was the thrust behind the Civil Rights movement to a similar indignation over the action of the United States government in Southeast Asia. And by advocating conscientious objection as a tactic of protest, SCLC remained consistent to its policy of nonviolent protest against what it considered immoral social and political practices. This strategic consistency and the international moral prestige of Dr. King stung the consciences of many Americans, especially liberals, and greatly assisted the legitimacy of the less well known New Left groups which were seeking to make the war their cause célèbre.

It was also in mid-April 1967 that the first of the defiant draft card burnings received national publicity. Over 150 persons burned their draft cards at the Sheep Meadow in New York's Central Park. The draft card burning was organized by the Cornell University We Won't Go, under the leadership of Tom Bell and Bruce Dancis. What made the draft card burning especially significant was the emergence from the spectators of a handsome, rugged-looking young man in a Green Beret uniform. The rigid, disciplined soldier cut his way through the press to the circle where the cards were being ceremoniously burned. Then he produced his own card and set it afire. Applause sounded and the press surged forward to interview the Green Beret. The young soldier was Gary Rader, who had served in the Special Forces and was then a student at Northwestern University. Two days after the Sheep Meadow rally, Rader wrote the commander of his company and resigned from the reserves. Later he became the leader and chief organizer of CADRE. The fact that Rader had served in the military and was now working against the draft and the war lent greater prestige to the New Left's position on the war and the draft.

The Resistance

The widespread demonstrations of hostility to the draft and the war which gained national attention in April 1967 were generally seen by the public as SDS and SNCC actions. But in fact they were only slightly attributable to these organizations. The protesters ranged from pacifists to draft resisters and many were not members of any organizations. However, there appeared in the spring of 1967 an additional national New Left organization specifically committed to antiwar and antidraft activity. The group called itself simply The Resistance. It originated with the leadership of David Harris in Palo Alto and Lennie Heller and Steve Hamilton in Berkeley. The former, who later married and divorced folk singer Joan Baez, had been student body president of Stanford University in 1966. Harris, a motorcyclist and "freak" (in the style of folk singers Richard Fariña and Bob Dylan), led the Stanford delegation to the National Student Association's Annual Conference in August 1966. His attempt to get the association to pass a resolution endorsing noncooperation with Selective Service came within two votes of passing. In January 1967, he turned in his draft card and the next month resigned as student body president. In March, he met with Lennie Heller and Steve Hamilton and the three men decided to stump the nation encouraging draft-age men to refuse induction.

It was not until the April 15, 1967 mobilization march against the war that their resolve became nationally known. At that march (in San Francisco), David spoke along with Eldridge Cleaver. Harris announced the existence of The Resistance and said that it was going to take national action on October 16, 1967. He called upon all men of draft age to turn in their draft cards on that day, and The Resistance circulated a leaflet entitled "We Refuse—October 16." "The Resistance is a group who are bound together by one single and clear commitment: on October 16 we will hand in our draft cards and refuse any further cooperation with the Selective Service. By so doing we will actively challenge the government's right to draft American men for its criminal war against the people of Viet Nam."

Most New Left organizations supported the first National Anti-Draft Day, October 16, 1967. Approximately 1,200 draft cards were collected in eighteen cities. Antidraft activities varied from city to city and on the West and East Coasts. On the West Coast they culminated in a violent Stop the Draft Week beginning October 16. On the East Coast activities culminated in a march to the Pentagon, where draft cards were supposed to be turned in, but many were burned instead.

Prior to the march on the Pentagon, the most publicized of the East Coast activities was the formation of the New England Resistance (NER). The NER was centered in Boston. Its most notable leaders were Alex Jack, a theology student at Boston University; Michael Ferber, a graduate student in English; William Sloane Coffin, chaplain of Yale University; Reverend George H. Williams, professor of divinity at Harvard, and Dr. Benjamin Spock, although the latter was not an organizer of the October 16 turn-in.

The New England Resistance took on a style of its own: intellectual, religious. Thus, on October 16, the turn-in was held at Arlington Street

Church (Boston), where William Ellery Channing had founded modern American Unitarianism 150 years previously. After the organizers had passed out 30,000 leaflets and there had been a rally on Boston Common with speakers Howard Zinn and Noam Chomsky, the turn-in began. Ferber spoke, Williams spoke, and Coffin received the cards. As cameras rolled, bulbs flashed, 60 men marched down the aisle and quietly burned their cards over a candle and 200 other men turned in their cards. Ferber, Coffin, and Spock were later indicted for conspiring against the administration of the Selective Service Act.

The SDS did not sponsor the subsequent march on the Pentagon of October 20, 1967, where cards were turned in and rallies held. But it specifically supported all activities surrounding the October 16 Stop the Draft Day. Its National Council passed the following resolution: "SDS encourages all chapters to seek out and support all men participating in the October 16 refusal to cooperate with the Selective Service and should aid them in further resistance to—that is, relevant obstruction and disruption of—the American war machine wherever vulnerable." Nor did SNCC *sponsor* the resistance activities. But once again it was SNCC that was *most militant about resistance*. While SNCC's leaders supported the styles both of NER and David Harris's Palo Alto Resistance, they clung to their own conviction of what resistance ultimately means. As the brilliant SNCC worker, Julius Lester, explained it earlier in the year:

To protest is to speak out against. . . . It is to say, "Sir, I protest" when you are slapped in the face.

To resist is to say NO! without qualification or explanation.

To resist is not only to say I WON'T GO. It is to say I'll make sure nobody else goes either.

To resist is to not go to jail when sentenced, but only when caught and surrounded and there is no other choice but death.

To resist is to make the President afraid to leave the White House because he will be spat upon wherever he goes to tell his lies. . . .

Have we forgotten? The man is a murderer. . . .

To protest is to dislike the inhumanity of another.

To resist is to stop inhumanity and affirm your own humanity.

One does not protest murder.

One apprehends the murderer and deals with him accordingly.[3]

Is it any wonder that at the time Julius Lester wrote this statement, seventeen staff members of SNCC were under indictment for refusing draft induction?[4]

By October 1967, then, the New Left, while in agreement about their disdain for the war and for the draft, offered no consensus about how to translate their disdain into effective action. This was evident in the differences between the antiwar activity in Washington, D. C. and antiwar activity in the Bay area. In Washington there was a march on the Pentagon and mass draft card burnings. In Oakland, California, the climax of the Stop the Draft Week became violent. The former was essentially nonviolent and heavily influenced by the New England Resistance and older participants, such as Spock and Coffin. The latter drew together many antidraft and antiwar groups, was more influenced by SDS and blacks, and divided hard-core New Leftists from pacifists.

The march in Washington, D. C. assembled 75,000 demonstrators, who were met by troops surrounding the Pentagon. It seemed that an unusually large proportion of the soldiers summoned to guard the Pentagon were black and very young. It was a highly emotional encounter between members of a single generation. The soldiers were obviously embarrassed, and many of them were sympathetic with the demonstrators. The latter pleaded with them to understand that the demonstrators meant no harm to them. Chants of "We are brothers and sisters. We love you! We love you! We love you!" echoed both day and night. Greg Calvert of SDS spoke to the soldiers with a bullhorn, endeavoring to divide them from their superiors. "The troops you employ belong to us, not to you. They don't belong to the generals. They belong to a new hope for America that those generals never could participate in." More draft cards were burned before the Pentagon on October twentieth and twenty-first than in any other demonstration against the war in Southeast Asia.

The Stop the Draft Week in the Bay area began on Monday, October 16, when 300 draft cards were turned in by The Resistance at the Federal Building in San Francisco. Approximately 120 pacifists were arrested at the Oakland induction center. On Tuesday, 3,000 demonstrators battled police at the induction center until, after twenty-five arrests and about twenty injuries, they dispersed. The climax came on Friday, when 10,000 demonstrators surrounded the induction center. They sported helmets and shields, built barricades, prevented buses from coming near the center, and painted slogans on the sidewalks.[5] Eventually the leaders of the Oakland episode were indicted as the Oakland Seven—they were later acquitted by a jury. Spock and others involved in the Pentagon rally and draft card burnings were convicted by a jury but acquitted on technicalities a year later.

On October 27, 1967, just after the episodes at the Pentagon and at Oakland, the Catholic Resistance made its dramatic appearance—or at least the press made it dramatic. Father Philip Berrigan, the Reverend James Mangel, Thomas Lewis, and David Eberhardt walked into the Selective Service offices in Baltimore and poured blood on their draft records. They were indicted for damaging government property and interfering with the administration of the Selective Service System. But Father Berrigan did not begin his term in prison until July 6, 1968. In the meantime he thoroughly outraged the government when, in May 1968 in Catonsville, Maryland, together with his Jesuit brother Daniel, Thomas Lewis, and six other Catholic priests and laymen, he helped destroy 378 draft files with napalm made from instructions in the *Special Forces Handbook* published by the United States Government Printing Office. Ultimately, all of the men were sentenced for destruction of draft records in what became the sensational trial of the Catonsville Nine.[6] Daniel Berrigan was released in early 1972 and Philip Berrigan was granted parole effective December 20, 1972.

From 1968 through 1971 there were massive antiwar demonstrations, and three more national draft card turn-ins. But the coherence of the antidraft movement diminished. The SDS, SNCC (by 1968 partially incorporated into the Black Panther Party), the NER, and The Resistance all remained in the forefront of the New Left, but their power of effective leadership of the antiwar movement decreased. The Catholic Resistance continued despite the imprisonment of the Berrigan brothers, but it suffered a setback in August 1971. In Camden, New Jersey and Buffalo, New York, in simultaneous raids, the government arrested twenty-eight members of the Catholic Resistance for alleged conspiracy to destroy government records. Several of those arrested were friends with the Berrigan brothers and had been devoted to the same genre of resistance.

In part, the decline of a unified antiwar movement can be attributed to the fact that the war as an issue went beyond the ideological bounds of these organizations. By the summer of 1968 the majority of the American people opposed American involvement in the war in Vietnam. But at the same time, most Americans were not prepared to follow the leadership of SDS, the Black Panther Party, or The Resistance to express their disapproval of the war. Nor were they able to view the war as racist, or imperalist, or genocidal, as did SDS and the Black Panther Party.

Furthermore, the extant political establishment was itself grudgingly incorporating some of the criticism which the New Left had previously monopolized. Senator Eugene McCarthy entered the race for the Democratic presidential nomination in December 1967. His platform and campaign were almost exclusively oriented toward ending the war and revising the Selective Service System. He drew thousands of young followers away from the militant New Left. In February 1968, Senator Robert Kennedy entered the race for the Democratic presidential nomination on a peace and civil rights platform. He, too, attracted youthful partisans who otherwise might have turned to or remained sympathetic with the student New Left organizations against the war.

There is at least one other crucial reason why the New Left failed to hold the national leadership of the antiwar, antidraft movement: the increasing rift between the older New Left organizations (SDS, SNCC) and the rapidly expanding, loosely connected movement created by David Harris, The Resistance. Students for a Democratic Society and SNCC became contemptuous of any sort of pacifism; they advocated militant, violent actions against the United States war effort, including the administration of the Selective Service Act. Following the Democratic National Convention of August 1968, and in the first quarter of 1969, SDS was at the zenith of its power, its activists estimated at between 70,000 and 100,000.[7] It welcomed participation from women's liberation groups, labor groups, and the Black Panther Party. And it became increasingly militant as it became increasingly factionalized. This prompted the NER and the resistance in general (after all, NER was Christian in orientation) to conclude that SDS was turning Maoist and doctrinal, and therefore leaving the mainstream of American radicalism (in fact, this was not true). The Resistance continued to be a single issue organization: military service. But SDS saw military conscription and the war as mere epiphenomena of a larger malady: monopoly capitalism, with all of its material, cultural, and psychological ramifications. And thus SDS and its followers dedicated themselves to political and social revolution; they considered themselves revolutionaries and tended to be intransigent, dogmatic, and at times elitist. This attitude divided them from The Resistance and from the majority of American students, who by 1969 began creating or accepting the leadership of other, less revolutionary, New Left organizations. This development will be more fully discussed in chapter 5.

Notes to Chapter 2

1. Christopher Bone, "The New Left: Its Nature and Future," *Connections* (March, 1971).

2. Cited in Jerome Skolnick, *The Politics of Protest* (New York, 1969), p. 44.

3. Published in *The Guardian,* August 19, 1966. Reprinted by permission of Julius Lester.

4. Michael Ferber and Staughton Lynd, *The Resistance* (New York, 1971), p. 127.

5. Oakland leads the nation in the number of men who do not serve in the Army. From October 1969 to April 1970, 4,463 men were ordered for induction at Oakland. Only 35 percent of them joined, 5 percent refused induction, 7 percent were rejected, and 53 percent never showed up. These statistics come from Ferber and Lynd, *The Resistance,* p. 283.

6. For an account of the trial (there are many, since almost every underground newspaper as well as the *New York Review of Books* covered it in depth), see Daniel Berrigan, *The Trial of the Catonsville Nine* (New York, 1970).

7. *The Guardian,* January 11, 1969.

III

The Emergence of a
Student New Left

Tin soldiers and Nixon's coming
we're finally on our own
this summer I hear the drumming
four dead in Ohio.
Gotta get down to it soldiers are gunning us down,
should have been done long ago
what if you do and find they're dead on the ground
how can you run when you know?
FOUR DEAD IN OHIO*

In the two years from 1965 through 1967, existing New Left groups came to focus their attention more and more on the war in Southeast Asia. Many new groups sprang up and joined the antiwar, peace movement, which seemed to rally all New Left groups. But, as was indicated in the previous chapter, the war in Southeast Asia, while initially uniting the New Left, came later to divide it. Nevertheless, the issue of the war or wars hastened the consummation of two trends within the radicalism of the early 1960's. First, it created a politically self-conscious student class. Students as a class engendered a culture centered around an underground press network and rock 'n' roll music. The culture was resolutely anti-Establishment, antiwar, and fiercely egalitarian. More important, because most students opposed the war by 1967, they found themselves pitted against the majority of the nation, who then supported the war. This lent a definite identity to students which distinguished them *politically* as well as occupationally and socially from the rest of the population. There was no precedent for this in postwar America. What the Civil Rights movement did for a minority of youth in the early

*Ohio, words and music by Neil Young. © 1970 by Cotillion Music and Broken Arrow Music. Used by permission of Atlantic Recording Corporation.

sixties (provided them with a political cause directly relevant to their generation) the Vietnamese war did for a majority of youth in the late sixties and
early seventies. The political identity given to students through the antiwar
movement had crystallized by 1970 in that students recognized themselves as
a political power at odds with the Establishment—be it over foreign policy,
ecology, civil rights, or university administration.

The emergence of a student New Left is evident when one notes the sharp
increase after 1965 in the number of student "left" organizations. Educational Testing Service reports that while in 1965 "student left" organizations
were present on 25 percent of campuses in the United States, by 1968
46 percent of American college and university campuses reported student
"left organizations." [1] In October 1968, SDS, the largest of the student left
organizations, claimed 7,000 dues-paying members and at least 35,000
members in over 400 chapters scattered throughout the country. [2] And as
has been previously noted, in January 1969 *The Guardian* estimated SDS
activists at between 70,000 and 100,000. Even discounting a score of civil
rights organizations, there were four national student left organizations which
had been founded since 1960. [3] Also, there were at least thirteen regional and
national New Left organizations working to end the war. Many of them
supported the New Left political parties such as the Mississippi Freedom
Democratic Party, the Freedom and Peace Party (FPP, New York), and the
Peace and Freedom Party (PFP, California).

Impressive as these statistics may be, by 1970, indeed even as of 1976, the
student left and the counterculture had produced only one broad, unifying
"institution." What had been created was not a political party or an organization, but a medium which remained almost unbesmirched by Establishment
assimilation and repression: the underground press. In addition to such large
pro–New Left periodicals as *The Guardian, The Liberated Guardian, Liberation, Daily World, The Militant, People's World, The San Francisco Phoenix,*
and *Ramparts,* there arose in the late sixties a huge underground press of over
500 newspapers which disseminated the values and philosophy of the
movement. The most significant of these were *Rolling Stone* (circulation
250,000), *Berkeley Barb* (circulation 90,000), *The Tribe* (circulation 60,000),
Los Angeles Free Press (circulation 90,000), *The Seed* (Chicago, circulation
40,000), *Space City* (Houston, 10,000), and *Great Speckled Bird* (largest
weekly in Atlanta, circulation 18,000).

In 1966, most of the underground publications combined into the Underground Press Syndicate (UPS), conceived by Walter Bowart and John Wilcock
(the latter was then editor of the *East Village Other,* which, while once having
a circulation of 60,000, went out of existence in 1973). Wilcock baptized the
UPS as being created "to facilitate the transmission of news, features, and
advertising anti-establishment, avant garde, New Left, youth-oriented periodi-

cals which share common aims and interests. Its members are free to pick up each other's features without remuneration."[4] The UPS was challenged in 1967 by the creation of the Liberation News Service (LNS). The latter is keenly political and militant. These two agencies continue to be regarded by partisans as counterparts to the Associated Press and United Press International.

The underground press is not confined to the United States. It has outlets in Britain, West Germany, Argentina, Colombia, Canada, Belgium, Switzerland, Sweden, Denmark, the Netherlands, Italy, Finland, and Australia, and its circulation has climbed each year. The Young Socialist Alliance (see chapter 5) has its own newspaper, *Young Socialist.* Similarly, the Black Panther Party has its own newspaper, *The Black Panther,* and its own Intercommunal News Service with headquarters in Oakland. Chicanos also have their own underground paper, *La Raz,* which was initially partly supported by the *Los Angeles Free Press.* And finally, there are several underground papers published by GI's. The most important of these seem to be *Fatigue Press* (Fort Hood, Texas) and *Shakedown* (Fort Dix, New Jersey). Using the formula employed by mass magazines (estimating six readers for each magazine), a readership of 9,000,000 is suggested. If one adds the high school, rock culture magazines, the Black Panther paper, the Chicano paper, and the armed forces underground, the estimate is 3,000,000 circulation, or 18,000,000 readers as of 1972.[5] Varied as these papers are, one cannot easily escape the conclusion of journalist Laurence Leamer that "To one degree or another, [underground] papers remain wedded to the vision of youth culture and Movement politics that brought *them* into the world and onto the streets."[6]

The point is that the New Left created a pervasive and strong indigenous press. Its newspapers have a definite political slant and offer readers information about virtually all happenings (including the Patricia Hearst affair in the Spring of 1974) and organizations affiliated with the New Left. It should not be surprising therefore that a United Nations study documented the influence of student "left organizations," including the underground press, and concluded that the student rebellion is the most important political and cultural revolution in the postwar world. The study notes that student organizations in 1968 were instrumental in the paralysis of France, Japan, Mexico, West Germany, Czechoslovakia, Italy, and Brazil, and that many of America's finest universities have been periodically obliged to discontinue services. The report's prognosis is that young people between the ages of twelve and twenty-five, numbering 750 million in 1970, will total one billion by 1980 and that these people will predominate in world affairs by 1980. "World opinion is going to become increasingly the opinion of the world's youth and the generational conflict will assume proportions not previously imagined."[7] In 1973 this conclusion was further refined by the Carnegie Commission on Higher Education, which estimated that despite declining enrollment in American four year colleges, enrollment will still average about 33 percent of the college age population until 1980, and there will be 3 million more students in colleges in 1980 than there were in 1970. And finally, these educated people will be channelled into positions of leadership.[8]

It is little wonder, therefore, that colleges and universities became targets of protest and recruiting grounds for radicals. As an organized political force, the student left first made itself known through the Berkeley Free Speech Movement in 1964. A close examination of the FSM indicates that it had its roots in the Civil Rights movement. CORE began activities in Berkeley and the Bay area in 1963 and sought equal employment opportunities for minorities. There were pickets, sit-ins, selective buying, and so on. After the Mississippi summer of 1964, in which some Berkeley people participated, the Civil Rights movement gained support on campus. Berkeley President Clark Kerr announced that the campus could not be used as a base from which to organize, publicize, or collect monies for civil rights political activities. This disappointed students planning a picket of the *Oakland Tribune,* then published by the conservative ex-senator William Knowland. It looked like Oakland was what the more militant civil rights writers said it was: a bastion of white supremacy which would step upon anything that challenged it. Even the most naive student was forced to give the civil rights exponents a second look when the great and powerful University of California forbade political dialogue on a campus which bordered upon one of the most sordid of America's black ghettoes. The issue as formulated by the students was the right of free speech on a campus where that right was presumably sacrosanct. Many groups therefore joined to form what became known as the Berkeley Free Speech Movement.

The FSM had the support of the Young Democrats, the Young Republicans, and socialist youth groups, but was predominantly led by two civil rights groups: CORE and the University Friends of SNCC. The movement took the form of sit-ins in December 1964—sit-ins until such time as President Kerr would allow "free speech" and drop disciplinary action against the leaders of the FSM. It soon escalated into a critique of the university itself— as a knowledge factory, a multiversity serving the research and development demands of corporations and the government, but not the students or the community. The criticism, led by Mario Savio, who had worked with SNCC during the Mississippi Summer Project, soon crystallized into an attempt to shut down the university. He led students to occupy the administration building and was the chief spokesman for the FSM.

A "free university" was founded and ultimately the students got their demands. But few people realized that the Berkeley FSM was to be the historical archetype of student protests in the 1960's or that the addition of the war (draft) would so exacerbate the situation that by 1968-69 student protest and demonstration on campuses would be the rule instead of the exception. Few perceived also that the pervasive disaffection of students from the University of California at Berkeley would spread to become a national phenomenon. Berkeley's undergraduate dropout rate was nearly 50 percent. And finally, few realized that what was eventually exhumed at Berkeley about the nature of a large public university would be found to be true of many public universities as well as most of the nation's great private universities and colleges: that the federal government has increasingly come to finance higher education and use it for manpower, research, and development. Quite expectedly, higher education has become research oriented, and graduate and professional services have taken priority over undergraduate instruction and even scholarship. "The national results of educational industrialization are the rise of publicly subsidized research-oriented universities, the decline of liberal arts colleges (which are starved for funds), and the appearance of factory-like community colleges to undertake routine manpower functions."[9]

After the FSM, student protests on the campuses became widespread when it was revealed that the CIA subsidized and for all intents and purposes controlled the National Student Association as well as many university research projects.[10] Demonstrations occurred at the Universities of Wisconsin and Chicago in May of 1966 against recruitment on campuses by the military and the CIA. In August 1966, SDS formulated its strategy of "student power" at its annual convention at Clear Lake, Iowa. That autumn it helped to organize demonstrations against military installations on campuses.

Similarly, the antimilitary, antiwar tenets of SNCC's black power philosophy articulated by Stokely Carmichael spread to black colleges and high schools. In March 1967 a Black Power Committee appeared at Howard University and initiated a demonstration against Selective Service recruitment on campus and against a visit by the head of the Selective Service System, General Lewis B. Hershey. When university officials attempted to discipline the leaders of the demonstration, the Black Power Committee stopped the hearing. At a black university or college in 1967, such resistance to administrative authority was literally unheard of and unthinkable. Howard University immediately expelled sixteen students and five faculty members who supported the Black Power Committee. But student resistance continued into the spring, when a boycott of classes was endorsed not only by the Black Power Committee, but even by the student government and the fraternities. The dispute between students and administration raged into the next year. After occupying the administration building, students were granted control of student funds, an independent newspaper, and an end to compulsory

ROTC. The latter point was of particular importance to blacks at Howard because the very name of the university reflects the influence of the military: the university was named after the Union general, O. O. Howard. And finally students were granted amnesty, hence the demand thereafter for amnesty by other protesting students at other universities and colleges.

In the winter and spring of 1967 large student demonstrations occurred at the University of California at Berkeley. These were directed against the recruitment on campus for the Marines, the CIA, and the Dow Chemical Company, manufacturers of napalm. There was fighting between police and demonstrators, resulting in many arrests. Demonstrations increased under the national leadership of the Spring Mobilization Against the War. Over 200,000 marched in New York City and about 65,000 in San Francisco. These demonstrators were not only students but housewives, executives, and working men. In New York's Central Park, several hundred draft cards were ceremoniously burned.

While the press acknowledged the magnitude of the marches, no official comment came from the White House. Comment ("shock and dismay") did come, however, during the explosive summer of 1967 when riots occurred in Newark,[11] Detroit, and other northern cities. During these the National Guard and police killed over eighty persons, almost all of them black. Although it is still generally believed the riots were "racial" (poor blacks against rich white capitalists), this was not the case—at least not in Detroit. Wayne State University psychologists interviewed over 400 persons arrested during the Detroit riot and discovered that 70 percent of the rioters had jobs averaging $115 weekly, and were unmarried. The interviewers concluded, "This was not a poverty riot, this was a protest riot."[12]

What was being protested was the same thing that engendered the student-led antiwar protests: the obsolescence of the cultural values and institutions that implemented policies based upon scarcity: racism, which guaranteed the white man a job, and imperialism, which guaranteed American economic hegemony in the world. Both policies were irrelevant to the reality of young people in the late 1960's and are not relevant in the 1970's, for they prevent the realization of a less repressed, more humane, generous, spontaneous life style. Institutionalized racism and military conscription are, of course, great impediments to the realization of such a life style. Consequently, there is great bitterness on the part of millions of blacks and whites, especially younger ones.

In 1968, the student left grew enormously, partly in response to the assassinations of two leaders sympathetic to the movement, Dr. Martin Luther King, Jr. and Senator Robert F. Kennedy. But the student left grew also because President Johnson announced in March that he would not seek reelection. This gave hope to many on the left who saw Johnson as the chief obstacle to change because of his resolute refusal to end the war in Vietnam. As might be expected, therefore, the zenith of student power in the 1960's came during March, April, and May of 1968. Columbia University was closed by students protesting the complicity of the university with the CIA and large corporations, as well as its unsatisfactory relations with the neighboring community of Harlem. Students held five buildings for a week and a dean for twenty-six hours. Almost simultaneously, riots broke out in Germany, France, and Italy. A temporary alliance between students and workers in Paris nearly toppled the French government by a general strike. Battles raged in the French capital for weeks. This in turn set off student demonstrations of solidarity for the French students and workers. Most impressive of these was in Berkeley, where fighting raged between police and students for four days. In later months General de Gaulle lost his majority in the French Assembly and resigned.

Probably more significant than the Berkeley street fighting was the outcome of the student New Left strikes in France. Their movement succeeded in at least limiting the oppressive, centralized, standardized, academic education in liberal arts which had been established by Louis XIV, eliminated during the Jacobin period by David, but later revived during the Napoleonic era. Anyone who has gone through this archaic system in France or read Jules Valles's description of it in the mid-nineteenth century would realize what an achievement the abolition of this system is. André Malraux, de Gaulle's minister of Culture, was obliged to announce that the École des Beaux-Arts itself would be decentralized and that nontraditional theories of architecture and design—that is, Japanese, Finnish, and American—would be taught. The École des Beaux-Arts, long the symbol of French academic insularity and establishment nationalism, was at last liberated in the eyes of thousands of European university students. Yet still, in the 1970's, with the exception of École des Beaux-Arts, the French student revolt has accomplished little of a concrete nature.

In the eyes of some, however, the student New Left was compromised when the Soviet Union and other Warsaw pact nations invaded Czechoslovakia in August 1968. In the United States, however, the result was the ostracizing of many of the Communist and Progressive Labor Party elements. Furthermore, it is necessary to point out that even before the impact of the Czechoslovakian invasion upon the New Left could be estimated, the catastrophe of the Democratic National Convention occurred. Millions of Americans and Europeans watched television as Chicago riot police beat demonstrators, bystanders, observers, and pressmen. Chicago's Loop area came under virtual siege by the National Guard and the police. Hundreds were beaten by police, hundreds arrested, and hundreds given summary trials. Within hours, confrontations again occurred in Berkeley between police and demonstrators expressing solidarity with Chicago's demonstrators.

The government moved rapidly to prosecute what it took to be the leaders of the Chicago demonstrators. Indicted for conspiracy and crossing state lines to incite riot were Tom Hayden of SDS; Jerry Rubin and Abbie Hoffman, founders of the Youth International Party (Yippies); Rennie Davis and David Dellinger, two incorrigible radical pacifists; John Froines, professor of chemistry at the University of Oregon; Lee Weiner, teaching assistant in sociology at Northwestern University; and Bobby Seale, cofounder of the Black Panther Party. These men became known as "The Chicago Eight."

The trial cost the government $2,000,000 and lasted five months. Seale, after being chained and gagged in the courtroom, was released after a mistrial was declared. He became immortalized in the song "Chicago" by Graham Nash, which told of his courage before the courtroom brutalities to which he was subjected. Froines and Weiner were acquitted on February 18, 1970. The others were convicted of crossing state lines to incite riots. They were sentenced to five years in prison and were fined $5,000 each by Judge Julius Hoffman. Finally, on November 22, 1972, they were acquitted by three Judges of the U.S. Circuit Court of Appeals. The judges ruled that the defendants' constitutional rights had been violated during their trial before Judge Hoffman.[13]

The final outcome of the trial of the Chicago Eight was viewed by radicals and many liberals as a victory for the New Left and civil rights. But the victory, while perhaps lending legitimacy to the New Left and to student-faculty activism, was at least partly vitiated by the stunning and bitter defeat of the movement at San Francisco State College. Here occurred the longest, most sustained student protest in the history of American colleges. In the autumn of 1968 a black instructor who was a member of the Black Panther Party was suspended. This set off four months of boycotts, minor riots, arsons, and pickets. At issue was the admissions policy of San Francisco State College and the attempt by blacks and other minorities to set up an ethnic studies program. A Third World Liberation Front, demanding open admission and ethnic studies, was set up after the suspension of the black instructor. The Front argued that since 54 percent of San Francisco's high school enrollment was nonwhite, at least 25 percent of the student body at San Francisco State College should be nonwhite. They pointed out that only 10 percent of the student population at the college was nonwhite and they charged discrimination in admission. Blacks particularly were affected, since admission of blacks to the college had dropped from 10 percent in the 1950's to about 4 percent in 1969.[14]

The general question was whether the college should have a definite responsibility of service to the community—whether a state college is so obliged. The American Federation of Teachers in the locality voted to support the student strike. They in turn were endorsed by the San Francisco Labor Council of the AFL-CIO. The Black Panther Party supported the strike, as did the Third World Liberation Front. In 1969, after the college had been paralyzed for months, its president, Dr. S. I. Hayakawa, signed an agreement with the Third World Liberation Front promising the creation of an ethnic studies program. But, in effect, he broke the agreement by firing Nathan Hare, who was the choice of the TWLF to direct the school of ethnic studies and to teach black studies. (Hare had been involved in the Black Power Committee at Howard University). This provoked a denunciation by Tom Hayden, who put the episode in a larger perspective of the New Left vis-à-vis the Establishment.

> Richard Nixon and Hayakawa ... are only saying that we have to throw out the protestors before we can deal with protest. They're saying the chief impediment to reform is the reformer! They're saying there should be or even *is* a black-studies program at San Francisco State, and it could get underway if only Nathan Hare would leave! If Hare, and Varnado, and Alvarado, and George Murray could be removed, they would go ahead with Third World studies.[15]

Hayakawa prevailed and got rid of Hare, and ultimately the student-faculty alliance gained none of their demands, although in 1970 a U.S. District Court of Appeals restrained Hayakawa from failing to pay striking faculty members and ruled in favor of Hare.

Despite the setback at San Francisco State College and the election of "law and order" Republican Richard Nixon as president in November 1968, student militance began almost the day of his inauguration. In January 1969 students, coordinated by a committee of five hundred, occupied the University of Chicago's administration building for fifteen days. The issue was the nonretention of a female sociology professor who "confessed" to being a Marxist and a women's liberation activist. Marlene Dixon, the sociologist, was offered an additional one year contract, but chose not to remain at the University of Chicago. Among those supporting her were radical historian Staughton Lynd and SDS organizer and University of Chicago sociologist Richard Flacks. The former has been almost entirely driven out of his profession. In the spring of 1969, the latter was nearly bludgeoned to death in his office above the library on the campus of the University of Chicago. The assailant was not apprehended. The University of Chicago expelled 42 students and suspended 181 others for their roles in the occupation and strike. As of 1976, that is a record for expulsions and suspensions from a white university. In terms of arrests, however, the record for all universities is held by Mississippi Valley State College. In May 1970, the college ordered 889 students arrested; they were all black students.

It was also in the spring of 1969 that students and street people (freaks, hippies) united in resistance to the University of California at Berkeley and to the California National Guard. There is not room here to describe adequately the infamous People's Park incident of May 1969. Suffice it to say that 200 policemen were summoned by the administration of the University of California to clear 50 street people from an area about half the size of a football field (the People's Park). These people had made the area a park for themselves and for their children. The students and citizens of Berkeley responded to the administration's order to evacuate by a march and rally of 3,000 in support of the People's Park. Six hundred police met them at the site of the People's Park, killed one student on a roof top, and blinded another. California Governor Reagan sent 2,000 guardsmen with fixed bayonets—they remained ten days occupying the campus. When groups of students assembled and denounced them, they countered by using helicopters to spray gas down upon the people. Estimates of injury to civilians vary from 30 to 1,000. Faculty turned against the occupation and demanded the removal of troops. Chancellor Heyns announced on TV that "we haven't stopped the rational process." But the People's Park was the great symbol of feeling over rationality or ownership. That the university owned the land was without question. But it had allowed people to use the land, and even the chancellor's own Advisory Committee on Housing and Environment had recommended that it be a community park. A student referendum showed 85 percent in favor of the People's Park. Still, the University of California refused to allow the people the land area and eventually succeeded in confiscating it.

Despite the fact that Berkeley's street people lost their park and the students gained nothing by their resistance to armed force, radical activism on the campuses did not decline during the summer of 1969. Indeed, it witnessed the creation of national organizations to prepare for antiwar demonstrations in the autumn. The result was the famous October 15, 1969 antiwar moratorium, which brought the largest number of demonstrators in the nation's history into the streets of American cities. President Nixon, even before the moratorium, indicated that he would not be influenced by it. This produced an intense bitterness in the ranks of the New Left and provoked criticism from the press. Although the president proposed and implemented a reduction of American troops in Vietnam, there arose a feeling of profound distrust of him by antiwar partisans.

The distrust was exacerbated with the ostentatious extension of the war into Cambodia in May of 1970. This, combined with the killing by the Ohio National Guard of four students at an antiwar rally at Kent State University and the killing of two more students at Jackson State College by Mississippi state militiamen, set off the first and largest national student strike in American history. (It also inspired the song "Ohio," by Neil Young, which sets off this chapter.) Students closed over 300 colleges and universities, initiated strikes and demonstrations on 760 campuses, and damaged at least 30 ROTC installations. But in so doing, twelve students were wounded by authorities at the State University of New York at Buffalo, and nine students received bayonet wounds at the hands of the National Guard on the campus of the University of New Mexico at Albuquerque.[16]

The eagerly awaited FBI report about the Kent State incident was published in November 1970. It stated that none of the students killed or wounded were in any way involved in radical activities or the protest demonstration itself. Further, the report found no substance to the national guardsmen's claim that their lives were endangered. Instead, the report established probable cause for filing criminal charges against some of the guardsmen. (Six of the guardsmen testified they did not believe their lives were in jeopardy.) Indeed, the only weapon found on any student present at the affair was a pistol carried by an undercover agent of the campus police.

Despite the FBI report, the Ohio Grand Jury indicted twenty-five students, one of whom was the student body president and an ROTC cadet. The general indictment was "second degree riot," which the grand jury defined as "being present in a riot or other tumultuous situation." To add insult to injury in the eyes of the students, not a single national guardsman was indicted. Finally, after an investigation by the Justice Department, former attorney general Mitchell concluded in August 1971 that no guardsman *would* be indicted and that the Justice Department would take no action regarding the Kent State killings.[17] Following the publication of the president's commissioned report on Kent State and Jackson State (*Campus Unrest*) in 1972, 10,338 Kent State students, as well as the president of Kent State University, Dr. Olds, petitioned President Nixon to convene a Federal Grand Jury to investigate the actions of the National Guard and to indict the guardsmen responsible for the killings. Over 40,000 other students and faculty from the entire country also petitioned the president for this purpose. The White House refused to reply, except to say in December 1972 that the petitions were received. This was particularly exasperating to students and radicals in general, for while the government would not convene a Federal Grand Jury upon their request, it had by January 1973 convened over twenty Federal Grand Juries to prosecute radicals, including leaders of the Vietnam Veterans Against the War who demonstrated against Mr. Nixon in August 1972 at the Republican National Convention in Miami. Not until the Watergate scandal thickened in the autumn of 1973 and the Nixon administration had gone through four attorneys general was a Federal Grand Jury finally empaneled, on December 18, 1973, to investigate the Kent State episode. The result was inconclusive.

Despite the bitterness of thousands of students toward the Nixon administration after Kent State and Jackson State, student radicalism was less noticeable in 1971–72. In part, this was due to the disintegration of SDS (this will be examined in chapter 5). But it was also attributable to the pervasive feeling among students and New Leftists that massive peaceful demonstrations, passive resistance or even civil disobedience were tactics of almost no efficacy against a conservative second Nixon administration and a weary American public. Accordingly, thousands of youth, mostly high school and college students, enrolled in an attempt to bring about the Democratic presidential nomination of Senator George McGovern. The latter, aside from the stalwart Senator Wayne Morse and the deceased Senator Ernest Gruening, had been the only politician of national importance who had loudly and consistently, and for many years, called for an immediate end to American involvement in the war in Southeast Asia. Hard core New Leftists such as Tom Hayden refused to cooperate with the Democratic Party, but the masses of students who once might have accepted the leadership of Hayden, Hoffman, Rubin, and others of the early New Left chose to try their luck at capturing the Democratic Party with George McGovern as their steed.

With the threat of widespread student militance apparently diminished, President Nixon concluded that a firm response to the North Vietnamese offensive of the spring of 1972 would provoke minimal domestic dissent. Hence he ordered bombing of military targets in and around Hanoi and Haiphong during April 1972. This provoked student demonstrations all over the country—as well as in Europe—but they were not of the virulence of 1970. Approximately 100 colleges and universities were compelled to close for a day. The most spectacular protests came from students at the University of Maryland and Stanford University. Maryland Governor Marvin Mandel ordered the National Guard to the University of Maryland to enforce a curfew after students disrupted traffic on U.S. Route 1 for three days and two thousand students fought police and broke university windows. In Palo Alto, police arrested 210 persons, some of them Stanford students, after they "trashed" areas along El Camino Real. But the student protests subsided, and they watched with fascination as the Vietcong continued to win their offensive despite American bombing and naval bombardment. In May, the Vietcong captured Quangtri, a provincial capital, besieged another provincial capital, An Loc, and had virtually severed ground routes to Saigon. President Nixon clandestinely ordered four squadrons of F-4 fighter-bombers to Indochina—bringing the total to 1,000. He also ordered the aircraft carrier *Saratoga* to join the Seventh Fleet off the coast of North Vietnam—bringing a total of six carriers and about 50,000 men stationed in the Gulf of Tonkin.

While these actions were reported immediately in the underground press, it was not until May 15 that the establishment press reported them. No significant student protests were provoked.

The student left, although busy with the McGovern campaign, made itself noticed the next week when President Nixon ordered the mining of Haiphong harbor and six other ports and the bombing of dykes in North Vietnam. Marches were mobilized in European capitals and many American universities were disrupted. In Santa Barbara, California, students attacked the Bank of America and blocked the airport. In Gainesville, Florida, they jammed a highway. In New Brunswick they stopped a train. And at the University of New Mexico, fourteen students were wounded by police shotgun fire; the university president declared a state of emergency. In Madison, Wisconsin, students went on a three day arson rampage, injuring three policemen who sought to arrest them. As might be expected, Berkeley erupted, with students attempting to tear up the asphalt which was laid over the People's Park in 1969. They were dispersed with tear gas, but 2,000 of them stormed the City Council to demand that the city of Berkeley sign a separate peace treaty with North Vietnam. These actions were of no avail in terms of influencing the president. Indeed, they partook of the protest of inefficacy. Hence the president of Amherst College, one of 475 persons arrested for demonstrating at Westover Air Force Base, announced: "What I protest is that there is no way to protest. I speak out of frustration and despair. I do not think words will change the minds of men in power who make these decisions."

And it was perhaps this lack of a way to protest, combined with the humiliating defeat of Senator McGovern for the presidency (subsequently in part attributed to President Nixon's Committee for the Re-election of the President), that accounted for the diminished activism of students when, on November 16, 1972, two students were shot and killed at Southern University in Baton Rouge by Louisiana sheriff's deputies and state troopers. Certainly, the fact that these students were black and male at an overwhelmingly black university tended to lessen the amount of media coverage of the incident. Nevertheless, in the underground press and in the *Black Panther* it was pointed out that this incident occurred at the largest black university in America and that it capped off a struggle by black students to influence the policies of their own black administrators. Black students, supported by the Black Panther Party, were calling for the resignation of the president of Southern University and the resignation of the dean at Southern University's New Orleans campus. The November sixteenth killings climaxed days of sit-ins, boycotts, and marches against the administrations of both schools. The predawn arrest of four student leaders, one female and three male, occasioned the occupation of the administration building. The subsequent clearing of the building by authorities upon the request of the president of Southern

University resulted in the violence. Governor Edwards summoned the National Guard and closed the university until after Thanksgiving. The only immediate student reprisal was the burning of two buildings, causing over $200,000 damage the afternoon of November sixteenth. Scattered student strikes occurred across the nation and memorial services were held at many universities, but there were no mass demonstrations and closings of institutions of higher learning as there had been after the Kent State and Jackson State killings. The cohesiveness of the student movement seemed at least temporarily in abeyance.

Though the "unfinished business" of Kent State brought the police again, in July 1977, carting off "demonstrators," the 1977 demonstrators were not exclusively a student movement.

Notes to Chapter 3

1. Richard Peterson, *The Scope of Organized Student Protest in 1967–1968* (Princeton, 1968).

2. Jerome Skolnick, *The Politics of Protest* (New York, 1969), p. 89.

3. Movement for a Democratic Society (MDS), Northern Student Movement (NSM), Southern Student Organizing Committee (SSOC), and SDS.

4. *East Village Other,* July 1966.

5. Laurence Leamer, *The Paper Revolutionaries* (New York, 1972), p. 15.

6. Ibid., p. 53.

7. Quoted in the *New York Times,* February 16, 1968.

8. Carnegie Commission on Higher Education, *Newsletter,* September 23, 1973.

9. Michael Miles, *The Radical Probe* (New York, 1971), p. 95.

10. Tom Hayden has revealed how SDS and SNCC students fought against the CIA in the National Student Association and finally quit the organization when it became clear that they would never be able to rid it of CIA control. "Ten Years from Port Huron," *Rolling Stone,* October 26, 1972.

11. For a really classic account of the Newark riot by a Newark dweller, see ibid.

12. *Newsweek,* March 11, 1968.

13. In December 1973, all of the Chicago defendants except Dellinger, Rubin, and Hoffman, were cleared of contempt charges pending from the original trial.

14. Miles, *Radical Probe,* p. 241.

15. Tom Hayden, "The Battle for Survival," in *The Conspiracy,* eds. Peter and Deborah Babcox and Bob Abel (New York, 1969), p. 167. Reprinted by permission of Dell Publishing Company, Inc.

16. The draft resistance movement was suddenly rejuvenated with the formation of Union for Draft Opposition (UNDO). During the two weeks immediately following Kent State and Jackson State, 10,000 draft cards and pledges to refuse induction were sent in nationally. Union for Draft Opposition started at Princeton University and spread rapidly on the East and West Coasts. As of November 1970, it was estimated that 35,000 young men had returned their draft cards or taken the pledge to refuse induction. See David McReynolds, "Striking the Draft," *War Resisters League News* (November–December, 1970).

17. There are two excellent accounts of Kent State. I. F. Stone's *The Killings at Kent State* (New York, 1971) includes the report by the Justice Department and the Ohio Grand Jury report. *The Report of the President's Commission on Campus Unrest* (New York, 1972) also deals in depth with the Jackson State killings.

IV

The Black Panther Party

If a man does not have knowledge of himself and his position in society and the world, then he has little chance to relate to anything else.
—Point 5, Black Panther party program

In the radicalism of the early sixties, a second trend whose development the war assisted was indigenous black radicalism. This was evident in Stokely Carmichael's leadership of SNCC beginning in May 1966. But by 1967 it came to be exemplified in the popularity, power, and pride inculcated by the Black Panther party (BPP). It became clear to most civil rights workers who moved with Dr. Martin Luther King, Jr. to Chicago in the spring of 1966 that the Civil Rights movement in the northern cities could not remain as it was in the South: a petition to the white power structure for juridical equality. Chicago's South Side and West Side ghettoes already had entrenched black power structures. Black leaders in these areas were not prepared to allow white radicals to usurp their power bases, even if the whites sincerely followed Dr. King's stratagems for the realization of black civil liberties. Constant police harassment of blacks could not be curbed effectively by politically powerless white rights workers, no matter how strenuously they tried. Thus, it is understandable that from Oakland, California (considered by rights workers to be the Chicago of the West), came the Black Panther party, an independent black radical organization.

The Black Panther party has undergone many changes, both in personnel and in political philosophy. (Even its name has been changed: it was originally called the Black Panther Party for Self-Defense.) The party was organized in October 1966 by Huey Newton (age 24) and Bobby Seale (age 30) the latter as chairman, the former as minister of defense. Newton and Seale became close friends in the early 1960's while attending Merritt Junior College in Oakland. They decided to form the party when they became disappointed with the efficacy of the Afro-American Association at the college. They named the party after the black panther in part to show the continuity of the black struggle for freedom and equal rights in white America. For the black panther was the emblem of the Lowndes County Freedom party organized in 1965-66 through the efforts of Stokely Carmichael. But they chose the name also because the black panther is reputed never to make an unprovoked attack, but to defend itself ferociously when attacked. In addition, the black panther precisely symbolized one of the basic teachings of Malcolm X and Frantz Fanon: self-defense in the face of police brutality.[1] It was the philosophy of these two black radicals that had the most profound effect upon Newton and Seale in the autumn of 1966. Later, they steeped themselves in the writings of Marx, Lenin, Mao, Ho Chi Minh, and Che Guevara.

The party was centered around a 10-point platform and program drafted by Newton and Seale in October 1966. (This platform was reendorsed and sent out again on March 29, 1972). In addition to stressing the defense of black people, the platform calls for black control of black communities, education, the right of jury trial for members of the black community, a demand for full employment, decent housing, and ample food for black people. By mid-1967 the party had its own newspaper, *The Black Panther,* and seventy-five members in Oakland, including Eldridge Cleaver and his wife Kathleen. Cleaver, a black radical, ex-Muslim and ex-convict, became minister of information. His wife became communication secretary of the party. By April 1973 the party claimed twenty-eight branches nationally and over 5,000 members.[2]

The party attracted immediate attention in Oakland, as armed Panthers trailed police cars and carefully observed their conduct in arrests and citations. The black community had never seen such boldness, and Newton and Seale became new black heroes. On May 2, 1967, the California state legislature began consideration of a bill to prevent the Panthers from carrying guns. Bobby Seale and thirty party members went to the legislature to protest that the proposal was a violation of the Second Amendment. All of them were arrested for disturbing the peace. Seale and several others were obliged to serve six-month sentences. But as Seale has pointed out, this was wise strategy, for it brought the party national attention. The party was thereafter able to set up offices in Los Angeles, Detroit, and New York.

National attention was again focused upon the BPP on October 28, 1967, when Huey Newton was arrested and charged with murder, assault, and kidnapping. This grew out of an episode in which one policeman was killed, another wounded, and Newton shot in the stomach. Newton insisted he had not done the shooting, that he had no gun at the time, and that he was unconscious when the officer was killed. Newton's trial lasted till mid-July of

1968, when he was convicted of voluntary manslaughter. He served until August 1970, when he was released after his conviction was overturned by an appellate court and a new trial was ordered. Finally, after a third trial, Newton was acquitted in December 1971. The trials attracted international attention because Newton was defended by the brilliant attorney Charles Garry, who raised touchy issues involved in the case: race, civil liberties, and imprisonment for political rather than criminal reasons.

While Newton was awaiting his first trial, two significant developments influenced the party. One was the short-lived merger with SNCC. The more militant officers of SNCC were given positions in the BPP. Stokely Carmichael, who delivered a speech at the rally, became prime minister, and James Foreman and H. Rap Brown were given positions. The influence of Carmichael upon the Panthers at this juncture is clear when one notices that he refused to accept a position in the BPP unless his title would refer to Africa. Accordingly, his official title was Prime Minister of the Black Panther Party of Colonized Afro-America.

But from the beginning the assimilation of SNCC into the Panthers was difficult. Many members of SNCC refused to accept it, and Julius Lester of SNCC wrote articles against the merger. In addition, Carmichael continued his insistence that black liberation could only come through united black fronts and that coalitions with white radicals ought to be avoided at all costs. He reiterated the view he held when he took over SNCC in May 1966. That whites inevitably seek to control all groups with which they work and that they would do so if the Panthers were to join with them at any point. Nevertheless, some SNCC veterans became active in the Panther party, and SNCC's effectiveness as a civil rights organization gradually diminished.

Following Carmichael's triumphant tour of Africa and his marriage to singer Miriam Makeba, the merger became extremely strained. Finally, from Guinea in July 1969 he resigned from the BPP, criticizing it for its dogmatism, its flirtation with white radical groups, and its failure to advocate cultural nationalism. Eldridge Cleaver, in an "Open Letter to Stokely Carmichael" published in *Ramparts* (September 1969), rebuked Carmichael and welcomed his resignation. Cleaver and the Panther party concluded that Stokely Carmichael, brilliant and impressive though he may have been, could also be too frightened of white people, too self-righteous, chauvinistic, and at times racist. Carmichael for his part remained virtually silent until June 1972. Then, in an interview, he reiterated much the same position he held in 1968: that black people in America are Africans, will never attain cultural and political satisfaction in the United States, and that their best strategy is to emigrate to Africa. As of 1976, this remains Carmichael's point of view, although he is far more of a Marxist than he was before he went to Africa.

Carmichael's defection from the BPP had little effect upon it, for during the short merger the party had gained a larger following because of a wave of violent confrontations with police. Bobby Seale, in February 1968, was arrested and charged with conspiring to commit murder. In June 1971, a judge dropped the case on the grounds that Seale could not receive an unbiased trial. But other members were not so lucky. On April 6, 1968, police surrounded a Panther meeting and, in an ensuing gun battle, one Panther was killed (Bobby Hutton) and Cleaver was wounded and arrested. David Hilliard, Chief of Staff of the BPP, was also arrested. Hilliard's appeal for parole or bail, made to the California Adult Parole Authority on December 12, 1972, was rejected. A new hearing for Hilliard was postponed until 1974. In 1976, Hilliard was released on parole. Earlier, Cleaver, also released on parole, became the 1968 presidential candidate of the Peace and Freedom party, a white radical party which formed a temporary alliance with the BPP. Cleaver, however, was suddenly ordered back to jail in the autumn of 1968, and he fled to Algeria on November 24, 1968.

Police repression against the Panthers continued with raids on Black Panther party headquarters in Los Angeles (December 8, 1969) and Chicago (December 4, 1969). In the latter raid, Fred Hampton, chairman of the Illinois BPP, was murdered along with fellow Panther Mark Clark. The Cook County Grand Jury later declared false the police argument that the Panthers fired first. Not till September 1971 was any legal action taken against the police involved.

As raids became more frequent, the party began to publicize the pattern of police activities against them. They listed twenty-eight Panthers killed between December 1967 and December 1969, and they claimed the government was deliberately attempting to destroy their leadership.[3] In addition, between May 1967 and December 1969, charges against eighty-seven Panthers were dropped because the authorities failed to prove their allegations. The Panthers' contention that the government was conspiring to destroy them was strengthened in February 1970, when Seattle Mayor Wes Uhlman disclosed that he refused a federal request that he be party to a raid on Black Panther headquarters. By June 1973, when it was revealed that the Nixon administration had sought FBI assistance in a huge federal plan to undermine all radical groups, the Panthers' contention emerged as truth.

But police action against the Black Panther party helped them gain the support of the Peace and Freedom party. It also brought the Panthers and SDS into an uneasy working alliance. Students for a Democratic Society was also subject to police harassment. Indeed, their Chicago headquarters was all but destroyed when police and firemen axed their way into it in 1969. In 1968 and 1969 officials of the BPP spoke more often at SDS meetings and participated more in its plenary sessions. When the BPP asked the assistance of SDS in the defense committees for Cleaver and Newton, support was given. Students for a Democratic Society set out its official position at its national council meeting in Austin, Texas, on March 30, 1969. "SDS declares its support for the Black Panther Party and their essentially correct program for the liberation of the black colony;—its commitment to defend the BPP and the black colony against the vicious attacks of the racist pig power structure." And SDS supported the defense of Bobby Seale when he was tried by Judge Julius Hoffman along with white radicals indicted for conspiracy during the Democratic National Convention of August 1968.

By 1970 the efficacy of SDS as a national organization was hard to deter-mine because it had gone underground. Nevertheless, some of its members or ex-members were active in the defense committees for black Marxist Angela Davis. Davis was indicted for murder in connection with the attempted escape of black prisoners in San Rafael, California, in the summer of 1970. A judge, as well as prisoners Jonathan Jackson, William Christmas, and James McClain, was killed in the attempt. The appeal of Angela Davis for the majority faction of SDS, the Weatherman, was her somewhat doctrinaire Marxism and her deep knowledge of the philosophy of Herbert Marcuse, her teacher. That particular brand of Marxism remains closely akin to the political posture of the Weatherman (now called Weatherpeople). Indeed, when Angela Davis was found not guilty by an all white jury in June 1972, both the Weatherman and the Black Panther party were jubilant. Their jubilation dimmed shortly thereafter, however, when it became obvious that Davis, though sympathetic to the goals of the BPP, preferred to work with the Communist party of the United States. Neither the BPP nor Weatherman have been able to work with the CPUSA; in fact, both have written small pieces against it.

The Black Panther party is best known for its many violent confrontations with law enforcement agencies (confrontations have continued in the 1970's: police ransacked the Atlanta Black Panther party headquarters and arrested eight party members on November 9, 1972). And it is generally considered by the public—and probably by most white radicals—to be the most powerful American New Left organization in the mid-1970's, although it is too early to estimate the power of the Symbionese Liberation Army (SLA) or the George Jackson Brigade. But the importance of the BPP is not that it will do armed battle with police. Rather, its importance is that it has developed a political philosophy which it is successfully putting into practice. That philosophy has gone through several phases and is still developing. So far there seem to have been at least three stages of philosophical development: (1) a philosophy of liberation primarily formulated by Eldridge Cleaver, but descended from Malcolm X and Frantz Fanon; (2) a version of international socialism derived essentially from Marx, Lenin, and Mao; and (3) a philosophy of "revolu-tionary intercommunalism" distilled and so named by Huey Newton. In

1974, the party reaffirmed its philosophy of "revolutionary intercommunalism," but as Newton himself has pointed out, there are vestiges of its previous philosophical emphases, and its 10-point program remains the same as when formulated in 1966.

Initially, the BPP viewed blacks in America as a "colony" and hence the emphasis was upon the liberation of the "colony." According to Cleaver, and documented in *Seize the Time* (1970), Bobby Seale's history of the early BPP, blacks are a colony, juridically and socially. That is, they are and always have been a subject people, legally, politically, and psychologically—living within the geographical confines of the United States as the mother country. Liberation means juridical, political, and psychological independence and equality of the colonized people vis-à-vis the mother country. Such independence cannot be *given* by the mother country to its colony any more than legally declaring a person an adult at age 18 can give him or her the self-confidence, savoir faire, and sense of identity of a person of fifty. Blacks must achieve for themselves such independence, such identity, such self-confidence as to say, "That is what I am, this is what I can do, this is my life, and this is how life works."

That there are white radicals and liberals who sincerely want blacks to achieve this has never been denied by the BPP. (Bobby Seale took pains to make it clear that the BPP is not racist.) Nor do the Panthers deny the legitimacy of white radicalism. But in the early philosophy of the BPP, its leaders argued that the radicalism of the late 1960's and 1970's was and is of a dual nature. "We feel," said Eldridge Cleaver, 'that there are two things happening in this country. You have a black colony and you have a white mother country and you have two different sets of political dynamics involved in these two relationships. What's called for in the mother country is a revolution and there's a black liberation called for in the black colony."[4] The Panthers saw correctly that white radicals are in revolt against their own system of government, which is intertwined with an exploitive economic and social order. Primarily, their revolution must be political they will have to alter the structure of the government and most institutions of power if they are to eliminate the economic and social exploitation inherent in the system.

But the Panthers also understood that, while they might assist in such a revolution, they would be altering a system they could never hope to control: the system of the mother country. It is therefore of first priority that blacks *create their own system.* That means liberating themselves from the present system of the mother country. This is the program of the BPP—black control of predominantly black communities. Hence Bobby Seale ran for mayor of Oakland in May 1973. The Panthers want to experiment with their own system, which would lean toward socialism if the BPP program were realized. Their socialist projects are not new: free breakfasts for children, community control of police, free clothing, free legal aid, cooperative markets, free busing to and from prisons for prisoner visitation, revolutionary trade unions, community employment programs, community schools from kindergarten through high school, and so on. What *is* new about these programs is that they constitute the first independent black socialist movement in America. Their precursors were always under white auspices in the Socialist party, the Socialist Labor party, or the Communist party of the United States. In this sense they are a truly revolutionary group and represent an authentic form of the New Left in America. Understandably, then, by 1970 Newton, Seale, and Cleaver were forging a more internationalist and avowedly Marxist-Leninist socialist philosophy. Indeed, Newton and a small entourage would visit Peking and meet with Chinese leaders in October 1971.

In describing the BPP's Marxist emphasis, it must be reiterated that Newton has repeatedly disavowed any connection with the Communist party of the United States. Newton and the BPP also disclaimed the Communist notion of the inevitability of violent revolution. This was made public with the "defection" of Eldridge Cleaver from the BPP in April 1971— although the party retained much of Cleaver's ideological contributions. Cleaver's contention that the BPP should be an armed revolutionary vanguard and go underground as did the SDS Weatherman faction was just too orthodox Communist for Newton and the other BPP leaders. Hence Newton wrote that "under the influence of Eldridge Cleaver the Party gave the community no alternative for dealing with us except by picking up the gun. . . . Eldridge Cleaver influenced us to isolate ourselves from the Black Community so that it was war between the oppressor and the Black Panther Party, not between the oppressor and the oppressed community." [5] And at the same time Newton rejected the whole vanguard theory so integral to orthodox Communism. Again justifying the "defection" of Cleaver, Newton argued that "we recognized that no party or organization can make the revolution, only the people can." If the BPP rejects the traditional vanguard theory and the use of violence, what sort of Marxist-Leninist philosophy are they espousing? The answer is that they adapted several Marxist-Leninist concepts to their own "colonized" situation.

Basically, the BPP took three general notions from Marxism: (1) Capitalism is the root of human exploitation; therefore, the party is adamantly anti-capitalist, including so-called black capitalism. (2) The greatest revolutionary potential comes from the most oppressed class. This is not the protelariat but the lumpenproletariat, of which blacks are the largest constituent. Hence the struggle is not based so much on race as it is on class. (3) History is a dialectical process, hence blacks are involved in resolving the dialectical contradiction within capitalism, which is now in its advanced imperialist stage. Hence the BPP recognizes itself as internationalist, since the contradiction is manifest in imperialism, which is by definition international. It should be emphasized that the BPP's interpretation of these Marxist conceptions *is an interpretation.* In short, at almost no point can one find an orthodox, doctrinaire, Marxist tenet. And this has been acknowledged by the BPP. Nevertheless, in Newton's comprehensive attempt at explaining BPP philosophy (a speech delivered at Boston College on November 18, 1970), he said, "The BPP is a Marxist-Leninist party because we follow the dialectical method and also integrate theory with practice." And it is also true that when he addressed the Revolutionary People's Constitutional Convention in Washington, D. C., on November 28, 1970, he said, "We foresee a system where all people produce according to their abilities and all receive according to their needs." So the point is that certainly in late 1970, Newton considered his party at least generally to have a Marxist-Leninist posture.

It must be remembered that Huey Newton had just been released from prison early in 1970 and that he was reestablishing his undisputed leadership of the BPP—hence the somewhat strong ideological statements. It was a time in which Newton was growing intellectually and formulating what he hoped would be an intelligible, coherent, flexible, yet genuine philosophy, which could serve as the glue of the party and which could help the party in the community. So for about two years, from early 1970 to early 1972, Newton was to experiment with a Marxist-Leninist socialism, both as a theory of society and as a guide for practical activity. Probably his most succinct description of what the party was doing during these years came at a press conference on September 5, 1970, held with David Hilliard, chief of staff of the BPP.

> . . . Stokely Carmichael . . . said that socialism is not the question, economics is not the question, but it is entirely a question of racism. We take issue with this; we realize that the United States is a racist country, but we also realize, . . . the roots of racism is based upon the profit motive and capitalism. . . . We believe that while socialism will not wipe out racism completely, a foundation will be laid. When we change the structure of bourgeoisie society; when we transform the structure into a socialist society then we're one step toward changing attitudes. The people then will have control of the mechanisms that shape attitudes. . . . But we say that the only way to start changing the racist nature of the society is to revolutionize or transform the institutions.[6]

It might be expected that since Newton and other Panthers visited China in October 1971 and met with Premier Chou En-lai, the philosophy of the BPP would have become even more Marxist or Maoist and certainly more internationalist. But this was not the case. When Newton returned from China he began more and more to enunciate a philosophy which he had been mulling over since late 1970: "revolutionary intercommunalism." And this seems to be the current philosophy of the BPP (although there are certainly aspects of Marxism and Cleaver's "colonized" people theory). In fact, it would probably have been impossible for Newton to have developed the idea of "revolutionary intercommunalism" without having worked his way through the ideas and practices of Marx, Lenin, Fanon, Malcolm X, Mao, and Cleaver.

Basically, the philosophy grew out of the conclusion made by Newton and others that the concept of nations no longer reflects historical reality. Nations no longer exist, because they have been overrun by the economic imperialism of American capitalism. As Newton put it:

> ... the United States is no longer a nation but an empire. However, an empire, by definition controls other countries, and in so doing transforms them. If a nation cannot protect its boundaries and prevent the entry of an aggressor, if a nation cannot control its political structure and its cultural institutions, then it is no longer a nation.
> ... Because of this new understanding we must ally ourselves with the oppressed communities of the world. ... We must place our future hopes upon the philosophy of intercommunalism, a philosophy which holds that the rise of imperialism in America transfomed all other communities into oppressed communities.[7]

Accordingly, says Newton, "the Black Panther party now disclaims internationalism and supports intercommunalism."[8] Hence the BPP newspaper is subtitled "Intercommunal New Service."

From the philosophy of "revolutionary intercommunalism" it follows that since America as a nation no longer exists, the state (government) no longer represents the nation, but rather the empire. Therefore, to try to capture the state either by violence or by national elections would be of no avail, for to capture the apparatus of the state would not help the people, only the empire. While this is not entirely logical, it is used as an operational principle. Hence the emphasis of the BPP remains "power to the people." This means local control of communities, for the ultimate unit from which to build is the community. It is a conception of history that envisages a struggle between oppressed communities and empires—with the most oppressive empire being the United States, and the most oppressed community North Vietnam (at least before the American withdrawal). Obviously, black Americans in this scheme of history can see themselves as comparable to North Vietnamese—both suffered heavily under the yoke of American imperialism. The first step then becomes to make it possible for your oppressed community to survive. ("Subscribe to Survive" is the motto of the BPP newspaper.) This means knowing *that* you are oppressed, *why* you are oppressed, and *by whom* you are oppressed. Then, it means careful and thorough organization to drive the oppressor out of your community. The preconditions for such community liberation are set down in the 10-Point Program of the Black Panther party. This remains their philosophy, despite the fact that Bobby Seale left the BPP for personal reasons in 1976 and Huey Newton fled to Cuba the same year. The leadership was then given over to Elaine Brown. She pursues much the same course, in consultation with the exiled Newton.

In July 1977, Newton returned voluntarily to the U.S.A. to "clear himself" by facing trial. (Bail was set, over defense objections, at $100,000).

Notes to Chapter 4

1. Newton got the actual idea of armed self-defense as a tactic from Robert Williams's book, *Negroes With Guns.* Williams was president of the Monroe, North Carolina chapter of the NAACP. He fled the country in 1961 and was not allowed to return until 1969.

2. Letter from Huey P. Newton to Christopher Bone, April 10, 1973. For a really complete history of the development of the BPP and a brilliant autobiography, see Huey P. Newton, *Revolutionary Suicide* (New York, 1973). All references to this book are by permission of Random House, Inc.

3. See "Evidence and Intimidation of Fascist Crimes by U.S.A.," *The Black Panther* (February 2, 1970). Also, Charles R. Garry, "The Old Rules Do Not Apply," in Philip S. Foner, ed., *The Black Panthers Speak* (New York, 1970), p. 258. All references to this book are by permission of J. B. Lippincott Company. In March 1974, the Department of Justice (after the death of J. Edgar Hoover) made public FBI memoranda supervising spying and harassment of several radical groups, among them the BPP.

4. Quoted in Foner, *Black Panthers Speak,* p. xxi.

5. Huey P. Newton, *To Die For the People* (New York, 1972), p. 51. Newton goes into great length explaining the "Cleaver Affair" in *Revolutionary Suicide.*

6. Newton, *To Die For the People,* p. 193.

7. Ibid., p. 40.

8. Ibid., p. 39.

V

The New Left in the 1970's:
A Precarious Coalition

Someone stood at a window
  and cried,
'One tear I thought that should stop
  a war
But someone is killing me'*

By the close of 1970, two things were clear about the New Left. First, it was divided between a white radicalism, led by no single national group, and an independent black radicalism, predominately under the national direction of the Black Panther party. Second, while white radicalism had seemed capable of sustaining unified action only around the single issue of the wars in Southeast Asia, the gigantic nationwide student strike following the Kent State and Jackson State killings revealed the existence of a self-conscious student class with enormous potential political influence. But it was also clear that continuation of the New Left's political influence in the 1970's depended (and still depends) upon the resolution of three major problems: (1) Can the Black Panther party and the student left continue to work together, especially on a national scale? (2) Can the existing New Left groups risk cooperating with and utilizing the tactics of the SLA? (3) Can the student left build an operational multi-issue national coalition?

As of this writing (1976) it is possible only to speculate tentatively on the resolution of these problems. The first problem is probably the easiest to consider. With the release of Bobby Seale and Huey Newton, the Black Panther party had renewed vigor and continued its policy of working with white radicals on some (mostly local) issues. (Panthers as well as white radicals

---

*Jefferson Airplane, "House at Pooneil Corners," words and Music by Marty Balin and Paul Kantner. © 1969 by Icebag Corporation. All Rights Reserved. Used by Permission.

claim responsibility for the bombings in September 1971 of government buildings following the attempted escape from San Quentin of Panther George Jackson.) But with the development of the philosophy of inter-communalism and the going underground of the Weatherman, national coordination seems very doubtful.

The second question has in part already been answered. The BPP, as well as Angela Davis, disclaimed the tactics of the SLA in allegedly kidnapping Patricia Hearst in February 1974. Still, the tactic is condoned by the Weather-people, and underground revolutionary cooperation between Weatherpeople and the SLA seems very conceivable. Indeed, Weatherpeople hid Patricia Hearst for many months before her capture in 1975. Clearly, however, the above-ground student left cannot risk much involvement with the SLA—at least not presently.

The third problem—whether the student left can build a national coali-tion—can best be understood after an analysis of the antiwar march and May Day demonstration of April 24, 1971. This march revealed the existence of what was perhaps the widest national coalition in the history of American radicalism. Approximately one-half million persons gathered in Washington, D. C., and a quarter of a million in San Francisco on April 24. This above-ground coalition persists (albeit precariously) into the mid-seventies.

In terms of the internal history of the student New Left, the April 24 demonstrations marked a turning point. For the demonstrations were *not* organized and led by older New Left groups, such as SDS and The Resistance. There were several reasons for this. The leader of The Resistance, David Harris, had been imprisoned for refusing the draft. This injured the organi-zation, which was, after all, designed to facilitate individual action against the Selective Service System rather than to stimulate nationwide action to end the war in Vietnam. But the April 24 demonstrations were run by new organizations primarily because SDS had become moribund and there no longer existed national student organizations with the kind of magnetism and leadership SDS had supplied in the 1960's.[1]

It has been argued that the demise of SDS came from its own factionalism. That is only partly true. Students for a Democratic Society was severely wounded by the persistent attempts at infiltration and disruption by the Progressive Labor party beginning in 1964. The PLP had defected from the Communist party of the United States in 1961 and developed a doctrinaire Maoist Communism. Its leaders were not students, but men in their forties. They were unable to gain a majority in more than a few chapters of SDS, notably in Boston schools. Attempts to infiltrate the Bay Area chapters failed, as did attempts to wrench the leadership away from Mark Rudd at Columbia University. At the 1969 SDS Convention in Chicago, although they held majorities in only a few chapters, the PLP members almost constituted a majority of the convention delegates. Despite profound philosophical differences, all other factions in SDS combined to expel the Maoist PLP. But the PLP refused to leave, contending it was the *true* SDS. (The PLP still claims, falsely, that it *is* SDS.) The remaining SDS membership split into two large factions: Revolutionary Youth Movement II, then led by Les Coleman and outgoing SDS national secretary Mike Klonsky; and Weatherman, then led by Mark Rudd, Bernardine Dohrn, Jeff Jones, and Bill Ayers. (Weatherman derives its name from a verse of "Subterranean Homesick Blues" by Bob Dylan—"You don't need a Weatherman to know which way the wind blows." [see chapter 13].) The Weatherman (Weatherpeople) absconded with the SDS mailing list and money, and temporarily retained the SDS national headquarters at 1608 West Madison, Chicago.

The Weatherpeople had reached the conclusion that it was time to dramatize the revolution by violence. Their hope was that the oppressed would follow their brazen, open, revolutionary actions. Hence they organized the "Days of Rage" which took place in Chicago on October 8–11, 1969. Ayers, Rudd, Dohrn, and other Weatherpeople toured college campuses in an attempt to recruit an army of volunteers to come to Chicago. Though thousands were expected, only a few hundred showed up. Hayden and Rubin gave implicit, though reluctant, support. It was a widely publicized "wargasm," so the Chicago police were waiting. Nevertheless, the Weatherpeople carried it off. They marched through downtown Chicago, "trashing" windows and cars and doing combat with the police. Bernadine Dohrn led a march to destroy the Chicago Military Induction Center (a task virtually impossible without a B-52 saturation bombing run). Her group was easily stopped; and most of the Weatherpeople had their heads beaten. When one was asked by newsmen for his estimation of the confrontation, he said "It's a bummer, man, the whole thing was a bummer." Boston and Washington, D. C. were also hit by the Days of Rage. But the only damage was to the Justice Department and the South Vietnamese Embassy on Connecticut Avenue. At that point, with the exception of Eldridge Cleaver, the Blac' Panther leadership withdrew public support for the Weatherpeople.

The Weatherpeople were still the strongest remnant of SDS. But this lasted only until January 1, 1970, for the final public meeting of Weatherman was in Flint, Michigan, December 27–30, 1969. This was a "National War Council," attended by about four hundred persons. They decided that a guerrilla war was needed, and hence Weatherpeople went underground to become bombers and subversives. Accordingly, their national organizational structure became unknown, and they ceased to exist as an above-ground national New Left student and youth organization. Shortly thereafter, a Federal Grand Jury in Chicago indicted Mark Rudd, Bernardine Dohrn, Bill Ayers, Cathy Wilkerson and others for conspiracy during the "Days of

Rage." They were to be arraigned before the famed Chicago Eight judge, Julius Hoffman. Utlimately, in January 1974, Judge Hoffman dismissed charges against twelve Weathermen involved in the "Days of Rage."

With the Weatherpeople died SDS as a recognizable organization and much of the élan which had created the student New Left and counterculture of the 1960's; for political realities became so harsh in the late sixties that the altruistic—often reformist—idealism which had bound the egalitarianism of the counterculture together with the loose structure of SDS, spent itself and foundered on the rocks of disappointment. The Weatherpeople incarnated all the feelings of failure which had grown out of the Civil Rights movement, the liberal Democratic reform effort, the urban community organization efforts, and the anti–Vietnam War effort. Theirs was a total disillusionment and a radical anger. Their choice to go underground alienated them from the Black Panther party and from the overwhelming majority of students. And it was their miscalculation (that the student movement was dead) that allowed other groups to capture the leadership of the student New Left. They recognized too late (after Kent State and Jackson State) that there was still a tremendous radical political potential in the student left.[2] And thus, for the most part, leadership of the student left has passed to two new groups: the National Peace Action Coalition (NPAC) and the People's Coalition for Peace and Justice (PCPJ). Their history is extremely complex, but may be summarized.

The National Peace Action Coalition is a descendant of the Student Mobilization Committee (SMC), which came into prominence in 1965. The latter (SMC) was created by the Young Socialist Alliance (YSA). The YSA was itself founded in 1960 as the youth affiliate of the Socialist Workers party, a Trotskyite Marxist political party.[3] The YSA was created with the intention of recruiting students and youth into programs for the socialist transformation of America and the world. When the war in Vietnam escalated in 1964, the Socialist Workers party and the YSA concluded that it was a capitalist war against a socialist country, and proceeded to create the Student Mobilization Committee as a student socialist group specifically dedicated to ending the war in Vietnam. The SMC competed with SDS for recruits and in general was dwarfed by the influence of the latter organization. Hence SMC repeatedly asked SDS to help them organize national strikes against the war. However, SDS, because it was a multi-issue organization, did not work with SMC or the YSA to organize antiwar strikes, but passed a resolution supporting demonstrations against the war.

Until 1972, the YSA and the SMC were able to argue that they were in large measure independent of the Socialist Workers party. That was not true, but it was the strategy of the YSA and the Socialist Workers party to minimize the connections. The result of this was the creation of another group—

the National Peace Action Coalition—in July 1970. So one must keep in mind that in fact the YSA and the Socialist Workers party created NPAC and held the key positions of leadership in the April 24, 1971 march, the demonstrations at the Republican National Convention in August 1972, and the march and rally in Washington, D. C. which attracted approximately 100,000 participants on the day of President Nixon's second inauguration, January 20, 1973.[4] Originally, the creation of NPAC was intended to attract all antiwar groups and organize them nationally. So the call went out for all such groups to meet at Cuyahoga Community College, in Cleveland. They were hosted by the Cleveland Area Peace Action Coalition. About fifteen hundred people showed up, including PLP'ers, Communists, women's liberation partisans, and others. The majority were from the SMC, and hence were prone to adhere to the YSA strategy. Out of this meeting came NPAC, originally led by Jim Lafferty of Detroit (independent); Don Gurewitz of SMC and also a member of the Socialist Workers Party; John T. Williams (vice-president of a Teamsters Union local in Los Angeles); Jerry Gordon (leader of the Cleveland Area Peace Action Coalition); and Ruth Gage-Colby (Women's Interntaional League for Peace and Freedom).

The other major sponsor of the march, the People's Coalition for Peace and Justice (PCPJ), has an elaborate and checkered history. It is the outgrowth of many mobilization committees from many localities. Some of these were dominated by the Communist party of the United States and the Progressive Labor party. It is therefore more prone to be ultra-leftist and multi-issue in orientation. By 1970, in addition to the above mentioned groups, it had contingents from SCLC, the American Friends Field Service Committee, and some supporters from the United Farm Workers. It vehemently insisted that it is impossible to separate the war in Vietnam from domestic oppression of nonwhite Americans and from the military–industrial complex. So it is possible to find individuals and groups within PCPJ who have widely differing views on tactics. There are those who favor supporting the Democratic party as well as those who are opposed to any participation in electoral politics. There are pacifist groups, groups which believe in disruption, groups which support women's liberation, and groups which argue that feminism "divides" the working class.

Cooperation between the PCPJ and the NPAC was agreed upon at a convention held at the Packinghouse Labor Center in Chicago, December 4–6, 1970. The convention was sponsored by NPAC, which subsequently came to have the greatest influence and responsibility for the march and for the maintenance of the nationwide coalition. There were fifteen hundred persons at the convention, representing 29 states, 34 labor unions, 150 colleges, 40 high schools, and hundreds of community peace groups. At the convention, the coordinators of the march were chosen and the means of financing the march was decided. Buttons, posters, advertisements, and donations at the demonstrations were to be the chief means of providing revenue. As it turned out, little money was raised except by the SMC, which contributed $60,000. This was sufficient to finance the San Francisco march, but the Washington, D. C. march cost about $250,000, only some of which was collected during the event itself.

It was agreed at the convention that for reasons of simplicity the march would be publicly billed as sponsored by the NPAC. The chief principles of the march were sent out to all contingents:

> The National Peace Action Coalition demands the immediate and unconditional withdrawal of all U.S. forces from and the dismantling of all U.S. bases in Indochina.

> . . . A basic principle of the NPAC is non-exclusion by which is meant all who oppose the war are welcome in the coalition irrespective of their views on other questions and regardless of other affiliations.

> . . . NPAC functions in a peaceful, orderly and disciplined fashion. Confrontational adventures hurt the antiwar movement by alienating otherwise sympathetic sections of the population, particularly labor and Brown people.

> . . . Mass demonstrations remain the NPAC's most effective method of communicating its message to and involving the largest numbers of people.

The march itself (meaning both San Francisco and Washington, D. C.) displayed the largest coalition yet achieved by the New Left. Among those to lend their names to it publicly were Senators Edmund Muskie, George McGovern, and Vance Hartke; Fathers Daniel and Philip Berrigan; Harold Gibbons, vice-president of the International Brotherhood of Teamsters; writer Norman Mailer; actor Alan Arkin; and academics Ashley Montagu and Howard Zinn. In both Washington, D. C. and San Francisco there were marchers representing contingents from such newly formed groups as Business Executives Movement for Peace, Hard Hats for Peace, Doctors for Peace, and the Gay Liberation Front. Third World groups, as well as Black Panthers, participated. But most impressive were the veterans' and women's liberation groups.

Within the coalition, the largest veterans' organization was the Vietnam Veterans Against the War, led by John Kerry. However, there was participation by many other veterans' groups, chief among which were the Ohio Veterans Coalition for Peace and the Chicago Vets for Peace. All these groups espoused a nonviolent strategy. They were in the front ranks of both marches and received more publicity than any of the other contingents. Their presence greatly enhanced the moral power of the antiwar movement, for they attempted to reveal the mistake they had made by serving in the war in hopes of dissuading other young men from making similar errors. At the rallies, they reiterated that participation in the war is a worse crime than refusing to join the armed services. They confessed atrocities, and many threw away their medals. This, along with an eloquent speech by John Kerry before a Congressional hearing, also contributed to the revitalization of the resistance movement.

The April 24 march was the first sizeable antiwar march in which there was large-scale organized female participation and leadership. While there were scores of women's liberation groups from all over the nation involved in the march, the women of Boston Female Liberation were particularly active in leadership positions. Participation of women in the march had first been discussed at the women's workshop during the NPAC Emergency Antiwar Conference in December 1970. At this meeting about 150 women met and decided to begin organizing a united women's movement, focusing on the effects of the war upon women. Following this initial meeting, over 250 women met on February 19-21, 1971, at the SMC National Student Antiwar Conference. While attending the "Women and the War" session of the conference, they passed the following four point proposal:

1. To endorse the April 24 demonstrations.

2. To endorse the ideal of independent women's contingents at the April 24 demonstrations.

3. To build this contingent by producing literature, buttons, posters, leaflets; sending women speakers on tour, and organizing mass distribution of literature.

4. To initiate local women's actions during the week of April 17–24 and to designate one day as "Women against the War Day" on which such actions could occur.

Thus the "United Women's Contingent" entered into the April 24 demonstration.

The presence of so many women, with insignia identifying their groups and their localities, was a surprise to even the most hopeful of the organizers. But the women made it clear that, while they were marching to protest the war, they were also marching to correct the misconception that the antiwar movement was led entirely by men. And they were marching to publicize how the war directly affected them: one million children left uncared for as soldiers served abroad, while demands for daycare centers went unheeded; hundreds of deaths from abortions because most states refused to make the operation legal; and lower pay than males, even though women often desperately need money for schooling or because they are the only support of their families.

The women's associations displayed an almost truculent attitude. They insisted upon autonomy and their own issues and they resolutely refused to be persuaded that there were larger issues of first priority. *They did not take the Vietnamese war to be of first priority.* Thus, as Nancy Williamson from Boston Female Liberation stated, "The women's movement, a separate movement, refuses to be submerged, subverted, and sabotaged as it has been in the past by not so well meaning male revolutionaries. People in the Antiwar Movement must understand that the women's movement is dedicated first and foremost to ending female oppression."

This fierce insistence upon autonomy, while notably an attribute of the women's liberation organizations, was also characteristic of many groups in PCPJ. Obviously, this threatened the continued existence of the national coalition of NPAC-PCPJ. Differences within the coalition were also evident when the more militant members of the Communist party and PCPJ participated in the attempt to shut down the Capital during the May Day protests. These were extensions of the April 24 march, but they were not endorsed by veterans' groups and were led primarily by Yippies. Tactics of civil disobedience and "mobile obstruction" (disrupting communications, transportation, etc.), were not endorsed by SMC and NPAC. Nevertheless, between May first and fifth, approximately 11,500 persons were arrested and detained. This divergence of tactics threatened the coalition, but as of 1974 the PCPJ continued to work well with the NPAC.

What makes this grand coalition so precarious is the fact that, in the final analysis, NPAC *is* (or at least still was, as of 1974) a single issue coalition, even though the YSA and SMC are not single issue organizations and their parent organization, the Socialist Workers party, has shown remarkable resilience since its founding in 1938. Still, many commentators believe that with the withdrawal of American armed forces from Southeast Asia the New Left would disintegrate. The author disagreed then and still does. The size of the New Left and the continued cooperation of NPAC, PCPJ, VVAW, Yippies, and SDS evident in the January 20, 1973 march in Washington, D. C.—after presidential assistant Kissinger announced that "peace is at hand" and a cease-fire was imminent—suggested the validity of disagreement. It is true, however, that NPAC diminished in strength after the fall of Cambodia in 1975. But the disintegration of coalitions is inevitable and certainly does not spell the end of movements. Indeed, the New Left is unique as a radical movement because it is multi-issue oriented and yet capable of organizing large coalitions around specific issues. Its strength is that its leaders and supporters, while seldom rallying to a do-or-die single issue, nevertheless perceive the interconnection of issues. Accordingly, civil rights organizations *do* support antiwar activities, and women's liberation and gay liberation groups *do* support NPAC. And these groups, while they currently form the backbone of NPAC constituency, are also vitally concerned with pollution, ecology, and freedom of the press. Furthermore, they continue to be the basis of a student left with the assistance and power of Ralph Nader's organizations, the Public Information Research Groups (PIRG's). Thus, while other radical American movements have died out with the waning of their central issue, this will not be the fate of the New Left.

The New Left, from its inception, has always beem polymorphic, composed of many movements, associations, and committees. Some of its organizations are structured and permanent, such as the PIRG's, others are temporary and work on single issues, but all of them are organized along decentralized lines. There simply are no "official" organizations of the New Left—especially since the "new" SDS is, as yet, ineffective as a national organization. Nevertheless, the New Left exists as a political and cultural position, a political and cultural manifestation of a larger phenomenon particularly rampant in the young: an impulse to radicalism. And one could argue, I think, that that impulse to radicalism would almost inevitably have gone through stages of formal organization as did SNCC and SDS, only later to go underground in cadres, as did the Weatherpeople and the SLA, and at the same time maintain a student base, like the PIRG's.

Moreover, it is important that the public as well as the youth realize that the New Left is *not solely a generational revolt.* Persons who consider themselves part of the New Left or counterculture are not all under thirty (David Dellinger, when indicted in 1969 for the Chicago "conspiracy," was 53). Not all of them are students, dropouts, or neurotic professors. And not all of them are engaging in youthful, immature ebullience. (Witness the support of New Left groups for the presidential bid of young Governor Edmund Brown, Jr. in 1976.) It is to the *advantage* of the current Establishment to pass off the protests and unrest as merely generational misunderstanding or jealousy. Tactically, this is what the government is trying to do. Consequently, as Richard Flacks has noted, radicals are put in jail for drug abuse, but it is the "official" policy of the government to work for reform of the laws on marijuana. Similarly, draft resisters were jailed while the government sponsored reform of the Selective Service System. Women's liberation is ridiculed, but legislators occasionally sponsor bills for reform of abortion laws and for day-care centers. Hippie-type communes in the cities are raided by police, but society provides fame, recognition, and fortune to rock music groups which are often spawned by such communities as Haight-Ashbury in San Francisco, the East Village in New York, and Watts in Los Angeles.

All of the above attempt to minimize the legimitacy of the New Left and the counterculture while acceding to many of their demands for improvements. "The hope is that if reforms can be made that will liberalize the cultural and social atmosphere, particularly in relation to sex, drug use, art music, censorship . . . the mass of youth will not become tempted by the message of the radical vanguard."[5] But this "liberalizing" just obscures the larger social, political, and cultural issues which are raised by the New Left and the counterculture. It is these issues which will be delineated in this book. The future of the New Left depends upon widespread understanding that it is in the interest of everyone, regardless of age, race, or sex, that we create a fully democratic social order which will provide meaning, both national and personal, to all our citizens. Between 1974 and 1975, over fifty million adults had been born in this country. They cannot continue to be treated as an isolated groups, nor can they continue to regard themselves as such. In order to survive, both political parties have had to move for the vote of the postwar generation. This is evident when one remembers that twenty-five million people under the age of twenty-five became eligible to vote in the presidential election of 1972. About eleven million of these were enfranchised when the voting age was lowered to eighteen in 1970. They were too young to have been affected deeply by the Civil Rights movement, Bob Dylan, the 1968 Democratic National Convention, and the Kent State disaster. But fourteen million of the new voters reached age twenty-one after 1968: they were affected. Yet despite the nomination of George McGovern as the Democratic presidential candidate, youth neither registered nor voted in substantial numbers. A Gallup poll indicated that there were still hundreds of thousands of young people who felt it best to remain aloof from politics. The question of the organization of their political potential remains in part the question of the political future of the New Left.

The New Left must be taken seriously, not only because of its political implications, but also because of what it means in the larger context of the history and development of American cultural values. Despite the changes it has experienced since 1960, the New Left draws support from leaders in academia, popular music, politics and literature, which is unparalleled in the history of any American radical movement. Indeed, one of the reasons the New Left must be taken seriously is that it has such a wide spectrum of support. Certainly one is hard put to understand the political and cultural affinities between SLA commander David De Freeze, philosopher Herbert Marcuse, historian Staughton Lynd, Freudian mystic Norman O. Brown, and communications expert Marshall McLuhan. It is difficult to see affinities between Zen advocate Alan Watts, drug narcissist Timothy Leary, and the progressive educator George Leonard, as it to see affinities between Supreme Court Justice William O. Douglas, language analyst Noam Chomsky, and gestalt psychologist Frederick Perls. It is even more difficult to find affinities between the above-mentioned public figures and rock stars like John Lennon, Bob Dylan, and Grace Slick, or between these men and women and writers such as Allen Ginsberg, Ken Kesey, and Jean Genet and political radicals such as Abbie Hoffman, Tom Hayden, David Dellinger, and Huey Newton. Understanding why these people support the New Left is further complicated by the fact that the philosophy and ideology of the New Left is never precisely defined. Part 2 of this book will, therefore, focus upon the common concerns shared by the wide spectrum of people who support the New Left.

Notes to Chapter 5

1. I do not want to give the impression that The Resistance was dead or that David Harris was not active in the April 24 mobilization. Indeed he was; he spoke at the San Francisco march. Also, there arose in 1972 a reconstituted SDS. It had few, if any, of the older SDS leaders, but had a working, albeit tenuous, alliance with the Yippies. Thus SDS was very much evident at the January 20, 1973 antiwar demonstration in Washington, D. C.

2. For a perceptive and accurate judgment of the Weatherpeople and the demise of SDS, see "An Interview with Tom Hayden," *Rolling Stone* (December 9, 1972).

3. I do not want to mislead the reader here. The Socialist Workers party, while a Trotskyite party, is an indigenous American party. It was created out of the Trotskyite Fourth International in the United States by James Cannon in 1938. Its membership in 1974 was approximately 1,200. But far more important than the SWP is its youth affiliate, YSA, which controls the SMC and exercises profound influence in NPAC. Still it must be forthrightly admitted that the student left and the antiwar movement were basically "captured" by the SWP via YSA, SMC, and NPAC by December 1970.

4. Indeed, at all of these radical activities a leading spokesman was Jerry Gordon of the original NPAC of Cleveland.

5. Richard Flacks, "Young Intelligentsia in Revolt," *Transaction* (June, 1970), p. 53.

Part 2

A Unity of Negation

Introduction to Part 2

> This unity of negation which characterizes the new protest does not go against the democratic values proclaimed by American rhetoric, but against the incapability of a society at the height of its collective wealth and technical development to bring about conditions of greater material and spiritual freedom.*

Although often difficult to perceive, there are common denominators linking the disparate followers of the left-wing radicalism which blossomed in the 1960's. One denominator would certainly seem to be generational. In the 1960's, the first postwar generation was engaged in a revolution against the spectacular achievements of the generation of the 1930's. That is, the generation which triumphed over a world depression, defeated a nation which attacked without warning, extirpated the racial cannibalism of Nazism, and went on to attain prosperity on a scale unknown in world history, also created rebels against the very society responsible for these accomplishments.

Yet, upon closer examination, it becomes evident that the crux of the radical impulse is not solely generational; it is a unity of cultural negation— a protest against the *values* which were instrumental to the achievements of the generation of the 1930's. Hence one can see a marked antirationalism—a revolt against leadership by the intellectual and professional expertise which society still holds as criteria for personal and social accomplishment. A pronounced antimaterialism is evident, both in the sense of material production and consumption and against materialism as a philosophy of reality. One can also detect a profound antitechnological bias, a rebellion against the technical knowledge and the technical approach to reality which the majority of Americans believe to be necessary for social improvement. And con-

*Massimo Teodori, *The New Left: A Documentary History*.

spicuous, especially when the United States was fighting in Indochina, there were strident antiwar and anticapitalist sentiments.

Superficially, the New Left in 1970 might have appeared to be a collocation of negative responses and attitudes with only one discernible demand: power. But what emerges upon a closer look is a philosophical potpourri. In politics, it is a radicalism bordering upon anarchism. In economics, it is municipal socialism in the cities and communities or cooperatives in the rural areas. In society, it is an absolute egalitarianism, communalist and somewhat anti-individualist. And omnipresent is a sensibility which makes it possible to see the radical impulse in its political and cultural manifestations as essentially a philosophy of idealism with utopian expectations, set against war and against the prevailing philosophy of materialism, with pragmatic rationalism defining its expectations. Accordingly, the following chapters of this book deal with the negative denominators: (1) antimaterialism, (2) antirationalism, (3) antitechnology, and (4) the system and the university. A final chapter on the single tangible factor, the demand for power, will describe the idealistic, moral emphasis of the radical impulse.

VI

Antimaterialism

The stakes are too great—an America gone mad with materialism*.

The New Left and the counterculture reject materialism, the philosophy which they believe underlies both American capitalism and Soviet Communism. Materialism generally has a double meaning, and so there is confusion about its exact usage. In a literal sense, it means that the totality of the world is solely matter. But by the New Left, materialism is used in a more limited sense—similar to the way Engels and modern American scientists used it—to mean the primacy of matter as an absolute substance involved in the constitution of the universe.[1] Materialism in this sense is not a theory of knowledge (yet it has come to automatically assume rationalism or a kind of pragmatism to be its theory of knowledge). Materialism in the sense of modern social science is really a *metaphysical* doctrine. It affirms that matter (or nature) is prior to spirit, or that spirit is an emanation of matter. Such metaphysical affirmation can neither be proved nor disproved—this was demonstrated by Plato, Kant, and in this century by Whitehead. It is really a question of faith—faith that the world is primarily or totally material (although few scientists and most Americans would not admit that their belief in the primacy of the material world is based upon faith).

For the members of the New Left and the counterculture, reality is neither solely nor even primarily material. And materialism most certainly carries no automatic theory of knowledge such as rationalism or pragmatism—indeed, these attempts at epistemology are perhaps the most lamentable attributes of a philosophy of materialism, no matter how vaguely conceived. But this will be examined in some length in the next chapter. What is strenuously protested is the organization of whole societies (and the individuals

*Allen Ginsberg, "Poetry, Violence, and the Trembling Lambs."

who live in them) around a materialistic conception of reality. This conception of materialism, the very foundation of the American social order to which all institutions are anchored, is the greatest defect in our civilization. Its harmful effects are almost masochistically dwelt upon by the New Left and youth, and they are scorned as the chief tenet of the American *Weltanschauung.*

The New Left argues that materialism is a deleterious philosophy because it denies the reality of the ideal world, the inner, or spiritual world, or, in political terms, because it denies the utopian dimension to human existence. It equates man, his behavior, his values, and his relations, with the material world and thus, to use the phrase of Herbert Marcuse, it makes man and society "one-dimensional." Or, in the words of that irrepressible veteran of postwar disillusionment, Allen Ginsberg, "Recent history is the record of a vast conspiracy to impose one level of mechanical consciousness on mankind and exterminate all manifestations of that unique part of human sentience, identical in all men, which the individual shares with his Creator." [2]

This may seem, at first glance, to be simply common philosophical dissatisfaction with materialism, neither new nor original. What is new is the scope of the attack mustered by the radicals against materialism. Few, if any, of the New Left theoreticians devote much energy to resolving the traditional arguments between materialism and idealism, or to attacking the inner logic of materialism as a philosophy. Rather, what is attacked are the corollaries, attendants, and effects of materialism. They attack what they believe are historical circumstances which result from organizing life around materialism. Here the beacons of radicalism are Herbert Marcuse, Allen Ginsberg, Gary Snyder, and Alan Watts, among others. Indeed Marcuse's illumination of the harmful influence of materialism (see *Eros and Civilization, One-Dimensional Man, Essay on Liberation, Counter-Revolution and Revolt, Negations*) is one of the keenest and most thorough discussions of this century. His books translate into philosophical terms the very thing that most social scientists have been unable or unwilling to grasp: that since the rise of science in the seventeenth century, materialism as a philosophy has become the foundation of practically *all* aspects of human life in the western world. This is easily stated but difficult to prove (because life is now so complex). To write or even to study the history of the growth of modern materialism is a monumental task. Yet, as more and more students are examining the history of science and intellectual history, they are finding that Marcuse's words (turgid as they are) are very relevant, and they give support to the struggle of the New Left against the stultifying and monolothic effects of materialism.

Generally speaking, the contention that the real is material can be attributed to the Roman philosopher Lucretius (96–55 B.C.). But the intellectual father of modern materialism is probably the English philosopher Thomas Hobbes (1588–1679). In his famous work *Leviathan* (1651), Hobbes contended that "the Universe; that is, the whole mass of all things are, Corporeall, that is to say, Body . . . and that which is not Body is no part of the Universe: And because the Universe is All, that which is no part of it, is Nothing; and consequently no where." [3] Since Hobbes, space and matter have generally been considered "final" reality. Hobbes asked for a reform of the English language to bring it in tune with material reality. The result has been a triumph of scientific language. Matter is assumed to be the ultimate reality; nothing can be added to knowledge except through the five senses or their mechanical extensions. The human soul and human emotions become epiphenomena of no real importance. One ramification of the triumph of scientific language is that whatever cannot be said in the language of the mechanics of matter is considered unreal, irrelevant, or illusory. This conclusion has since been contested by many trenchant philosophers, from Hume through Wittgenstein, and, as we shall see, it has also provoked a bitter reaction from New Leftists and counterculturists.

The problem posed for young people growing up with this materialist conception of reality is the same as it is for the poet or artist: what is imagination? Is the imagination unreal, or is it merely the random association of images? Is imagination an untrue or unreliable guide to human affairs? Is imagination just a socially permissible escape and are its artistic expressions merely elegant toys, rather than vehicles of truth? Or, in philosophical terms, can there be no such thing as metaphysics except the vague materialist metaphysics we already have? This is, of course, an old question, and the sudden vogue of European poets such as Blake, Shelley, Coleridge, and Rilke, and, recently, of American poets Allen Ginsberg, Gary Snyder, and Rod McKuen is due in some measure to their rigorous defense of the imagination. Listen to Ginsberg from his famous poem "Howl":

> What sphinx of cement and aluminum bashed open their
> skulls and ate up their brains and imagination? [4]

The fact is that the utilitarianism prevalent in America and the Communism prevalent in the Soviet Union are thoroughly materialistic and offer no freedom to the imagination except where it can be specifically used by the Establishment for political purposes (more will be said about this in chapters 7 and 8).

The hazard of a materialist world view and a materialist language is not simply that they make no room for imagination. It is also that they imply a determinism; materialism as we know it implies that everything that happens, everything that is, has been "caused." There is no spontaneity; everything, every event, has been caused by a prior event, a prior cause. This carries with it a moral determinism, a kind of puritan hubris. Human actions become viewed as being caused, not by choice, but by circumstance. This has led many young people, especially teenagers, to a pathetic reliance upon mechanical systems of judgment, and to placing the onus of moral decision on historical circumstance, progress, science, or necessity. Hence the unfortunate proclivity of many who have relinquished their potential as moral agents to accept a political leader as a moral prophet. (Recall the moralistic fervor with which partisans below the age of twenty-five presented Senator Eugene McCarthy in 1967–68 and Senator George McGovern in 1971–72.)

Another dangerous effect of materialism as a philosophy is that it can offer no legitimate scheme of value judgments. The world of material things does not automatically create a system of ethics—there is no correlative analogy; a description of the world of material things will not allow us to deduce human value judgments. Most natural scientists and social scientists acknowledge this, but how does that help the young man or woman trying to "get it together"? The failure of materialism to accommodate values and ethics absolves most of our finest and best-trained minds from the responsibility of delineating or even considering the world of values. Natural scientists and social scientists are allowed to hide beneath the guise of a value-free approach to reality (science). This value-free approach creates a civilization which is largely devoid of values, and is only logical if one subscribes to the notion that reality is material and matter has no values sui generis. Thus, the disciplines that deal with values—the humanities, particularly English and philosophy—are so dwarfed in the public's mind by the accomplishments of the sciences that they are considered frivolous activities for neurotic intellectuals. The inclination of a materialistic culture is definitely toward a value-free conception of the world. Indeed, the chief thrust of—and the highest value of—knowledge itself, is the gathering of more knowledge about the operation of the material and social world. While this is assumed to be objective, value-free knowledge, it is simply knowledge for the technical management of the natural and material worlds.

Accordingly, persons who consider themselves part of the Movement would probably agree with Marcuse's statement that materialism, "which has led to the explication of nature in terms of mathematical structures, quantification, has separated reality from all inherent ends and, consequently, separated the true from the good, science from ethics."[5] Teleology, the conviction that there is an overall design or purpose to the world, whether in the human world or in the natural world, ceases to exist: scientific objectivity replaces teleology. This also means that the ideas that were integral to the Greco-Christian world—ideas of beauty, good, and justice—are "unscientific," not amenable to objective verification, and therefore illusions. But these concepts *are value categories,* and members of the New Left argue that human beings must have them as ingredients of their existential reality. Without a general consensus about ideas such as good, evil, honest, beautiful, ugly, right, wrong, love, and hate, there is no meaningful freedom. That is, freedom exists in the same realm as the ideas, and if *they* do not exist, neither does *freedom.* And finally, the argument runs, if a person does not have freedom in the sense described, he or she has not achieved Being.

The dominance of materialism as a philosophy has led to a moral relativism and an unhealthy solipsism which most young people find unmanageable. It is one thing to see that our judgments are valid in relation to our own particular problems—this is a necessary part of the pursuit of generality. But right, wrong, and beauty have shared the fate of "scientific truth," until by a curious combination of attitudinal non sequiturs, people have come to feel that nothing is good or beautiful unless a purpose can be defined or calculated. And since we *have no* teleology and no purpose, we begin to feel that nothing is good or true or beautiful at all.

Materialism ridicules the spiritual and casts doubt upon the validity of value judgments while encouraging scientific or objective assessment. This has always been the case, although young people are just now discovering it. Far more disturbing, and a major grievance of the radicals, is what a materialist cosmology does to human relationships. The logical result of materialism is an empirical approach to reality as a whole. That is, if a material (physical) object is a component of the larger concrete universe, then a physical object, such as a human being, must also be a component of the concrete universe; in this way, humans are divided from and bracketed out of the larger Being of the universe. Hence, both physical and psychical entities become objects whose field of being is extremely truncated. Relations between all "things" become patently artificial. Indeed, Being as a cosmological concept ceases to exist in any meaningful sense. In short, the feeling is that materialism and science have made men into "things," objectively spiritless under the purview of science. Thus people become "things" in the eyes of the civilization and are required to regard other people as "things"—polled, surveyed, categorized, and computerized. And it is no consolation "if the thing is animated and chooses its material and intellectual food, if it does not feel its being-a-thing, if it is a pretty, clean, mobile, thing." [6]

The quantitative approach used by science, when translated into a political and social dimension, seems crude and inhuman. For it has created a society in which numbers (measurements of quantity) also measure morality (right or wrong). This was abundantly clear in the Vietnam War, which was largely justified on the basis that a substantial number, once the majority, supported it. It follows that the American government could and did substitute numbers for morality—which really means the elevation of convention and conformity to the rank of morality. But counting noses is not a system of measuring value; it is a method for measuring effective demand. And what the majority of people believe, technologically managed as it is, is not necessarily true, or good, or beautiful. In the words of the too-little-known poet-philosopher Michael Roberts: "A superstition does not become true through being widely held; and an activity such as the publication of inaccurate, trivial, and mildly pornographic newspapers does not become valuable through being awarded a million pounds and a peerage." [7] Is it any wonder, therefore, that the *Heard Report on Campus Disorders,* which was presented to President Nixon in July 1970, concluded that 78 percent of the students polled believed that the United States lacked a sense of values and was too conformist and too materialistic? [8]

The current zenith of a scientific and materialistic approach to living is to be found in the branch of philosophy which is dominated by analytical philosophy, a glorification of the logical positivism of the 1920's and 1930's. This approach studies the syntax of words and word-symbol constructions as if they were pieces of reality. The quest for the meaning of reality or of the elements in reality is reformulated as the quest for the meaning of words. Metaphysical problems of good, evil, beauty, soul, and God become illusory, problems of words and semantics, not of life or reality.

In the view of the New Left, materialism as a philosophy of reality and science as the explicator of that reality seem to have incarcerated man in a social and personal nightmare. In addition, the argument that there is room for personal conscience and belief appears specious to many in the postwar generations. In grammar schools, high schools, and colleges it is taught that Christian cosmology is false according to the standards of astronomy. The biblical story of creation is ridiculous according to the models of biology. The miracles of the New Testament are impossible according to the laws of physics. Therefore, students are led to believe that nothing is ever miraculous. In college, a student finds that the study of comparative religions makes it difficult to believe strongly in any one religion. And later in life, the psychological investigation of spiritual states is berated as a form of neurosis, devoid of dignity and reduced to the level of pathological problems. It is not unusual, then, that Bob Dylan was so popular with young people when he sang in the mid-sixties:

> Disillusioned words like bullets bark
> as human Gods aim for their mark
> Make everything from toy guns that spark
> To flesh colored Christs that glow in the dark
> It's easy to see without lookin' too far
> That not much
> Is really sacred.

. . . .
Although the masters make the rules
For the wise men and the fools
I got nothin' ma
To live up to.[9]

And is it any wonder that six years later (1972) after scream therapy to resolve the same problem mentioned by Bob Dylan, ex-Beatle John Lennon could sing a song in which he disclaimed belief in, among other things, magic, the I Ching, the Bible, Hitler, Jesus, Kennedy, the Gita, Yoga, Elvis, Zimmerman (Dylan), and the Beatles? Lennon could only conclude quietly but resolutely, "I just believe in me."

It is generally accepted since Marx, and since then supported by many sociologists such as Max Weber and anthropologists such as Claude Levi-Strauss, that the organization and direction of a tribe, society, and even a large imperial civilization reflect the conception of reality of the unit examined. And it is generally conceded that such theories of reality (scientifically or magically verified) are actually surface rationalizations of metaphysical beliefs about the nature of the world. These beliefs are models of reality constructed in human minds; these models, which are passed down for decades and sometimes for centuries, neither truly find nor accept, but rather create the contours of the external world. This is no less true of a materialist philosophy. In the view of the New Left, capitalism and all its concomitants—marketing, advertising, efficiency, rationalism, and centralization—are part of a materialist world view, or a "materialist historical project," as existentialists have termed it.

However, the New Left sometimes argues that while a materialistic philosophy defines the boundaries of a society's historical project, any given project (such as capitalism) is one project of realization among others. Hence, it is not inconsistent for members of the New Left to argue that capitalism can be altered or possibly abolished even if materialism temporarily remains the established philosophy of reality. To support this theory, the New Left points to Sweden, which appears to be a more successful project, though one still anchored in materialism. But at the same time it is recognized that, as Marcuse says, "Once the project has become operative in the basic institutions and relations, it tends to become exclusive and to determine the development of society as a whole."[10] And so the effort of the committed member of the New Left is to liberate society from its own narrow, unimaginative realization of one materialist historical project: capitalism. This means fighting "the system." Thus, capitalism and all it has created to perpetuate itself are obvious targets for the New Left.

Notes to Chapter 6

1. By materialism is meant the current broad, popular understanding of the term. Certainly, the Marxists in the New Left are quick to point out that Marx's philosophy of materialism is *not* the same as what I refer to here as materialism. The point is that most persons in the New Left contend that neither Soviet nor Chinese Communism lives up to the theoretical materialism of Karl Marx. Rather, they too have degenerated into the "bourgeois materialism" of which Marx was so critical.

2. Allen Ginsberg, "Poetry, Violence, and the Trembling Lambs," in Thomas F. Parkinson, ed., *The Case on the Beat* (New York, 1961), p. 24.

3. Quoted in Michael Roberts, *The Modern Mind* (London, 1937), p. 69.

4. Allen Ginsberg, *Howl and Other Poems* (San Francisco, 1959). Reprinted by permission of City Lights Books.

5. Herbert Marcuse, *One-Dimensional Man* (Boston, 1964), p. 146. All references to this book are by permission of Beacon Press.

6. Ibid., p. 33.

7. Michael Roberts, *The Recovery of the West* (London, 1941), p. 100.

8. Excerpted from *The Heard Report on Campus Disorders by the American Council on Education* (Washington, D. C., 1970), p. 10.

9. "It's Alright Ma (I'm Only Bleeding)," words and music by Bob Dylan. © 1965 by M. Witmark & Sons. All Rights Reserved. Used by permission of Warner Bros. Music.

10. Marcuse, *One-Dimensional Man*, p. xvi.

VII

Antirationalism

We ain't never, never gonna grow up. We will always be adolescents; we ain't never gonna be rational. Fuck rationality. This school turns you into rational beings so you're capable of becoming bureaucrats in Wall Street, able to become politicians, able to become Pentagon generals. We're irrational. We are everything they say we are.*

According to the New Left, the chief means by which materialism as a philosophy defines or sets the limits of this society's historical project is its epistemology, its theory of knowledge. Rationalism is considered by the New Left to be the epistemology of materialism. Rationalism is defined as the general rules and criteria by which society determines the accuracy of human cognition. As a general approach to reality, rationalism tells us what sorts of statements about the world deserve to be called knowledge, and it supplies norms that enable us to distinguish between questions which may and may not be raised (questions or approaches that are worth considering and those that are not). This kind of approach is normative and as such defines what the scope of reality is. Reality is experience which may be rationally explained and in great measure controlled. The fundamental constituent of reality is matter, and knowledge must have some demonstrable relation to matter and the material environment. There are obvious oversimplifications in this explanation of rationalism as an epistemology; nevertheless, using this conception of rationalism, the New Left and the counterculture have developed a comprehensive critique of education and the way the Establishment (and society as a whole) operates.

A prime characteristic of rationalism as a cognitive method is that it

---

*Jerry Rubin, reported in *Yale Daily News* (May 2, 1970). Reprinted by permission of *Yale Daily News.*

demands the "ordering" of reality. That is, we cut up into segments the continua of space and time in which we live. This means that we are predisposed to think of our environment as consisting of a multitude of separate things belonging to named classes. Similarly, we are inclined to think of the passage of time as sequences of separate events. Our manner of dealing with reality, which segments, categorizes, and objectifies the world, does the same thing when it organizes a civilization and defines a culture; that is, we segment and order our social and cultural world in the same way that we order the natural world. Since we approach the natural world by means of categorization, differentiation, and objectification, we also approach the world of the human being by the same means. But Being, in the human sense, demands an understanding of, or at least an awareness of and participation in, essence. A pragmatic epistemology cannot sui generis assist us to achieve Being, for pragmatism is specifically designed to deal with function, not with Being or essence. The aim of our epistemology (call it empiricism, positivism, pragmatic rationalism), is *regulative*—to ascertain the regularity of behavior of whatever subject matter—*not constitutive*—to find the essence or Being of a subject or perceptual field. Therefore, the epistemology of rationalism will always fail to achieve Being and thereby curtail freedom, since freedom is a salient ingredient of Being.

In other words, the segmentation of the human mind required by contemporary rationalist epistemology breaks up the continuum of the world, both in a personal and cultural sense. If Being includes an awareness of and participation in the continuum, our entire social order and our entire world view are a hindrance to Being. Alienation is a byproduct of the failure to achieve a continuum (and thereby Being). One solution to alienation is to reject rationalism, and the entire epistemology of the contemporary technological world. This would mean (in the parlance of the Establishment) to "drop out," to become a freak, a hippie, or a yippie. In so doing a person becomes a walking "counterenvironment," sharing a certain "liberated" intersubjectivity with his or her peers. This of course entails a conspicuous display of clothing, language, and lifestyle, which makes a freak, a hippie, or street person appear out of line with the present cultural and social norms. But this is precisely the point of the counterculture. It is a counter-reality, a living, visible vitiation of the fundamental, self-evident principles of the day—the principles of rationalism.

It should not be surprising, therefore, that a major constituent of postwar youth radicalism is its antirationalism. Most New Left radicals (with the possible ambiguous exception of the Black Panther party) do not subscribe to the notion that reason and the intellect, rather than the senses, provide the primary source of knowledge. Some members of the New Left and the counterculture reject the fundamental precept of rationalism that a person can make inferences from facts and draw conclusions from these inferences that enable him or her to understand the world and to correlate this knowledge with the attainment of personal or common ends. In reaction against the categorization of rationalism, the New Left has no established program or philosophy. Indeed, a movement suffused with antirationalism could hardly be expected to articulate a rational program! But it should be recognized that the antirationalism of the Movement is itself a philosophical commitment. *The radicals are antirational because they take rationalism to be the epistemology of materialism.*

The criticism of rationalism is bolstered by a distinguished list of thinkers: philosophers like Nietzsche and Bergson, poets like Blake and Rilke, as well as contemporaries like Alan Watts and Timothy Leary. For most American members of the New Left, however, the most influential critic of rationalism is Herbert Marcuse.[1] Rationalism, Marcuse contends in *One-Dimensional Man* and *Negations,* is by necessity the child of materialism. With great skill, Marcuse demonstrates that rationalism reduces the world to a single dimension—the material. In so doing, rationalism also reduces man to one dimension, because it proceeds from the assumption that the outer world of matter is real while the inner world of spirit is illusory. The scientific approach to reality which is today the mainstay of a highly technological society has evolved out of rationalism epistemology. Its central tenet is a complete empiricism which reduces the subject matter to units which can be predicted, understood, and, if not totally controlled, highly manipulated. The world then becomes a functional world; its operation takes on a mechanistic impression: it has working parts. This is done by rational differentiation, the creation of categories which divide reality according to how it behaves.

Rationalism can be seen in virtually all the larger forms of social activity. As political scientist Theodore Lowi has observed: "In production we call it technology. In exchange it is called commerce or markets. In social structure we call it differentiation. Rationalism applied to social control is administration."[2] A world perceived with such an epistemology is a Kafkaesque nightmare, a reality in which everything is presumed to be functioning for some portentous but unknown reason.

Rationalism so viewed is, thus, stultifying, one-dimensional, and palpably antiutopian. Furthermore, it is an injurious epistemology on at least two other grounds. One, it reinforces the problem implicit in materialism—the sustaining or ascertaining of operational moral, human values. Two, it contributes to, if not causes, alienation. The problem of morals is deceptively simple. A rationalist materialism, because it reduces the world to "things," cannot provide moral values from its own system. "Things" are neither inherently good nor bad, but are only judged that way. People are the sole creators of values, and if they too are regarded as "things," having no inherent value in themselves (no inherent capacity for the creation of values), then it becomes illogical to expect a human "thing" to have moral values while contending the rest of the "things" in the universe do not. In order to support moral values (and rationalism certainly claims to), rationalist epistemology must implicitly divide reality between material things and human things. However, rationalism is not divisible; its applicability by the nature of its system is universal; it is a unified epistemology which presumes a unified reality. If morals exist in reality, rationalism must posit them, but since morals do not participate in material reality, rationalism cannot logically or legitimately derive morals from its system.

In order to cope with the problem of values, Anglo-American rationalist epistemologies have introduced a rather clumsy deus ex machina: a kind of rational utilitarian calculus of values. Gigantic social and personal efforts have been taken to avoid or prevent situations where obvious and serious value judgments would have to be made. In short, great efforts and expenditures are made to *avoid conflict* as a fact of life and to engender a roseate optimism surrounding a paradisiacal notion of "harmony." Utilitarianism has become a kind of rationalist adjunct, providing a philosophy of ethics not evident in rationalism itself yet which we feel *ought* to be there. Hence, our society is rooted to the conviction that human conflicts can be traced to insufficient knowledge and that better public education will result in a rational organization of the political and economic order, while simultaneously resolving conflicts between individuals. At the same time, it is contended that this approach to social organization will facilitate the greatest possible individual freedom in a large, industrialized society. This can only work, however, if human individuals are treated as abstract and basically uniform elements in the society or within any institution. In this system, the individual is considered the embodiment of the abstract essence of man, along with a modicum of personal preferences which differentiate him from others. He is free to exercise his personal preferences *as long as his freedom does not interfere with the rational interests of others.* Man, then, is the totality of his generic needs. It is believed that these needs can be satisfied by intelligent social organization while reducing man's private needs (some of which may be "antisocial") to a point where they will not interrupt the efficient and harmonious operation of society. The individual is thus packaged and placed in a larger mechanism known as society—a society that proceeds toward goals that few, if any, individuals can specify. But to a New Leftist, this attempt at gleaning or salvaging the realm of values from a materialist philosophy with a rationalist epistemology fails.[3] The reasons for its failure will be made clear in the chapters entitled 'Man, the Player" and "Being."

Rationalism and utilitariansim debase mankind; the utilitarian man, the rational man, is an empty intellectual abstraction, not a human being with a full range of responses. The notion that a rough, empirical approximation of the characteristics of human beings will allow individuals the freedom to create many of their own values while supplying them with absolute moral guidelines—such a notion is repugnant as well as intellectually indefensible to any member of the New Left. It is the notion of the conforming man, the organization man, the bureaucrat, and the Watergate man; it is the butt of jokes by underground newspapers and hundreds of rock songs. Utilitarianism leads to a uniformly lifeless existence, with uniform physical needs satisfied by uniform goods, and with man's inner self repressed by sedatives or by su· gery. Ultimately, this world view spawns a creature under constant mechanical control from incubator to incinerator. And if this is our goal, only one question remains. As Roderick Seidenberg said in *Post-Historical Man:* "Why should anyone, even a machine, bother to keep this kind of creature alive?"

The contention that rationalism engenders alienation is also a salient aspect of the radical critique. Members of the New Left believe that rationalism categorizes and differentiates life in order to facilitate domination and control of reality. Hence, implicit in rationalism is the notion that man is in a hostile relationship with the natural world—a world so hostile that, if man is to survive, he must subjugate the natural world. This is a consequence of a historical project grounded in materialism and sustained by rationalism. It also brings with it acceptance of the conviction that the scientific and technical relationship of subject to object and, consequently, of man to nature, is the only valid one. This engenders alienation of man from man and man from nature. As one New Left historian remarks: "While the art and literature of our time tell us . . . that the disease from which our age is dying is that of alienation, the sciences, in their relentless pursuit of objectivity, raise alienation to its apotheosis as our *only* means of achieving a valid relationship to reality."[4] If man continues to see himself surrounded by "things"—whether human or material—to use, to control, or to possess, he may perceive the world rationally, but he will perpetuate his alienation from it. Accordingly, radical Tom Hayden has drawn attention to the fact that "loneliness, estrangement, isolation, describe the vast distance between man and man today." And ". . . these dominant tendencies cannot be overcome by better personnel management, not by improved gadgets, but only when a love of man overcomes the idolatrous worship of things by man."[5]

Older radicals and members of the counterculture are especially convinced that rationalism produces alienation because it is too narrow a channel for the perception and enjoyment of reality. These older radicals would agree with the American philosopher, William James (1842-1910), that "our normal waking consciousness, rational consciousness as we call it, is but one special type of consciousness, whilst all about it, parted from it by the

filmiest of screens, there lie potential forms of consciousness entirely different." And they would also concur that "no account of the universe in its
totality can be final which leaves these other forms of consciousness quite
disregarded. . . . They may determine attitudes though they cannot furnish
formulas, and open a region though they fail to give a map. At any rate they
forbid a premature closing of our accounts with reality."[6]

Just as James used nitrous oxide and Aldous Huxley used mescalin to
"open the doors of perception," today many use marijuana, or synthetic
chemicals like LSD and psilocybin. Others use the vibrations of rock music
combined with weird light shows. The general aim is the same: to pass
beyond the one-dimensional reality of materialist philosophy and rationalist
epistemology. And this aim has philosophical and ecological foundations.
After all, physicists Einstein and Heisenberg, philosophers Hegel and
Whitehead, and anthropologists Mead and Levi-Strauss, have all moved
toward a conception of man as an organism, inseparably part of a larger
organism (the rest of the universe). Levi-Strauss, perhaps the most celebrated
anthropologist in this century, has contended that a definite characteristic
of man's being is that whether primitive or modern, he never conceives of
himself as a totally isolated ego. "There is no I that is not part of a 'We.' "
And again, "Man is not alone in the universe, anymore than the individual is
alone in the group, or any one society alone among other societies."[7]

Yet most people of the Western tradition believe strongly in the isolation
of the personality, estranged from the cosmos around it. The rationally
organized social order sustains this supposition and thereby reinforces the
feeling of estrangement—the belief that there is an inseparable difference
between the inner world of human consciousness and the outer world of
nature. But LSD, mescalin, and to a lesser extent marijuana, provide an
immediate awareness of the unity of inner and outer worlds and of the person
and all he or she perceives. There is joy and relief experienced in realizing
that one is not alone and not a prisoner of the ego. Consequently, works
by psychologists such as Abraham Maslow, Paul Goodman, and Rollo May
enjoy a popularity among young radicals, as do the ideas of Timothy Leary,
Norman O. Brown, Ken Kesey, and Susan Sontag. To varying degrees, these
writers uphold a mystical primordial consciousness which they contend is the
real unifying base of the universe and man.

In addition, they cast doubt upon the separation, commonly made by
rationalism, of mind and body—that the two are distinct and never merge.
In the view of the New Left particularly, such a philosophical dualism rele-
gates freedom and self-realization to an inner world of the spirit and takes
the external world of material culture and human relations to be somehow
irrelevant to true human fulfillment, a realm of inevitability, necessity, and
misery. Many New Left radicals also have doubts about the Christian concept

that the mind is a prisoner of the body, doomed to be constantly at war because the body is material and the mind is spiritual. As the philosopher Wittgenstein once remarked: "What is troubling us is the tendency to believe that the mind is like a little man within." Or to paraphrase Norman O. Brown, there is no longer any reason to believe the Christian notion that the soul is life's prisoner of the body.

To a member of the New Left, then, the distinctions made between mind and body and man and nature are artificial and among the most deleterious aspects of rationalist epistemology. This is because *the distinctions themselves facilitate an experience of alienation.* As Alan Watts puts it, there

> ... has always been at least an obscure awareness that in feeling oneself to be a separate mind, soul, or ego, there is something wrong. Naturally, for a person who finds his identity in something other than his full organism is less than half a man. He is cut off from complete participation in nature. Instead of being a body he "has" a body. Instead of living and loving he "has" instincts for survival and copulation.[8]

Viewed in this way, alienation seems to explain many of the "hangups" of modern life. The more philosophical leaders of the New Left view self-consciousness in much the same manner as do Alan Watts and Norman O. Brown: self-consciousness is a symptom of alienation and is caused largely by the separation of the self from the rest of organic life. This separation is exploited by capitalism through the glorification of competition—competition to survive and to excel. Yet there is no place for such separation, such competition with reality, in the idealist philosophy of the counter-culture. Detaching the self from the rest of reality is consciously obstructing reality, and one becomes aware of this as acute self-consciousness.

In the view of a member of the New Left, therefore, the consciously, carefully planned individual action which is so exalted in the modern capitalist ethos is really just a morbid celebration of alienation, a kind of repetitive compulsion to overcome the isolation of the individual. But as long as man perceives the world as discrete categories as defined by rationalism, alienation will never be overcome. If we are to overcome alienation, politics must cease to be the rational adjustment of would-be conflicting groups; rather, politics must have to do with overcoming the personal alienation caused by the artificial divisions imposed upon men by their mistaken rationalism. As Tom Hayden explained it: "Politics has the function of bringing people out of isolation and into community.... Channels should be commonly available ... so that private problems from bad recreation facilities to personal alienation are formulated as general issues."[9]

Finally, the radical objection to rationalism is that it leads people to believe that life is a struggle between and among species, between elements in reality which must be controlled for survival. This is a shallow perception of life. It eliminates other, more joyous, modes of looking at life, and, more often than not, fails to achieve much human happiness. It does not allow a person to see life in its fullness. The fullness which the young radicals insist is inherent in life is described by Alan Watts in *The Joyous Cosmology:*

> Life is basically a gesture, but no one, no thing is *making* it. There is no necessity for it to happen, and none for it to go on happening. For it isn't *happening* to anyone. . . . Time, space, and multiplicity are complications of it. There is no reason whatever to explain it, for explanations are just another form of complexity, a new manifestation of life on top of life, of gestures gesturing. . . . There isn't any substantial ego at all. The ego is a kind of flip, a knowing of knowing, a fearing of fearing. It's curlique, an extra jazz to experience, a sort of double-take or reverberation. . . .[10]

The point stressed by Watts is that to appreciate life, rationalism, with its insistence upon reducing reality to functional instrumentalities and to mathematical and word symbols only, is a hindrance, not a help. Consequently, there is an impulse even among less philosophically inclined radicals to repudiate rationalism and to stress the importance of intelligence and the whole organism in order to appreciate the interrelatedness of the world. Let us "rediscover the universe as a distinct from a mere multiverse."[11] For this task, rationalism is simply not enough. There is, accordingly, an emphasis by the first two postwar generations upon the nonintellectual capacities of the mind. Increasingly, we may expect to witness the continued development of a certain ecological sensibility, an instinctual faith in the phenomenology of the universe and a faith in the interrelatedness of the world that will be a giant step toward overcoming human alienation and toward giving man greater and more constant joy.

Notes to Chapter 7

1. While Marcuse's critique of rationalism is compelling, a brilliant historical account of the development of rationalist epistemology from Hume through Dewey is by the Polish philosopher, Lesek Kolakowski, *The Alienation of Reason,* trans. Norbert Guterman (New York, 1969).

2. Theodore Lowi, *The End of Liberalism* (New York, 1969), p. 27.

3. While this is the vulgarized pragmatic epistemology of most Americans, I do not suggest it is the epistemology of the most famous pragmatist philosopher, William James. Nor do I suggest that the philosophy of American pragmatism inevitably had to degenerate into the rationalism we now have. Indeed, in the view of the New Left, a more relevant epistemology has been formulated by the great American pragmatist philosopher, John Dewey (1859–1952). Certainly, if his philosophy of "instrumentalism" had become the dominant one in American society, the New Left would be less critical of American corporate liberalism, for Dewey's instrumentalism asks that philosopher, citizen, and government analyze the social effect resulting from the acceptance of given policies, ideals, political institutions, etc. The practical applicability of these is the standard of value and criterion of truth. There is no difference between cognition and knowledge, for knowledge as a whole is valuation, an attempt to describe the reality of the "good" from the point of view of practical behavior. Usefulness becomes social usefulness, and truth ceases to be a means to personal ends; it becomes, rather, an "instrument" of social action. Truth is still clearly relative, but relative to a broadly conceived, collective national interest. Although certainly not satisfying the New Left's quest for Being, Dewey's philosophy would allow enough freedom so that it would be acceptable to many in the New Left.

4. Theodore Roszak, *The Making of a Counter Culture* (New York, 1969), p. 232.

5. From "The Port Huron Statement," reprinted in Paul Jacobs and Saul Landau, *The New Radicals* (New York, 1966), p. 155.

6. Quoted in Alan W. Watts, *The Joyous Cosmology* (New York, 1962), pp. x-xi. All references to this book are by permission of Random House Publishers.

7. Claude Levi-Strauss, *Tristes Tropiques* (Paris, 1955), p. 398.

8. Watts, *Joyous Cosmology,* p. 6.

9. From "The Port Huron Statement," quoted in Jack Newfield, *A Prophetic Minority* (New York, 1966), p. 91.

10. Watts, *Joyous Cosmology,* p. 72.

11. Alan W. Watts, *This is It and Other Essays* (New York, 1967), p. 58.

VIII

Antitechnology

There is a time when the operation of the machine becomes so odious, makes you so sick at heart that you can't take part; . . . and you've got to put your bodies upon the levers, upon all the apparatus, and you've got to make it stop. And you've got to indicate to the people who run it, to the people who own it, that unless you're free, the machine will be prevented from working at all.*

In the eyes of a Left radical, inextricably interwoven with the philosophy of materialism and an epistemology of rationalism is the development of *technique*. *Technique* means "the totality of methods, rationally arrived at and having absolute efficiency for a given state of development in every field of human activity."[1] *Technology* means "the institutionalization of utilitarian norms," featuring "the application of rational principles to the control and reordering of space, matter, and human beings."[2] Consequently, the gigantic extension of a technical approach to life since World War II is, in the view of the more philosophical radicals at least, the outgrowth of a materialist and rationalist historical project. And therefore there is a tendency among some radicals to be antitechnology. But there is by no means unanimity regarding technique. Perhaps it would be most accurate to say there is a pervasive fear of technique, especially as it is now used.[3] Among the members of the New Left, there are many who believe technique can be controlled and redirected for democratic and almost utopian ends.

Nevertheless, the immediate reaction of the younger radicals is to shy away from anything technical and to refuse to participate in anything managed by technicians, administrators, bureaucrats, and the like. The reason for this response is that the postwar generations find themselves growing up

*Mario Savio, leading students to occupy the administration building of the University of California during the FSM.

in the most technological country ever known. The country as a whole, with its poverty, its inflation, its energy shortages, its undeclared wars, its moon shots, and its phase I–IV presidential socialism, moves in a direction that young radicals do not understand, from a starting point in history which they cannot locate, and toward a destination nobody seems able to predict. Tom Hayden brilliantly captured this impression: "... there is astute grasp of method, technique—the committee, ... the lobbyist, the hard and soft sell, ... but, if pressed critically, such expertise is incompetent to explain its implicit ideal. Theoretic chaos has replaced the idealistic thinking of old— and unable to reconstitute theoretic order, men have condemned idealism itself." [4]

In addition, technique as an approach to life and reality seems to per- petuate itself. There is never really a challenge to the *method* of technique. The question is always whether the technique works to solve a problem—a problem which is formulated strictly in technical terms. The social problem of riots, for example, is reduced to controlling the causes of the riots. The simplest technical solution is to control the agents of the riots (people). This can be done, according to technique, by strengthening police forces with sophisticated weapons and surveillance. Hence, sociologist Morris Janowitz, in his study of riots, concluded that only surveillance and covert penetration are effective techniques to manage riots. [5] And yet both the Kerner Commis- sion and the report of the National Commission on the Causes and Prevention of Violence have argued that there are *no* technical means for controlling riots. Furthermore, "An approach that gives equal emphasis to force and re- form fails to measure the anticipated consequences of employing force: and it fails to appreciate the political significance of protest. If American society concentrates on the development of more sophisticated control techniques, it will move itself into a destructive and self-defeating position." [6] Yet, we still rely so heavily on rationalism and technique that problems which cannot be formulated in technical terms—such as alienation, happiness, justice, and relevance—become nonproblems. These are among the problems that cause riots and protests. But individuals and the society as a whole tend to discount problems such as alienation and relevance as purely personal concerns and therefore unworthy of society's attention or the taxpayer's money.

It is little wonder then that Herbert Muller's book on technology, *The Children of Frankenstein* (1970), struck such a receptive response among college students and New Left radicals. Muller's title refers to the postwar generation of youth who have grown up in a superindustrial, technological society, symbolized by what may be seen by many as a Frankenstein monster: the computer. And, indeed, children of the postwar generation are programmed in their education by computers, subscribe to literature by computers, watch moon exploration controlled by computers, see bombing and missile combat done by computer, and learn "computer science" in institutions of higher learning. Indeed, the computer may seem something like a Frankenstein—a machine able to outwit man himself, at least to make his mental capacity and his human capacity superfluous or obsolete. Of course, to someone even slightly knowledgeable about computers it would hardly seem justifiable to compare them to Frankenstein. However, the computer has implications we do not yet know and it can go astray. For example, an omission of a hyphen by a programmer at Cape Kennedy made it necessary to destroy a rocket costing $18,500,000. Even though no one was killed, it wasted the taxpayer's money and, possibly, deprived a few hundred people of material aid.

But the horror of the computer as a symbol is that it has been made the servant of a materialist conception of reality and a rationalist theory of knowledge. Hence, it processes only quantitative or factual information, not qualitative judgments or social, cultural values. While it is true that computers can translate languages, they are unable to give an accurate rendition of the connotative, emotional, or spiritual overtones of linguistic communication. For example, when a computer was asked to translate "The spirit is willing but the flesh is weak" into Russian and then back into English, what resulted was "The ghost is ready but the meat is raw." [7] The point here, of course, is that a computer is not a human being, and, while the computer is assigned to regulate more and more of people's lives, the result is the *abstraction of personal relations.* Computers make no value judgments, nor can they communicate values with human intensity. The fear is that they will further alienate people from each other rather than facilitate a solution to alienation. As yet, the problem of alienation has neither been submitted to a computer nor has merited accepting the answer. There is much truth to Senator Robert Kennedy's statement that the computer measures "neither our wit nor our courage, neither our wisdom nor our learning, neither our compassion nor our duty to our country. . . . It measures everything, in short, except that which makes life worthwhile." [8]

Accordingly, many young people seem to be at the stage of historical evolution where everything that is not technique is being eliminated. And the challenge to a country, to an individual, or to a system appears to be solely a technical challenge. Consequently, there is widespread belief, particularly among college students, that there is no room for an individual today unless he is a technician. This is an ironic situation. While technology has clearly broadened the range of opportunities for enjoyment and has created more leisure recreation, it has at the same time demanded that the college graduate become an occupational specialist. And specialization means to become technically proficient at a specific, usually technically relevant, profession.

This requires a cultivated technocratic mentality, a uniformity of approach to one's job, and, usually, a standardized life style. The result is that people feel dominated by technique and that their horizons are controlled by whatever technical problems are formulated by the government and business. This is why a society whose horizon and whose historical project is formulated in purely technical terms is viewed with such horror by the radicals. For in such a society, whether George Orwell's *1984,* Ken Kesey's *One Flew Over the Cuckoo's Nest,* or Anthony Burgess's *A Clockwork Orange,* the point is the same: technocracy, no matter how pure, produces a world which perpetuates and increases the continuum of spiritual repression. Man's inner world, his spiritual or nonintellectual dimension, is controlled. For technique, as sociologist Jacques Ellul has noted, results in "the lack of spiritual efficiency of even the best ideas. The very assimilation of ideas into the technical framework which renders them materially effective makes them spiritually worthless." [9]

Many people in the postwar generations have grown up in this kind of technology-dominated world. It is the world so vividly described by biologist George Wald in his famous speech at the Massachusetts Institute of Technology in March 1969: an America of gigantic technocracies created during and after World War II—the Pentagon, a standing army of 3.5 million, a huge defense establishment within a civilian economy, a clandestine, apparently impregnable Central Intelligence Agency, and a mysterious, very powerful Atomic Energy Commission. It seems to be a world where everything is "managed" or "administered" (euphemisms for technically controlled).

The main reason for this situation is that technique pursues no end; there is no purpose or plan that is being progressively realized. There are labor relations boards, community relations boards, church relations boards, racial relations boards, human relations boards, student relations boards, farm relations boards, ad infinitum—all of them technical agencies to facilitate the harmonious functioning of individuals and groups, but for no discernible reason except to perpetuate a national life of producing, buying, and selling at a cost of outrageous toil and human suffering. In postwar America, man has become an *administré.* And so society seems, as Ken Kesey put it: "like an old clock that won't tell time but won't stop neither, with the hands bent out of shape and the face bare of numbers and the alarm bell rusted silent, an old worthless clock that just keeps ticking and cuckooing without meaning nothing." [10]

Especially disturbing to radicals is the impact of a technical approach upon politics and government. Increasingly, since the days of President Kennedy and Secretary of Defense McNamara, the government has become a technical apparatus which promotes technical programs to solve technically formulated problems, from race relations to Vietnam. Politicians and their staffs have become, in the jargon of the New Left, "technicians of power." This has resulted in a short circuit between the people and the power, the latter becoming an amoral administration. The paramount criterion for deciding the governmental course of action is no longer whether it is constitutional, or moral, but more often what technique can best solve a problem. (The classic example was the decision to injure the Democratic party in 1971-72 by illegal political espionage—Watergate.) Efficiency of execution, rather than justice of application, has become the issue of judgment. Thus, as George Wald has pointed out, the morality of producing napalm—whose *only* known use is as an antipersonnel weapon—is not an issue. The issue is whether it can kill people who seek refuge in cellars or in underground fortifications. What has sprung up, the radicals argue, is a creeping technical totalitarianism. This weakens the legitimacy of the government because as it seeks to disencumber itself of the role of master planner, it delegates technical (administrative) powers to bipartisan agencies whose origins are technical, not moral, and whose responsibility is to the state, not to the electorate. This has produced a feeling of frustration and helplessness in the poor and particularly in the young. For many people, it has inaugurated an age of individual ineffectiveness, for there is a suspicion that we no longer possess any means of combating or substantially influencing the "technicalization" of society. Countless Americans share the feeling of the great poet W. H. Auden that

> We are lived by powers we pretend to understand:
> They arrange our loves; it is they who direct at the end
> The enemy bullet, the sickness, or even our hand.[11]

There is, then, a definite radical impulse against technique and, to a lesser extent, against technology. It is directed against what seems to be a world run by invisible men high in office buildings whose employees hide behind IBM computers, punch-cards, and production lines. It is against systems engineers and business executives who exploit honest workers and whose imaginations are unable to grasp a microscopic fragment of the horror which results from faithfully serving machines. The antitechnology sentiment is aimed against the dehumanization of these workers and the sickening spectacle of their nightly recovery with their wives, martinis, "pills," and TV. And it is aimed also against the directives of smug administrators, directives issued and passed on by men whose moral judgment is too often diseased by an idolatrous worship of power, such as was the case in the Watergate affair.

Such a situation is, of course, a nightmare. But for most conscientious members of the New Left, it does not mean the repudiation of technique, modernity, or the seeking of pastoral bliss in a neo-Fascist paradise. It means that we draw the obvious conclusion that American society has chosen to accentuate technological change, to regard it as perhaps its most creative expression, and most certainly to view it as the power behind economic growth. If this is the case, the crucial issues are how to use technology and who participates in deciding how we use it. The answers to both of these questions are contingent upon convincing millions of citizens and hundreds of "technicians of power" that we cannot achieve an environmentally safe country without combining transportation, manufacture, land use, waste disposal, pollution control, and population planning into a single global or "whole earth" perspective. This means that no significant social or economic decisions should be made without a global perspective. As William Ruckelshaus, ex-head of the Environmental Protection Agency, put it, we must stop the policy of "waste now—pay later."

In this view, technique is clearly not to be feared; indeed, it is to be seen as an instrument of hope for mankind. At least that is the interpretation still held in the 1970's by the majority of members of the New Left:

> Is it still necessary to state that not technology, not technique, not the machine are the engines of repression, but the presence in them of the masters who determine their number, their lifespan, their power, their place in life, and the need for them? Is it still necessary to repeat that science and technology are the great vehicles of liberation, and that it is only their use and restriciton in the repressive society which makes them into vehicles of domination? [12]

And it is Marcuse who, backed by educator George Leonard, economist Robert Theobald, and psychologist Paul Goodman, insists that "All the material and intellectual forces which could be put to work for the realization of a free society are at hand." [13] These intellects are supported by a study done by the National Commission on Technology, Automation and Economic Progress, which reported that "if America were to take all its productivity gains from 1965 to 1985 in the form of increased leisure, it would then be able to choose between a twenty-two-hour week, a twenty-seven-week year and retirement at thirty-eight." [14] Thus, it does not seem unrealistic that many in the New Left argue: "Utopian possibilities are inherent in the technical and technological forces of advanced capitalism and socialism: the rational utilization of these forces on a global scale would eliminate poverty and scarcity within a very foreseeable future." [15]

Although the more optimistic members of the New Left see technology as a virtual panacea, many are less starry-eyed about it. These people are usually dubbed "ecofreaks"—ecology freaks. They generally consider themselves part of the movement, but are quick to point out that we cannot restore the earth, or this country, to what it was when only the Indians lived here. To these ecology-oriented radicals, the priorities, the real moral decisions, are ecological, and they argue that no generation until this one has been confronted by such portentous decisions. Therefore, we must consider the ecological impact of all our activity: the detergents we use, the cars we drive, the no-return cans and bottles we use, the air conditioners which demand so much power, the noise of our industrial engines, and the pesticides and herbicides which kill irreplaceable wildlife (over 200 species have become extinct since 1600 A. D. and over 100 vertebrates since 1700).

It is the "ecofreaks" who parade the slogan "The population bomb is everybody's baby." For they are convinced (and can prove it statistically) that a human population that increases geometrically will ultimately doom all private and public efforts to save the earth and probably make it impossible to sustain our present standard of living. As Mr. Ruckelshaus has indicated, each new baby will dump 38,000 pounds of sewage into our rivers and bays during his lifetime. He or she will pollute 30 million additional gallons to keep him in food and services. He or she will own three or four cars in his lifetime and burn 21,000 gallons of gasoline. And yearly he or she will add 200 pounds of waste paper and 480 cans and bottles to his heap of solid trash, not to mention several hundred pounds of plastic refuse.[16] So, these "ecofreaks," many of whom take their guidelines from Ralph Nader and the student PIRG's, point out that there can be no significant environmental control, no real progress on the uses of technology until we limit the users of technology, the human population. Since most of the human population is of childbearing age, the "ecofreaks" and young people carry a weighty responsibility. (Even if married couples average the replacement level—2.11 children—the population of the United States will keep on rising until 2037 A.D.) That would be just about when the first postwar generation itself will have in large measure perished. That would mean an additional 70 million people or an American population of 275 million. Despite the clamor of both the antitechnologists and the utopian technologists in the New Left, it is the "ecofreaks" who first predicted the energy shortage and perhaps one day may gain the majority following.

Some unanimity is evident in the attitudes of the New Left and the counterculture toward technology. Members of the New Left agree that technology is not being used to end poverty, to facilitate more humanistic education, to develop sources of power which do not pollute and which are not controlled by a small coterie of corporations, or to create life styles more amenable to recreation. Indeed, we have been so unimaginative that we have done little to apply technique to pleasure, to community recreation, or to the aesthetic dimension of man. Indeed, whatever we have to sustain much interest among young people has come about purely by accident: rock 'n' roll music and multi-media concerts. In the United States, the present monopoly of capitalist culture prevents technology from being applied to more imaginative purposes. For example, to apply technique with a serious

intent of eliminating air pollution is difficult because the ten largest corporations in the United States sell either cars or gas. Unfortunately, the direction
of technology, particularly if it is to come from industry, will hardly be
changed unless new uses of technology are made attractive for our large corporations. This is especially important when one considers that according to
the Senate Subcommittee on Anti-Trust, in 1975, 300 corporations owned
75 percent of the industrial assets of the world.[17]

Consequently, the use of technology is a rallying issue for many radicals.
As Abbie Hoffman put it,

> . . . we have the capabilities and the technology for relieving a great
> deal of human suffering in the world and we don't use these tech-
> nologies, and that makes us pissed. You see it's not only the attitude
> that we're living under a state of repression, but also the fact that we
> have a vision that could be achieved, that could realistically be achieved
> and that there are blundering old menopausal dinosaurs who control
> the power in this country, and are not allowing that.[18]

And so, what the radicals want, even the more skeptical ones, is a redirection
of technology, but with a more humane view of man and a far more planetary
ecological perspective.

It follows that technology will have to be utilized in accordance with a
new sensibility. And, of course, the New Left and the counterculture are
vitally concerned with that new sensibility, that new perspective toward the
world and technology. They argue that using technique for sheer economic
growth is not enough, indeed, it is not as important as the growth of the
human spirit, of kindness, and of decency. The beginnings of such a sensibility were evident during the Woodstock Festival of Life in the summer of
1969. This new sensibility would have to reflect that pain, ignorance, injustice, hunger, and cruelty are no longer inevitable or acceptable as
existential conditions as they were fifty or even twenty-five years ago.
Finally, such a new sensibility would manifest the humility and resilience so
eloquently expressed by I. F. Stone. "The problems of war, racism, bureaucracy, and pollution are everywhere. No society has solved them; their roots
are deep in the ancient conditioning of man and in his inability to control
technology. Man himself is obsolete unless he can change. That change
requires more altruism; more kindness—no one need be ashamed to say it—
love."[19] With these changes, we might be on our way toward achieving a
technology of liberation. But liberation can never happen until that ill-
defined monster called "the system" has been slain or at least neutralized.

Notes to Chapter 8

1. Jacques Ellul, *The Technological Society,* trans. John Wilkinson (New York, 1964), p. xxv.

2. Robert A. Nisbet, *The Social Bond: An Introduction to the Study of Society* (New York, 1970), pp. 244-45.

3. See William Braden, *The Age of Aquarius: Technology and the Cultural Revolution* (Chicago, 1971).

4. From "The Port Huron Statement," in Paul Jacobs and Saul Landau, eds., *The New Radicals* (New York, 1966), p. 153.

5. Morris Janowitz, *Social Control of Escalated Riots* (Chicago, 1968), p. 21.

6. Jerome Skolnick, *The Politics of Protest (A Task Force Report to the National Commission on the Causes and Prevention of Violence)* (New York, 1969), p. 346. Reprinted by permission of Simon and Schuster.

7. Herbert Muller, *The Children of Frankenstein* (Bloomington, Indiana, 1970), p. 92.

8. Quoted in ibid., p. 12.

9. Ellul, *Technological Society,* p. 245.

10. Ken Kesey, *One Flew Over the Cuckoo's Nest* (New York, 1962), p. 53. Reprinted by permission of Viking Press, Inc.

11. W. H. Auden, "In Memory of Ernest Toller," *Collected Shorter Poems 1927-1957* (New York, 1966), p. 144. Reprinted by permission of Random House, Inc.

12. Herbert Marcuse, *An Essay on Liberation* (New York, 1969), p. 12. All references to this book are by permission of Beacon Press.

13. Herbert Marcuse, "The End of Utopia," in *Five Lectures* (New York, 1970), p. 64. All references to this book are by permission of Beacon Press.

14. Quoted in Michael Harrington, *Toward A Democratic Left* (Baltimore, 1969), p. 28. Reprinted by permission of Macmillan Publishing Co., Inc.

15. Marcuse, *On Liberation,* p. 4.

16. See William D. Ruckelshaus, "Commencement and Ecommencement," A Commencement Address delivered at Butler University, June 6, 1971.

17. Harrington, *Toward A Democratic Left,* p. 28.

18. Abbie Hoffman, "Freedom and License," in *The Conspiracy,* eds. Peter and Deborah Babcox and Bob Abel (New York, 1969), p. 73. Reprinted by permission of Dell Publishing Co., Inc.

19. *I. F. Stone's Bi-Weekly* (March 5, 1970). Reprinted by permission of the author, I. F. Stone.

IX

The System and the University

Once the religious, the hunted and weary
Chasing the promise of freedom and hope
Came to this country to build a new vision
Far from the reaches of Kingdom and Pope
. . . .
But though the past has its share of injustice
Kind was the spirit in many a way
But its protectors and friends have been sleeping
Now it's a monster and will not obey*

Probably the most vocal and most consistent criticism heard from the radicals of the New Left has been against that amorphous monster referred to as "the system." The term has come to encompass all the harmful effects of capitalism—the administrative establishment which maintains capitalism, the military and industrial complex, the imperialism in Southeast Asia, Africa, and South America, and the reduction of the citizenry to a position of virtual powerlessness. Perhaps all of these effects cannot be directly attributed to capitalism, but they are the historical concomitants of postwar America which claims its chief glory to be a capitalist economic system. Hence, when the New Left radicals attack "the system," they recognize that they are not just attacking the economic theory of capitalism (as for instance an orthodox Marxist would). The attack is upon the whole spectrum of problems which may not be directly *caused* by capitalism, but which may be sustained or perpetuated by capitalism. Capitalism here is defined as the theory that commodities should be produced, distributed, and serviced for individual profit.

When radicals do criticize capitalism as an economic philosophy, however,

---

* "Monster," words and music by John Kay and Jerry Edmonton. Reprinted by permission of ABC/Dunhill Music, Inc.

the critique, whether it comes from veteran SDS member Greg Calvert, philosopher Herbert Marcuse, or radical economists Paul Baran and Paul Sweezy, is generally the same: capitalism is obsolete. That is, capitalism as an economic theory does not correspond to how the economy works, and it does not facilitate individual freedom. All of these leaders seem to agree that the era of individualism and private enterprise is over. We now have a corporate or monopoly capitalism at work which since World War II has increasingly become a business arrangement between the government, universities, the military, and a few favored and often multinational corporations. The claim that the American economy is one of free enterprise is considered a palpable lie by most radicals.

At no time has private enterprise or free enterprise been possible in America—in the sense of having *unlimited* right to start a private business. In the eighteenth and nineteenth centuries, private enterprise (as a form of capitalism) did have meaning because it differentiaed the American system from the vestiges of European mercantilism and the dying guild system. Now, however, such a conception of capitalism is meaningless. Now we have monopolistic capitalism in which a few corporations almost totally control the economy and wield proportional power in politics. Some examples may be illustrative. At the time of this writing, Radio Corporation of America (RCA) has large holdings in the publishing business: namely Random House, which itself owns Alfred Knopf, and Pantheon. The Columbia Broadcasting System (CBS) has interest in the New York Yankees baseball team and stock in General Motors, Ford, and Chrysler; CBS owns outright Holt, Reinhart and Winston, the publishers. Time, Incorporated owns Little, Brown & Co., previously an independent publisher. Time also owns some TV stations, as well as publishing *Time* and *Fortune* magazines. But probably the most illustrative example of monopolistic capitalism is General Motors, the world's largest corporation. It has an annual revenue larger than any government except the United States, the USSR, and the United Kingdom. It sells over half of all automobiles sold in the United States and, since the second devaluation of the dollar in February 1973, it has sold an even greater percentage of automobiles in the United States. Clearly, it is in a monopolistic position. And finally, International Telephone and Telegraph (ITT) is a conglomerate of 433 separate boards of directors and gets 60 percent of its income from holdings abroad (it had holdings in 40 countries in 1971). It ranks as the ninth largest industrial corporation in the United States and derives one-half of its domestic revenue from the United States government via defense and space contracts.

Monopoly here is not defined as primarily having one firm as the single seller of a product, but as having few sellers dominate the markets for products which are more or less satisfactory substitutes for each other.

Thus, monopoly lessens, rather than increases, competition. Liquid and material assets which might be used to facilitate more equitable competition among many more firms are now controlled by means of mergers and outright acquisitions. This has been a major development in the economic structure of this country since World War II. It is not as it was in the period 1870–1930, when large trusts in a few large firms dominated a single industry. Now a few firms dominate several industries. The trend was set and continues to be set by petroleum companies. Subsidized by tax credits abroad and depletion allowances at home, they have practically taken over the fertilizer industry. They are also very influential in the coal industry, chemicals, plastics, trucking, auto parts, and nuclear power. Hence, it is not surprising that 4,550 firms disappeared by merger in 1969 and about 6,000 by merger and acquisition in 1970.[1]

Furthermore, the argument used by large firms that bigger enterprises are more efficient and thereby lower consumer prices is untrue—at least that was the conclusion of the Senate Subcommittee on Anti-Trust and Monopoly in 1970. It was reiterated in a different manner by Robert Townsend, former chairman of the board of Avis and author of *Up the Organization:* "Excellence and bigness are incompatible!" So New Leftists contend that we are witnessing the substitution of a monopolistic price system for the traditional competitive system. Accordingly, radicals are sure that free enterprise, individual initiative, and the essence of American capitalism, are today anachronisms, Establishment shibboleths. But in fact *capitalism is no longer even an Establishment shibboleth.* The United States government no longer pretends to espouse capitalism, but while decrying the system we *do* have, the government does *almost nothing* to improve it. Hence, former President Nixon's attorney general, John Mitchell, warned against the growth of monopolistic capitalism in a speech on June 6, 1969:

> In 1948, the nation's 200 largest industrial corporations controlled 48% of the manufacturing assets. Today these firms control 58% while the top 500 firms control 75%. The danger that this super concentration poses to our economic, political, and social structure cannot be overestimated. Concentration of this magnitude is likely to eliminate existing and future competition. It increases the possibility for reciprocity and other forms of unfair buyer-seller leverage. It creates nationwide marketing, managerial and financing structures whose enormous physical and psychological resources pose substantial barriers to smaller firms wishing to participate in a competitive market.
>
> And finally, super concentration creates a "community of interest" which discourages competition among large firms and establishes a tone in the marketplace for more and more mergers.[2]

To the New Left radicals, concomitant to corporate or monopoly capital-

THE SYSTEM AND THE UNIVERSITY

ism is the concentration of profits in an industrial-military complex which is so powerful as to constitute a state within a state, a society within the larger society. And this has curtailed rather than facilitated the liberty of the majority, for it continues to make more and more people dependent upon the complex (the system) for their survival. In brief, it makes more and more lives dependent upon the policies of the government and the military while offering the people no real control over the making and implementing of policies such as war, space exploration, highway, and public project construction.[3]

This criticism is not new. The potential centralization of economic and political power in the hands of a military-industrial clique was pointed out by President Eisenhower just before the inauguration of his successor, John F. Kennedy, in 1960. "In councils of government we must guard against the acquisitions of unwarranted influence, whether sought or unsought by the industrial-military complex. The potential for the disastrous rise of misplaced power exists and will persist." Nevertheless, Kennedy took office three days later and increased military spending; he increased the number of army divisions by 45 percent, the number of Polaris submarines by 50 percent, the number of Minuteman missiles by 100 percent, and ordered a 100 percent increase in the number of nuclear weapons in our strategic alert forces. This, as Secretary of Defense McNamara pointed out, enabled us to fight (as we did in Southeast Asia) without general mobilization. What has arisen in the 1970's is a military and industrial economy run primarily by the Department of Defense. The latter has become, to a great extent, the real master of the nation's economic resources. And this economy is most certainly political, *not* guided by independent private enterprise.

The Department of Defense owns 39 million acres of land, employs 7½ million persons directly (including soldiers)—that is 10.3 percent of the national work force—and spends over 80 billion dollars yearly.[4] The spectacular concentration of power (economic and political) in the Department of Defense can be understood if one notes that the Pentagon budget of 1972–73 was larger than the entire federal budget for 1957–58. This means that the Pentagon is richer and more powerful than any small nation on earth. Its property (in 1976) and plant and equipment are worth over $202 billion (10 percent of the total assets of the United States). This makes it the largest planned economy outside of the Soviet Union. And the point that the radicals make is that it *is* a planned economy—that is to say, not private enterprise, but socialist in nature. This economy is managed by approximately 15,000 persons in the government (mainly in the Department of Defense). They arrange for the renewal of contracts and the assignment of new contracts with business corporations.[5] In 1968, two-thirds of Defense Department contracts went to fewer than 100 companies, and five of these received over one billion dollars worth. "In the case of 10 of these firms, AVCO, Collins Radio, General Dynamics, LTV, Lockheed, Martin-Marietta, McDonnell, Newport News Shipbuilding, Northrop, and Raytheon, these government orders exceeded half of their sales volume."[6]

So it should not have surprised anyone when Lockheed asked for and received $250 million from the government when the firm was approaching bankruptcy in August 1971. Lockheed's economic failure and its request for a government "loan" were by no means unique. General Dynamics was rescued from bankruptcy by the Pentagon in 1962 when it was awarded the Department of Defense contract for the F-111 tactical fighter. The contract was awarded despite the superiority of design and earlier delivery date promised by Boeing Aircraft Company. Subsequently, after losses of several F-111's in Vietnam, the plane was grounded, brought out in an updated model, and then again grounded because of its heavy losses. Also, it should be noted that in January 1973, the Navy bought $1.7 million worth of stock in the Gap Instrument Corporation, thus rescuing it from bankruptcy due to cost overruns similar to Lockheed. Until Gap can buy back the stock (which as of 1976 it had not done), the Defense Department will be the largest stockholder in the corporation.

For these firms and for smallers ones, the government has great control over what they produce; often the Defense Department owns most of their means of production. In addition, the government assumes a major role in research and development by paying most of the cost. The government also supplies much of the plant equipment and working capital. "The cost of government-supplied property exceeds the amount of company-owned property reported on the balance sheets of major military contractors."[7] For example, LTV owns less than one percent of the 6.7 million square feet of office-lab-factory space used for defense work; the rest is owned by the government. It must be remembered also that it is not just aerospace and military contractors that receive government subsidies in one form or another. It was estimated in 1970 that the government spends over $6 billion yearly on direct subsidies to "private enterprise."[8] Some examples are in order. In 1970, "the very Congress that failed to provide a food stamp program to feed hungry children voted $199.5 million in subsidies to ship builders. . . . Congress also voted $193 million in increased subsidies for ship operations, mostly to help pay the salaries of crews." And finally, perhaps of immeasurable value as a form of subsidy, "the big defense contractors get the rights to patents they developed with government funds."[9]

Clearly, this sort of economic arrangement can hardly be called capitalism in the private enterprise sense. It is common knowledge to almost anyone working at the higher levels of the government, business, and academia that the federal government has supportive programs via subsidies, research and promotional contracts, tax shelters and write-offs, and protections from competition, and that these are used to perpetuate the corporate mission of profit and sales maximization. Although the government has virtual control of only several firms, it can exercise "regulation" of business not only by statute, but also by unilateral exercise of its monopolistic market position. In 1968, for example, General Dynamics and Lockheed got over $4.1 billion from government contracts (four-fifths of this money was for military objectives). This amounted to nearly 85 percent of their business. In certain geographic areas where defense industries are large employers, tens of thousands of persons are at the mercy of contracts. It has been estimated that in Washington, Oregon, and California, over 26 percent of the working population is employed in defense-generated occupations.[10] In the Seattle-Tacoma area, site of the Boeing Aircraft Company, at least 40 percent of the employment is defense related. Hence, the unemployment rate climbed to 13 percent in 1970 when Boeing reduced its employment from 101,500 persons in 1968 to 38,000 in 1970. In the autumn of 1970, Senators Magnuson and Jackson of Washington repeatedly warned of the disaster to the Seattle area that would result if Boeing were not awarded the Supersonic Transport (SST) contract. The same year, economist Seymour Melman estimated that nationally the industrial-military complex directly influences the lives of 3.5 million soldiers on 2,257 bases, 1.2 million civilian employees, 3 million workers directly employed in war production, and an even larger number in defense-related production. There are millions of persons who must cooperate with "the system" in order to survive. Another economist, Robert Heilbroner, estimated that if the Department of Defense closed down it would result in a total national unemployment of 15 percent—as high as during the Great Depression of the 1930's.[11]

But, according to radicals, this is not simply a dangerous economic situation; it is an even more dangerous political situation, because politics and the industrial-military complex are inextricably related. Funds for the industrial-military complex must be voted by Congress, so there is tremendous pressure on politicians. Since congressmen are not above making good investments, it is not surprising that in 1969 at least sixty congressmen owned stock in aerospace and related industries.[12] Since many white and blue collar workers depend on contracts which Congress approves, it is also not surprising that "some four or five million votes come under the influence of aerospace funding."[13] Hence, millions of citizens have a personal stake in the direction of the defense and space policy. Accordingly, the radical finds it difficult to make headway against "the silent majority," many of whom were partisans of the war in Southeast Asia, who made their livelihood off the war, and who continue to make their livelihood off military spending generally. For it is the military machine, backed up by the fantastic productive capacity of American technology, which has created six tons of TNT for every inhabitant on earth. It is the military machine that, by September 1973 (seven months after the ceasefire), dropped 7.4 million tons of bombs on Southeast Asia. This was three times the total bomb tonnage dropped by the United States in both the European and Pacific theaters of World War II. And until February 1973, it was the policy of the United States government to spend $2.5 billion each month for military activities in Southeast Asia. Moreover, it was the use of very sophisticated weapons and hundreds of thousands of men, backed up by an enormous amount of research and technology, that caused the nations of the *world* to increase their total expenditures for armaments in the postwar era. The United States Arms Control and Disarmament Agency reported that by 1969 the nations of the world were spending over $182 billion yearly for armaments, or an average of $53 for every man, woman, and child on earth—more than many of them have to live on. The Disarmament Agency also estimated that the world will spend $4 trillion on armaments by 1980. This is the price tag for a "security" which, in a nuclear age, no nation enjoys, including the United States, the leading spender.

It is against this kind of "system," this kind of social and economic organization and its perpetuation, that the New Left protests. "We call it free enterprise. But it is a vastly restrictive system of oligopolistic market manipulation, tied by institutionalized corruption to the greatest munitions boondoggle in history and dedicated to the infantilizing of the public by turning it into a herd of compulsive consumers."[14] It is a system interlocked with politics, industry, war, individual employment, and, as will be seen, the universities. Its priorities are morally outrageous. The Pentagon budget for 1969–70 was $82 billion, or 40 percent of the federal budget, while housing and community development received only $2.8 billion, or 1.4 percent of the budget (even the reduced 1974 budget of $79 billion was 30 percent of total federal spending). To make a specific comparison, the amount spent on military housing facilities from 1965–67 was more than the total spent by the government on public housing. Thus, former Justice William O. Douglas calculated, for the first annum of the 1970's, "we will spend 2 billion dollars for development of ABM, which is more than we will allocate to community action and model cities combined; we will spend 2.4 billion on new Navy ships, which is about twice what we will spend on education for the poor; we will spend 8 billion dollars on new weapons research, which is more than twice the current cost of the medicare program."[15] At the same time we allow 13 million American families to make less than $3,000 yearly and 5 million families to make less than $1,000.[16] It is little wonder that this is "the system" which Allen Ginsberg calls "Moloch" and the rock group Steppenwolf names "The Monster."

What is particularly irksome to the student radicals is the wholesale infiltration of many of the nation's great universities by the military-industrial complex. Since World War II, universities have been orienting themselves toward the production of knowledge for specific government projects, from counter-insurgency training at Michigan State University to defoliant research at Columbia University. Universities have become increasingly dependent upon government grants and corporate investment. The trend is for increased government financing of colleges and universities. In the 1960's, the government financed approximately 13 percent of higher education through the allocation of national research and development projects. This amount was raised to 21 percent by special provisions of the Education Acts of the Kennedy and Johnson administrations in the mid-1960's. It is estimated by the Carnegie Commission for Higher Education that the federal government will finance about 33 percent of higher education by 1980.[17]

Increased participation by government and business in the financing of higher education has altered the emphasis of education and resulted in a new kind of university administration: more secretive, less involved with students, and more responsive to business and governmental magnates. Bluntly stated, the moral and cultural authority of the universities has been compromised as universities have become mainstays of the system—the current military-industrial economic structure. Indeed, the very structure (the operational organization) of most large universities has taken on the form of the larger industrial order, i.e. the conglomeration, or the multiversity, to use the term coined by ex-President of Berkeley, Clark Kerr. Hence the classic, but by no means dated, description by James Ridgeway:

> A conglomerate corporation is a profit-making enterprise, while a university is not. But modern management techniques, such as input-output analysis, make it possible to run a multiversity on precisely the same principle as a business corporation: return on investment. A university is centered in the education field, while a conglomerate purports to operate in a wide range of non-related activities. But most of the largest conglomerates are heavily into one market—military-aerospace—while the universities also run non-educational enterprises, including university presses and investment trusts, weapons research and riot-control projects, poverty programs and counter-insurgency studies, real-estate offices and cigarette-filter promotions. Both are dependent on the "public market"—state and federal contracts and subsidy, especially for military-aerospace operations. Both are going international.[18]

The only basic operational difference between universities and industrial and governmental conglomerates is that the former are nonprofit and the latter profit-oriented institutions; both depend on the same market—servicing, maintaining, and advancing a larger military-industrial economy. Furthermore, with the introduction of military-aerospace research and development projects on college campuses, the distinction between working for the government, private enterprise, and academia has all but vanished. It is not surprising, therefore, that it has been estimated that 63 percent of the nation's scientists, engineers, and technicians work on defense projects of one kind or another.[19] Many of these people are either on the staffs of universities or maintain relations with universities. Increasingly, it appears that, with the exception of small liberal arts colleges, universities are essentially repositories of knowledge and processing institutions for government agencies and key businesses. This has been pointed out repeatedly by Tom Hayden, Ralph Nader, and by the radical chemist, Professor John Froines.

The student revolt at Columbia University in 1968 revealed the extent to which the university was a part of the "system." At that time, the Central Intelligence Agency directly funded five foundations at Columbia, partially funded three others, and participated in the funding of twelve others. Seven of the university's highest administrators had direct ties to business corporations which contributed generously to Columbia. Among these were Lockheed Aircraft and General Dynamics—corporations which received 10 percent of all military contracts ($3.6 billion) in 1968. At that time the president of Lockheed was also chairman of the government's Institute for Defense Analysis, which was located on the campus of Columbia. In addition, a trustee of Columbia's Riverside Research Institute was also the consultant for the Defense Department on atomic energy and a director of three private corporations heavily dependent on the government for military contracts. President Grayson Kirk himself had been on the board of directors of Mobil Oil, which was a substantial contributor to Columbia University. And, of course, several of the banks which invested in business corporations affiliated with the university were represented on the board of directors of the university itself.[20] Finally, it was revealed after the whole episode—which ended with the closing of the university, the prosecution of 1,100 persons, and the suspension of several hundred students—that 40 percent of Columbia's budget came from military research and development projects and that half of these were secret.

Another illustration of a university's role in the "system" is the Stanford Research Institute (SRI). Until students occupied the Applied Electronics Laboratory in 1969, the SRI was owned outright by Stanford University as a "subsidiary," whatever that meant. The SRI ranked among the 100 leading military contractors, including "private" corporations. It clandestinely ran a counter-insurgency program in Thailand and even had the audacity to have an office in Bangkok. Its board of directors was appointed by the Stanford University board of trustees, thus making a mockery of the latter's statement that they had no idea of what the SRI was doing. As the student demonstrations increased in militancy, it gradually became clear that Stanford University was incredibly involved with the military-industrial complex—probably more so than any other university on the West Coast. The SRI was conducting chemical biological warfare research for the Department of Defense.

In addition to the SRI, there existed a multitude of "front" institutes affiliated with Stanford University, using university personnel and equipment, and receiving money from governmental agencies, to undertake classified research and to do projects of a clandestine nature. It was discovered and verified, however, that the Atomic Energy Commission was "contributing" about $30 million to research and development projects done at the Stanford Linear Accelerator Center, that the Stanford Electronics Laboratory received close to $2 million for classified research, and that the Department of Defense gave Stanford University $16 million in contracts in 1969.

But it was not just the presence of the swank, clean, air conditioned SRI and other institutes that aroused student interest about Stanford. It was the realization that the military-industrial complex controlled or was in a position to control Stanford University itself—that Stanford University was being run at its top levels by corporate and military power for the benefit of the military-industrial complex and that the university's complicity in the American war effort in Indochina was deep and unfathomable in precise terms.

It was finally discovered that the SRI (which happened to be doing counter-insurgency work in Thailand) had Malcolm MacNaughton on its board of directors; Mr. MacNaughton was president of Castle and Cooke, which, as of 1972, still had controlling interests in Thai-American Steel. The SRI also had Edgar Kaiser and Fred L. Hartley on its board of directors; Kaiser was part owner of the Thai Metal Works and Hartley was part owner of Union Oil, which had drilling rights off the Thai coast.

All of these men were appointed by the Stanford University Board of Trustees, which was the governing body of the university. As it turned out, several of the trustees were also conspicuously involved in the military-industrial complex; one of these was William Hewlett, president in 1969 of Hewlett-Packard, a military aerospace company doing $34 million in Defense Department contracts. And the co-founder of his firm, David Packard, was then serving as undersecretary of defense. Subsequently, it was discovered that Hewlett was also a director of Chrysler Motor Corporation, which was doing $146 worth of Defense Department work. The plot thickened when it was divulged that another member of Stanford's board of trustees was the chairman of the board of General Dynamics; another was president of Northrup Aircraft Company; and still another was a director of Lockheed Aircraft Company, which was doing almost $2 billion worth of contracts for the Department of Defense.[21] And to cap it off, the president of Stanford University, Kenneth Fitzer, was a director of the RAND Corporation, which had publicly acknowledged its projects undertaken and paid for by the Department of Defense. Students closed Stanford and trashed the university as well as many of the institutes.

Student radicals know that such a situation, such penetration by the "system," is not confined to Columbia and Stanford. The Pentagon alone gives over $400 million yearly to colleges and universities—often through agencies like the Institute for Defense Analysis, the Rand Corporation, or the Agency for International Development (AID). By 1970, the latter had formed AACT (Academic Advisory Council for Thailand). Over thirty colleges and universities participate in AACT, which was designed to help counter-insurgency forces in Thailand. Some of the nation's foremost academicians receive financial aid for their services to AACT. It is no wonder that Justice William O. Douglas pointed out that the Pentagon, the CIA, and the AEC all have research and development projects on many college campuses including MIT, the University of Washington, Johns Hopkins, Stanford, Columbia, and Michigan. But it is not so much the increasing power of the government in the universities, or that private corporations use and influence the universities, it is the *form, the structure, and the nature* of the influence. It is that the governmental and industrial conglomerates *have allowed themselves to become militarized*, apparently without compunction—or does the profit motive in capitalism ever allow for compunction? The answer given by the New Left is a resounding no! Thus, we are faced with a military-industrial, monopolistic capitalism.

It is now common knowledge that federal and industrial support of universities in the postwar era did not come from a long range master plan. Nor did it come from any known form of socialism. Nor did it even come from any tenable, codified national philosophy. It came from the military demand for weaponry, counter-espionage, defoliants, and so forth. The whole research and development policy of the federal government is a product of the postwar era. What arose to deal with the cold war was a military technology engendered by an unlimited arms and space race. After the Soviet Union launched their satellite Sputnik I in 1957, President Kennedy announced the missile gap. Then came the aggressively counterrevolutionary foreign policy of Kennedy and then the practical needs of war in Southeast Asia—including pacification, chemical defoliants, and laser beams. In the early 1970's, President Nixon endorsed expenditures on weapons delivery systems and nuclear technology. By the end of the 1960's, the federal government subsidized 70 percent of all research and development and the government militarized it: 85 percent of the monies went into the fields of defense, space, and atomic energy.

It must be remembered that 12 percent of the total federal budget goes into research and development; this assures military security and economic stability by encouraging continued growth. Quite simply, the system works as follows: The federal government provides a market for the product made through research and development—thus eliminating economic risk for "private enterprise." The public puts up the tax money, Congress appropriates the funds and a federal bureaucracy supervises the operation. The government is the prime contractor and, ultimately, the boss. As Professor Michael Miles has concluded, "the purpose is public, but the operation is for profit."[22]

And it is impossible to discern who is ultimately responsible, since managers operate their individual agencies, companies, and programs, and do not question the overall logic of the system. It is clear, however, that most of the funding is administered by the Department of Defense. It is also clear that only a few corporations are involved in this military-industrial complex— 300 corporations do 97 percent of federal research and development, and they also do 91 percent of all private research and development. "All of these 300 are military contractors, and many of them are predominantly military-aerospace. If the social priorities shift, the military-aerospace companies will be ready with their organized knowledge, their appreciation of the "complex" and their game optimism."[23] What this means is obvious: *The return to a peacetime economy does not substantially alter the structure of our economic system.* Those persons in academia and business who, during the war in Southeast Asia, sincerely believed they were doing their country a service by allowing their occupations to become temporarily militarized, did the opposite: the military-industrial complex is now entrenched in our society and will be here for the foreseeable future.

Furthermore, the universities may well have lost their original position of cultural and moral authority—for the universities will be part of the military-industrial complex for a long time to come. When the universities cannot be objectively critical of industry, government, and society, when they cannot effectively sustain the intellectual and emotional values of our culture by championing free inquiry and free speech, and when the universities cease to have the power and authority of free speech, then there remains no institutionalized agent of ferment in our society. The universities produce the knowledge which our society utilizes, and when universities are denied the right to be critical of how knowledge is used, or when they are economically so dependent upon the military-industrial complex that they dare not refuse to do technical projects for the government, then the demise of the culture is imminent. Many students and faculty believe that the situation is critical now. Most academicians would agree with Paul Goodman that "it is almost

unheard of for the univerisities or scientists to say Veto, whether to pesticides, or the causes of smog, the TV programming, the military strategy,
or the moon shot." [24]

Radicals are willing to stand and fight on the college campuses because
they see the universities becoming factories which produce technicians, not
men and women; they see the universities becoming bastions of conformity,
creating or at least engendering an establishment mentality—seldom asking
questions, pursuing a job, and abdicating its freedom to be a morally responsible agent. As Tom Hayden expressed it, experience in the "universities has
not brought us moral enlightenment. Our professors and administrators
sacrifice controversy to public relations. The questions we might want
raised—what is really important? Can we live in a different and better way? If
we wanted to change society, how could we do it? . . . are brushed aside." [25]
So the "system" spawns its own super-rationalist mentality, which is really its
own cultural value—and it is a business-as-usual attitude, a purely functional
approach to the life as a whole. As Paul Goodman says,

> It operates like an Establishment: it is the consensus in politics, the
> universities and science, big business, organized labor, public schooling,
> the media of communications, the official language; it determines the
> right style and accredits its own members; it hires and excludes, subsi-
> dizes and neglects. But it has no warrant of legitimacy, it has no tradi-
> tion, it cannot talk straight English, it neither has produced nor could
> produce any art, it does not lead by moral means but by a kind of
> social engineering. . . . The American tradition . . . is pluralist, populist,
> and libertarian, while the Establishment is monolithic, mandarin, and
> managed. And the evidence is that its own claim, that it is efficient, is
> false. It is fantastically wasteful of brains, money, the environment, and
> people. It is channeling the energy and enterprise to its own aggrandize-
> ment and power, and it will exhaust us.[26]

Finally, in the eyes of the radicals and the counterculture, the system of
managing social relations to facilitate profit and power has reduced man to
a state of virtual powerlessness. Capitalist centralization and hoarding are
known to create poverty, but it is not only the poor who are powerless in
this system. Rather, it is the majority of the populace—from the university
professor to the milkman. The decision-making process does not give the
power of decision to those most affected by it. The military-industrial
complex has, at most, fifteen thousand persons making decisions on contracts which will directly influence the lives of approximately 7 million
Americans and an unknown number of other people throughout the world.
And, of course, defense priority directly affects the lives of hundreds of
thousands of students who are just getting by, and it affects millions of blacks
and Chicanos existing in misery in the richest country the world has ever

known. It is estimated that one-half of the 6.5 million Chicanos in America live and die in poverty. In Texas, the average completion of school by Chicanos is 4.8 years—that is, education to the fifth grade—to age nine and one-half.[27] The fact that nothing is being done to decentralize power and thus to mitigate the evils of a monopolistic capitalist society is blamed on the current political-military-industrial technocracy and the materialistic complacency it sells as success and happiness. "For in reality," writes Herbert Marcuse,

> ... neither the utilization of administrative rather than physical controls (hunger, personal dependence, force), nor the change in the character of heavy work, nor the assimilation of occupational classes, nor the equalization in the sphere of consumption compensate for the fact that the decisions over life and death, over personal and national security are made at places over which the individuals have no control. The slaves of developed industrial civilization are sublimated slaves, but they are slaves. . . .[28]

And this is of course precisely the point made by the Black Panther party.

It is little wonder, then, that the claim that America is a democracy brings either scornful laughter or a stinging epithet from a radical. The overwhelming majority of Americans do not have any meaningful control over the decisions which shape their lives. The radicals argue that individuals have no control over their lives because politicians are not responsible to their voters. Rather, a politician is responsible to the monied interests behind him—not to the propertyless, to the poor, or even to the majority. In the eighteenth century, it was meaningful to say that America was a democracy because it then distinguished a republican form of government from the prevailing monarchical forms in Europe. Today, however, the operation of government is oligarchic, not democratic. This has been pointed out by myriads of critics and is accepted as fact by the New Left. Even if the majority of Americans still believe they are in control of their own decision making, the radicals remain convinced that they are powerless against the system. Grace Slick of the rock group Jefferson Airplane sums up the disenchantment felt by radicals in discovering that the great American system they were taught to venerate, the democracy and the individualism they were taught in school, are empty shams:

> When the truth is found
> to be lies,
> And all the joy
> within you dies,
> Don't you want somebody to love?[29]

Notes to Chapter 9

1. Jerry S. Cohen and Morton Mintz, *America Incorporated: Who Owns and Operates the United States?* (New York, 1971), p. 41. All references to this book are by permission of Delacorte Press.

2. Ibid., pp. 16-17.

3. Unfortunately, there is not space in this book to discuss the Highway Trust Fund, a "lobby" group with large capital behind it and a direct influence on the allocation of billions of dollars ($5 billion in 1972), making it "the second most powerful *de facto* coalition in Washington—ranking behind only the massive military-industrial complex." This is quoted from the letter of Denis Hayes published by the *Forum for Contemporary History* (July 28, 1972). The contentions of Mr. Hayes, Fellow in Energy Policy Studies at the Woodrow Wilson International Center for Scholars, were the subject of a spirited debate between Mr. Hayes and John W. Volpe, Secretary of Transportation. See *The Journal* (October–November, 1972).

4. Patrick Morgan, "Politics, Policy, and the Military-Industrial Complex," in Omer L. Carey, ed., *The Military-Industrial Complex* (Pullman, Washington, 1969), p. 58. These figures are little changed by the 1974 Department of Defense Budget, which was $79 billion.

5. See Seymour Melman, *Pentagon Capitalism: The Political Economy of War* (New York, 1970), passim.

6. Murray L. Weidenbaum, "The Military-Industrial Complex: An Economic Analysis," In Carey, *Military-Industrial Complex,* p. 33.

7. Ibid., p. 35.

8. Herbert Muller, *The Children of Frankenstein* (Bloomington, Indiana, 1970), p. 180.

9. Cohen and Mintz, *America Incorporated,* pp. 70-71.

10. Samuel Huntington, "Vested Interests and Public Interests," in Carey, *Military-Industrial Complex,* p. 12.

11. Robert Heilbroner, "Military America," *New York Review of Books* (July 23, 1970). See also John Kenneth Galbraith, "How to Control the Military," *Harper's* (June, 1969).

12. Morgan, op. cit., p. 58.

13. Ralph Lapp, "The Military-Industrial Complex," in Carey, *Military-Industrial Complex,* pp. 44-45.

14. Theodore Roszak, *The Making of a Counter Culture* (New York, 1969), p. 16.

15. William O. Douglas, *Points of Rebellion* (New York, 1970), p. 44.

16. Ibid., p. 71.

17. Michael W. Miles, *The Radical Probe* (New York, 1971), p. 140. I am in debt to Professor Miles for much statistical information and I recommend his book highly.

18. James Ridgeway, *The Closed Corporation* (New York, 1968), p. 13.

19. Heilbroner, op. cit.

20. See *Who Rules Columbia?* (New York, 1969). I have used statistics from the aforementioned which have been excerpted in the main from Massimo Teodori, *The New Left: A Documentary History* (New York, 1970), pp. 69-71, 335-45. See also Jerry L. Avorn, *Up Against the Ivy Wall: A History of the Columbia Crisis* (New York, 1968).

21. Miles, *Radical Probe,* p. 48, 160.

22. Ibid., p. 151.

23. Ibid., pp. 152-53.

24. Quoted in Henry Silverman, ed., *American Radical Thought* (Lexington, Massachusetts, 1970), p. 314.

25. From "The Port Huron Statement." Quoted in Paul Jacobs and Saul Landau, *The New Radicals* (New York, 1966), p. 153.

26. Paul Goodman, *Like A Conquered Province* (New York, 1967), p. 141.

27. Douglas, *Points of Rebellion,* pp. 45-47.

28. Herbert Marcuse, *One-Dimensional Man* (New York, 1964), p. 32.

29. "Somebody to Love," words and music by Darby Slick. © 1967, by Irving Music, Inc. (BMI). All rights reserved. Used by Permission.

X

The Singular Tangible: Power

The dissent we witness is a protest against the belittling of man, against his debasement, against a society that makes "lawful" the exploitation of humans. This period of dissent based on belief in man will indeed be our greatest renaissance.*

> Wandering between two worlds, one dead,
> The other powerless to be born.†

Accompanying the criticism of materialism, rationalism, technology and the system (a unity of negation) is one demand: power. This may, at first, seem to be a contradiction: how can a movement which is united only in its negation seriously expect to be granted power? The demand for power, however, provides us with the key to understanding the unity of negation. The demand for power is the one tangible form of negation that everyone recognizes, although few see it as *the* ultimate negation and therefore quite consistent with other characteristics of a movement of negation. The New Left is a movement of negation because it is utopian—it seeks to change the present state of affairs. It must be clearly understood, however, that negation is *not* the opposite of construction. Rather, it is the opposite of affirming existing conditions. The New Left cannot be criticized for being a destructive rather than a constructive movement because, logically, every act of construction is an act of negation toward the status quo. In short, every constructive act implies that the status quo is not good enough and must be improved upon—the status quo is thereby negated.

Seen in this light, the singular *positive* which the New Left seeks is power,

---

*William O. Douglas, *Points of Rebellion.*
† Bruno Bauer, in William J. Brazill, *The Young Hegelians.*

the power of utopia, the power, of construction, the power to negate the existing order of things. Hence, the hallmark of all radical groups is an insistence that they be given power—people power, black power, woman power, student power, Chicano power, Indian power. For in a technocratic society, operating under the current system and utilizing enormous bureaucratic and administrative hierarchies, human dignity can only be achieved with power. Dignity and power are inextricably intertwined. Accordingly, the manifesto of the California Peace and Freedom Movement (founded in 1968) seeks to make it clear that the "demand for human dignity is at root a demand for power—and that the people will have this power only when we all can democratically assure that our economy works to fulfill human needs rather than to increase the power and profit of a small minority." [1]

But because the New Left, especially in the 1970's, was prone to at least a subcutaneous utopianism, it suffered the pangs of disillusionment and despair. Hence, by 1972 even some of its founders, such as Richard Flacks, were pessimistically proclaiming it a dead movement. And clearly the demise of the original SDS and the rise of the frantic guerilla tactics of the Weatherpeople are results of the fragility inherent in a movement which is based on utopian assumptions and expectations. The author has witnessed utopianism among members of the New Left which was almost messianic in certainty. Certainly Marcuse's utopian vision of technology helped to fan the flames of impatience on the left. There are many in the New Left who do not share the utopian belief in an ultimate scheme of things that will eliminate conflict, duplicity, struggle, jealousy, and so forth. Indeed, such hopes in some measure smack of liberal utilitarianism—that it is possible to eliminate conflicts, that really serious moral choices with grave consequences will not arise —in a word, to divest the world of dilemmas. But it is impossible to understand the negation of the Movement without observing its chief ingredient, utopianism, and the tangible form of that utopianism—the demand for power.

Accordingly, it is this demand for power, endemic to all radical groups, which is perhaps the most significant contribution to be made by the Left. For the question the radicals are asking is the most crucial question that can be raised in a highly sophisticated and very advanced technological society: precisely what do we hope to achieve with our almost limitless technological powers? Or, to put it another way, what is going to be the common purpose of our technological society?

Unfortunately, the question is complicated, or at least obscured, by the philosophical consideration of what constitutes power. Historian Leonard Krieger has suggested that "Power in its general usage, is an original faculty of individuals and a simple substance of societies." [2] The dictionary defines power as the capacity to act on a person or thing. This implies that power is an elemental phenomenon, that it is generic, ultimate, and a fact of life. In philosophy and political science the precise nature and legitimacy of power have been a source of debate since Plato and Aristotle. Indeed, much of the current argument over the legitimacy of political power stems from the legacy of the idea of power, a legacy which began with Plato and Aristotle. Plato identified power with a moral purpose. Power meant the exercise of the will to achieve the Good, and Good was itself an absolute truth of the ideal realm.[3] Power, according to Plato, was inextricably linked with the Good; indeed, it served only to achieve the Good. Hence, power was always described in an ethical context.

Aristotle, on the other hand, argued that power could be used to achieve almost any end; it was not confined to exercising the will to achieve the end of Good, but was conceived as exercising the will to realize "potentialities." It was a constituent of all reality, for it was the teleological striving of all things in the world.[4] This meant that power is applicable to the original materials of reality and is itself a principle qualitatively different from the end it is directed toward. In this interpretation power is not (as Plato would have argued), solely an aspect of the realization of the "Good." Furthermore, the characteristics of power could vary according to the ends that one sought to achieve. This same interpretation also seems to indicate that power is more understandable as the material means than as the moral end it might seek to achieve, for the moral end exists separate from and outside of the power itself. In addition, Aristotle assigned physical force to moral power in a zealous way, thus making power seem more physical than moral.

Nevertheless, the Greek legacy of the idea of power appears to be that in order for power to be considered legitimate it must have the capacity to realize good ends. To a philosophical member of the New Left, just as for the Greeks, this means that *political power, as a category of legitimate power, does not exist.* A member of the New Left would agree with Professor Krieger's contention that the Greek legacy carries a conviction that "there is only a political application of a general ethical power employing as a means a political force, which when divorced from this moral direction becomes impotent and illegitimate."[5]

Despite the fact that the Romans initiated a notion of distinctive political power, valid in its own right, there is still the belief that power realizes a moral end and has—or should have—a moral purpose. However, political power no longer seems to be pursuant of or linked to a moral purpose or end, but rather to a demonstrable temporal and usually material effect. Power has become associated more with providing the means to the physical trans- formation and control of the world than with facilitating the knowlege and achievement of Good. And, as a philosophical corollary, notes Professor Krieger, there is a "finite tendency of potentiality (power) in its original sense, to surpass every stage of itself until its end becomes, in the political context, the tendency of power, bereft of its purpose, toward infinite expansion of itself."[6] In short, power, especially political power, does not seem related to moral ends, but *to itself, by essence.*

The debate over the nature of power, which was begun by the Greeks, continued in the Middle Ages. This debate sharpened in the fifteenth and sixteenth centuries as monarchies developed more sophisticated means of political and economic control, and the Reformation challenged the manner in which spiritual power was related to political power. From this debate arose the belief that power is of two kinds: political and ethical, and that Their relationship was cloudy at best. Thus, Machiavelli contended that political power was itself legitimate but had to borrow its spiritual values, while Luther argued that spiritual power was legitimate but had to borrow its physical means from politics. The merging or reconciliation of the two kinds of power has been facilitated in modern times through the efforts of such men as Spinoza, Locke, and Rousseau.

Jean Jacques Rousseau (1712–1778) in particular helped to resolve the Plato-Aristotle debate. Rousseau suggested that power was in fact an element of the individual will, the will that did know the Good and could achieve it, and that political power was power by consent of the individual moral agent. There was, therefore, an ethical source of power (the individual) directly connected and theoretically antecedent to the political vehicle through which it was exercised. Nevertheless, the legacy of the French Revolution and of the nineteenth and twentieth centuries would lead one to conclude that the source of power has gradually become politics, the state. The price for territorial sovereignty and the nation-state system has been the tacit, reluctant acceptance, as scholar Hannah Arendt has indicated, that power is force and that the state is the repository of force and not about to surrender it if the people withdraw their consent.[7] We now have a situation where individuals, especially those exercising power, feel responsible *to* power; that is, responsible *to* the institution of power, not to its theoretical base, the people.

In the eyes of the radical, this means an Establishment—a "Watergate" mentality, a conscious effort to delude oneself into believing that institutionalized power has no other justification, responsibility, or source than *itself.* The rhetoric of the New Left—"technicians of power," "crisis managers," "capitalistic pawns," "pigs"—is used to describe those who possess political power. Implicit in this rhetoric is the assumption that, however technical and material in its operation, political power still incorporates a spiritual relevance that should make it accountable on a scale of universal morality. To those in power, this assumption is utopian and naive. To those in the Movement, the justification for power can only be moral, and this means that power is ultimately and always responsible to the sovereignty of the people. The Establishment insists that there is a responsibility of the individual *to* power. In response, the New Left addresses itself to the real issue, which is the responsibility *of* power *to* its fundamental, ethical source: to facilitate the highest good, happiness. The radicals argue that when political power is used primarily to perpetuate itself or for ends clearly antithetical to good, then political power is illegitimate. Here radicals agree with the conclusion of Abraham Kaplan in his classic essay on ethics and power: "There is no autonomous political obligation distinct from moral obligation and its legal offspring. Democratic political theorists from Locke to Laski have insisted on this moralizing of power, in contrast to the totalitarian practice of politicizing even morality."[8] Thus, in the view of the radicals, the military exercise of American political power in Vietnam became increasingly illegitimate in the late 1960's when it was learned that the Gulf of Tonkin incidents had been vastly misrepresented to the American people, and that the United States was not fighting to establish free elections, but had consistently opposed them.

The disillusionment about the way the United States exercises power is compounded by a blatant paradox. As the base of American power becomes more democratized, at least for students and blacks, the cry for the political realization of moral ends increases. Yet these ends—broad individual freedom, a national cultural identity, and a common brotherhood of citizenry—are ends which seem to the Establishment *independent* of political power. Thus, political scientists Edmund Stillman and William Pfaff have warned against "the burdening of politics with expectations and responsibilities that actually are far larger than politics—and weightier than politics can bear." It is a mistake, they argue, "to expect that political action can resolve issues of social and cultural integrity and creativity, even of philosophy and religion—eschatological issues concerning the purpose of individual life and society itself."[9] But to the radicals, politics and power are most certainly instruments to be used for the pursuit of happiness, which is considered a moral good. The irony, the radicals point out, is that while Stillman, Pfaff and others decry using politics for moral or spiritual ends, they admit that "Politics is the vehicle of our culture, our only universal system—the only universal system—the only common language possessed by the expanded Western society of the 1960's."[10]

In the 1930's and 1940's, such a paradox was not as serious as it is today, and it did not provoke the pervasive alienation in young people it provokes today. For during Franklin D. Roosevelt's administrations it was possible to claim that political power could only and would only be used to achieve the limited collective ends which condition the human capacity to achieve a moral ideal. But now that the political apparatus (the system) has technological capabilities to build hydrogen bombs and put men on the moon, it has become in effect total, and it resists the application of values of individual freedom, human brotherhood, and the like—values it dismisses as nonpolitical. The radical thus sees no real values attached to the political power apparatus escept self-perpetuation and vague national interest slogans. This leads the radical to conclude that, given the total political means of the society and the lack of human values to guide those means, only a confrontation can come about. The Establishment argues in return that allowing everyone to "do their own thing" means anarchy of human goals, with the result that political power becomes directed toward a hedonistic collapse rather than a moral end.

This philosophical stalemate brings us to the heart of the matter—where the New Left finds itself today. The New Left is faced with the problem of relating the individuality (which is still our final goal), with the generality of what we can achieve with our total political means. Or, seen from a slightly less abstract perspective: how do we settle upon an ethos of happiness, at least communitywide, without gravely damaging what appears to be a necessarily total political apparatus? There is currently no consensus among New Left radicals on how to resolve this problem. Rather, what is emerging is the awareness that before we resolve the problem of power, we must have a clearer idea of the nature of our ultimate goal—happiness. And this, of course, requires a philosophical consensus. This consensus, which is gradually emerging within the New Left and the counterculture, is that happiness is an attribute of something larger and more elemental: Being.

Notes to Chapter 10

1. Quoted in Massimo Teodori, ed., *The New Left: A Documentary History* (New York, 1970), p. 443.

2. Leonard Krieger, "Power and Responsibility: The Historical Assumptions," in Leonard Krieger and Fritz Stern, eds., *The Responsibility of Power* (New York, 1967), p. 3.

3. This, it seems to me, is the general thesis of Plato's dialogues.

4. See Aristotle's *Metaphysics*.

5. Krieger, "Power and Responsibility," p. 18.

6. Ibid., p. 10.

7. See the last chapters of Hannah Arendt's *The Origins of Totalitarianism* (Cleveland, 1958).

8. Abraham Kaplan, "American Ethics and Public Policy," in Elting Morison, ed., *The American Style* (New York, 1958), p. 71.

9. Edmund Stillman William Pfaff, *The Politics of Hysteria* (New York, 1964), p. 244. Reprinted by permission of Harper and Row Publishers.

10. Ibid., p. 243.

Part 3

A New Philosophy
For a New World

Introduction to Part 3

you are as sticky as peanut butter, united states of amerika
you stick to the roof of my mouth
you make me want a drink of pure water
to wash away the shit that you have left in me
but jesus christ all the water is fucked up
it is filled with little ugly death colored pieces of you
the graven images of usa, anointed with ddt
your language:
it's a bundle of sticks that shape letters that shape words
do you know what you are saying?
what have you given me to believe?
so you really think I want to pledge allegiance to a flag?
who are you, flag?
you are supposed to be me
where is the resemblance?
you are supposed to be nixon, too
nixon and the flag and I are not one
I am being educated to be part of this system
I am being honed and milled and sharpened and dulled so
    that I'll fit
but I don't
where I am, there are all sorts of sharp poking things
why are you so full of sharp poking things, amerika?
you are educating me to be happy
I am not happy
my brothers and sisters aren't happy
is anyone happy?
why do you have toothpaste grins on your faces?
why does killing make you happy?

is to be happy to kill?
then I don't want to be happy
I want to be very sad

—Kate Pickens, Age 20, June 1971

The dissatisfactions mentioned in part 2—the unity of negativism, and the demand for power which characterize the New Left and youthful radicalism—stem from a unique vision of man, reality, and happiness. There is a genuine love of man at the base of the radical movement. Georges Sand once said that "indignation at the wrongs of humanity is one of the most passionate forms of love." The vision of the young radicals is not invalid simply because the young radicals did not formulate nineteenth-century utopian blueprints of their vision. In an age in which everything is scrutinized analytically and thousands of critics, academicians, and politicians make their livelihood by debunking utopian schemes, one could hardly expect an antirational movement to proffer a rational apocalypse. More important, few decades of history have a clear set of alternatives—certainly Franklin Roosevelt had none in 1932. The general coherence and the general spirit of a generation is illusive, amorphous, intuited, and rarely a perfect articulation.

Nevertheless, it is possible to sketch with broad strokes the positive outlines of the counterculture. The members of the New Left and the counterculture *do* have a philosophy. This philosophy is based on a conception of reality which gives priority to the metaphysical, the spiritual; the philosophy conceives of man as a player, an organism that creates and manipulates symbols. And the philosophy has a certain "idea" of happiness as unpremeditated joy, aesthetic response, and natural interaction with man and things. Part 3 of this book will examine these philosophical foundations of the radical impulse.

The historical significance of this philosophy is that it signals the end of an epoch of rational symbolism and the beginning of an epoch of nondiscursive symbolism. This is already evident in the complaint of students that knowledge (communicated in rational symbols) is irrelevant. It is also evident in the nondiscursive symbolism which young people have created, especially in rock 'n' roll music. Accordingly, there are in this section separate chapters dealing with (1) man as a player, (2) the idea of happiness, (3) the crisis of relevant knowledge, (4) the meaning of rock 'n' roll music and the counterculture. The conclusion brings together the diverse strands which constitute this postwar radical impulse.

XI

Homo Ludens: Man the Player

It is only into the game of life that we have lost the power to enter.*

In 1969, Abbie Hoffman wrote, "We have underground press. We have underground newsreels. We have underground theater. We have a whole philosophy."[1] He was neither exaggerating nor bragging. That philosophy, too often obscured by the negativism and cynicism of the young and the minorities, is nevertheless intuitively understood by them. It *is* in the underground newspapers, films, and theater. But it is also apparent in the life style, the long hair, the use of drugs, the be-ins, the love-ins, and the festivals of life (like Woodstock); and it is widely apparent in its own medium, rock and folk-rock music.

The philosophy of the youth movement is to some extent the historical realization of the ideas of such perspicacious thinkers as Friedrich Nietzsche, Rainer Maria Rilke, Alfred North Whitehead, Suzanne Langer, Marshall McLuhan, and William Thompson.[2] They have suggested repeatedly that the end of a historical epoch comes with the exhaustion of its motive concepts. And that is precisely what the young sense—that the motive concepts of materialism, rationalist epistemology, competitive individualism, and social, national, and racial differentiation are no longer generative values. Put in a broad historical perspective, this signifies that the era of mathematical, verbal (discursive) symbolism is giving way to a new era of nondiscursive symbolism. This means that the New Left considers the verbal and mathematical symbols of rationalism as neither final nor definitive. Indeed, there is a pronounced tendency to reject discursive thinking entirely and to rely upon occult means of experiencing the world. Hence, Philip Kapleau, in his popular book *The Three Pillars of Zen* (1965), is able to state categorically: "Your enemy is

*Antoine De St. Exupéry, *Wind, Sand, and Stars*.

your discursive thinking, it leads you to differentiate yourself on one side of an imaginary boundary from what is not you on the other side of this non-existent line." [3]

In addition, there is a tendency to reject the prevalent attitude that discursive symbolic systems represent the pinnacle of man's intellectual development. The Movement contends that systems of discursive symbols do not provide the ultimate tools for man to deal with his world. Rather, they constitute a rational, discursive complex of abstractions which has mistakenly come to be mistaken for the real world itself. But, in fact, the only reality that systems of discursive symbols actually provide is the reality that man acclimates and orients himself to the universe by *making* symbols. The important thing about man then becomes not so much *what* he symbolizes (what he can know using discursive symbols), but *that* he can symbolize.

What emerges, then, is the philosophical conviction that man is essentially a symbolizer, one who transforms experience into mental stuff. The transformation of the world into mental stuff is the particular tropism of man. But this transformation need not take the form of discursive symbolism only—that is an Enlightenment prejudice which reached its modern zenith with Hegel. As philosopher Susanne Langer points out, "the basic need, which certainly is obvious only in man, is the need of symbolization. The symbol-making function is one of man's primary activities, like eating, looking, or moving about. It is the fundamental process of the mind, and goes on all the time." [4]

Radicals Alan Watts, Timothy Leary, Abbie Hoffman, Jerry Rubin, Tom Hayden, and Huey P. Newton have, in their own ways, come to the same conclusion (although they have faded as leaders in the mid-1970's). The end of symbol making is usually some sort of activity. This can mean forming ideas, communicating orally, or even dancing: in fact, any behavior. Individuals as philosophically removed from one another as Alan Watts and Erich Hoffer have indicated that there is little evidence that the human organism is engaged in purposeful activity. Man is simply the transformer (for no reason except, perhaps, pleasure) of whatever he senses. In short, man does not necessarily approach the world with a predisposition to utilize it for rational purposes. We know that the temple and palace preceded the utilitarian house, that ornament preceded clothing, and that work, especially teamwork, derives from play. It has been contended that the bow was a musical instrument before it became a weapon, and some authorities believe that fishing originated in a period when game was plentiful. In the words of Erich Hoffer, "it was the product not so much of grim necessity as of curiosity, speculation, and playfulness." Finally, "we know that poetry preceded prose, and it may be that singing preceded talking." [5]

It has now been documented by such diverse authorities as Susanne

Langer, A. D. Ritchie, Noam Chomsky, Mircea Eliade, Kenneth Burke, and
Claude Levi-Strauss that singing did precede talking. We know also from
Freud and Levi-Strauss that ritual is not capable of being understood em-
pirically, but is most certainly intelligible both psychologically and anthro-
pologically. Indeed, it has been contended that discursive language itself
originated in "purposeless lalling-instincts, primitive aesthetic reactions
. . ."[6] From Levi-Strauss, Chomsky, and others it is possible to put together
a tentative theory regarding the evolution of language: from lalling, to image,
then to icon, later to sign, and presently to syllabic writing (words and
grammatical constructions). But as Marshall McLuhan has pointed out, it
was a long evolution from aural sounds to written language using verbal
symbols.[7] And with the development of electric circuitry, the relevance and
adequacy of the word symbol and the mathematical symbol has declined.

All of these observations reinforce an idea of man held by many in the
New Left and by most of the freaks and hippies—man as the symbol-maker,
player, Homo ludens, jester, or even "merry prankster," to use Ken Kesey's
term. And so Abbie Hoffman wrote that "the aim is *not* to earn the respect,
admiration, and love of everybody—it's to get people to do, to participate,
whether positively or negatively. All is relevant, only the play's the thing."[8]
And this is neither frivolous philosophizing by Hoffman nor another one of
his put-ons (although he is master of the put-on). It is a truth accepted by
many psychiatrists, among them T. S. Szasz, that *the play is the thing*. Szasz,
in his now famous books *The Myth of Mental Illness* (1961) and *The Manufacture of Madness* (1970), argues persuasively that what people need most in
life is not wealth, or self-image, but games worth playing. The most important
ingredient of psychic health, according to Szasz, is participation in a game
which a person feels is genuinely worth playing.

It is the view of members of the New Left and the counterculture that
there are basically two kinds of games to which people commit themselves.
The game a person chooses reflects his or her level of inner development (one
is less or more highly developed, in the language of the counterculture).
Less developed games are object games—arrangements of human relations
with the implicit goal of attaining material things. Highly developed games are
metagames—arrangements of human relations to attain intangible spiritual
states of mind. Object games predominate in our civilization; they are played
by the Calibans. Metagames predominate in the counterculture and are played
by the Prosperos. While this may seem fanciful, it is also the general message
of writer J. R. R. Tolkien and anthropologist Carlos Castaneda. No game, no
aim. Obviously, the system is a game too, albeit a less developed one.

In the late sixties and early seventies Abbie Hoffman consistently articulated this philosophy of Homo ludens better than any other famous radical.
He was truly a quintessential freak. His escapades during the long trial follow-

ing the 1968 Democratic Convention (wearing a black robe like the judge) and later appearing at a party given by Tricia Nixon as the "bodyguard" of Grace Slick of the Jefferson Airplane, dramatized the prank instinct. Hoffman was absolutely serious when he said, "our alternative fantasy will match in zaniness the war in Vietnam. Fantasy is freedom. Anybody can do anything. The Pentagon will rise 300 feet in the air." [9] And he was brilliantly disarming to the Establishment with these tactics. In August 1968, while in Chicago, Hoffman and other Yippies nominated a pig for president of the United States. Chicago's police apprehended it, and Hoffman, with acerbic gravity, announced that "next time we're going to nominate a lion." The result was that guard duty was doubled at Chicago's Lincoln Park Zoo. When Hoffman announced through the underground press that the Yippies intended to put LSD in Chicago's water, the reservoir was cordoned off by national guardsmen. When pressed to explain the "rationality" of his tactics, he answered: "It's all a myth, man. Yippie's a myth. The Pig's a myth. I am a myth; who ever heard of a commie-anarchist-terrorist with a color television?"

Many did not understand; *many others did.* For Hoffman was just articulating the same philosophy of play that had inspired the following: hexes, "make love not war" slogans, flower power, flowers dropped down the barrels of soldiers' rifles, the Kool-Aid acid tests of Ken Kesey and the Merry Pranksters, demands by Indian groups to negotiate with the Bureau of Indian Affairs in a teepee, thousands of outrageously decorated freak trucks and vans which grace America's roads, and the "streaking" across campuses and on television during the Academy Awards. These are all attempts to illustrate that man is a player—even in the face of a totally different philosophy sustained by the "silenced majority." [10]

What resulted was, and still is, direct confrontation between radicals and the Establishment—but on the radicals' own terms. It is "psychic guerrilla warfare." The tactic is essentially to encourage imaginativeness, lack of seriousness and playfulness, not to encourage physical encounters with the Establishment. This is what Abbie Hoffman meant when he said *he* believes "in the politics of ecstasy." When asked "can you explain that a little more," his answer was "No, but I can touch it, I can smell it, I can even dance it." [11] Accordingly, Richard Neville, Australian editor of the underground newspaper *Oz,* concluded rightly that "There is one quality which enlivens both the political and cultural denominations of Youth protest; which provides its most important innovation; which has the greatest relevance for the future; which is the funniest, freakiest and most effective. This is the element of play. . . ." [12]

Consequently in this philosophy, life is to be fun, an enjoyment of symbolic interaction with the world. This is why Marcuse reiterates the necessity of viewing life and the world as "potential," as "transcendence." By that he means the world is full of experiences which man can transform symbolically (aesthetically and/or materially). The imagination and the senses will almost automatically and naturally transform the world. Consequently, Marcuse asks that we recognize that the world "intends qualities which surpass all particular experience." These qualities "persist in the mind, not as a figment of imagination nor as more logical possibilities, but as the 'stuff' of which our world consists." The human organism knows intuitively that, as long as it lives, its natural potential for symbolizing will never be exhausted. "Thus the concept of beauty comprehends all the beauty not yet realized, the concept of freedom all the liberty not yet attained." [13] In this view, reality becomes transcendent and all the senses interact simultaneously—playing and transforming all. Man becomes an artist and, as Professor Erich Heller explains it, "the *symbol* [italics mine] becomes the body of that which transcends, the measure of the immeasurable and the visible logic of the heart's reasoning." [14] And so, radical Christopher Reiner as well as Abbie Hoffman can seriously assert the contention of Marcuse and Nietzsche that "life is an undifferentiated aesthetic continuum."

This conception of transcendent reality and of man as a player emphasizes the aesthetic dimension of man. Man the player is man the transformer, the metamorphoser—for his own delight, for fun. Creativity is thus greatly encouraged. Hence, homemade clothes, bizarre dress, unorthodox mannerism, magic trinkets, and strange art forms are in vogue in the counterculture. These activities dramatize the dictum of Nietzsche, one of the counterculture's heroes: "Only as aesthetic phenomenon is the world forever justified." And the justification of man is simply that he interacts, that he aesthetically transforms the world. And that *is* the purpose of life according to this philosophy. Thus, to stare into space for hours, to get stoned, or to sit and contemplate in a meadow *is* doing something, and is absolutely justified. As one student put it:

> Climb with a caterpillar
>   or
> a mountain goat.
> Ride with Grand-daddy long legs
>   or a mule
>   a snake or a mouse
> It doesn't matter how, just get there, get there now. [15]

To "get there" means, as the Beatles say, to "get back" to the world of imagination, to put oneself again in the reality of potential, of the world gesturing and happening, miraculously and delightfully. To "get back," in short, means to retain many of the playful characteristics of childhood even while living in the "grown up, established world." And this is commensurate with radical Freudian Norman O. Brown's conclusion in *Life Against Death:* childhood is the real goal of man.

Philosophically and/or politically, such a change in the world view of thousands of young people is disconcerting to many people, for it would mean the ascent of the aesthetic principle as the form of the reality principle. In other words, the real would not be regarded as rational, and certainly not material, and therefore the society would have to cease to organize itself around such notions. This would mean a cultural and probably sociopolitical revolution. The vision of life as aesthetic response and playful symbolization of the senses, when translated into the present "straight" world, is interpreted by the Establishment as fantastically unoperational, dysfunctional, utopian, and irrational—a kind of inspiring hallucination. And it is all of these things— precisely because it *cannot* be realized and translated perfectly into everyday political and social life using traditional, rational, political, and technological means.

Such a philosophy would bring a kind of life and society that would be radically different from the current one, anchored as it is in materialism and rationalism. Marcuse, in his *Essay on Liberation* (1969), *Five Lectures* (1970) and *Counter-Revolution and Revolt* (1972), has probably best sketched the outlines of the sort of life it might be.

> Released from the bondage to exploitation, the imagination, sustained by the achievements of science, could turn its productive power to the radical reconstruction of experience and the universe of experience. In this reconstruction, the historical *topos* of the aesthetic would change: it would find expression in the transformation of the Lebenswelt— society as a work of art. . . . In other words: the transformation is conceivable only as the way in which free men shape their life in solidarity, and build an environment in which the struggle for existence loses its ugly and aggressive features. The Form of Freedom is not merely self-determination and self-realization, but rather the determina- tion and realization of goals which enhance, protect, and unite life on earth. . . . The beautiful would be an essential quality of their freedom.[16]

But the essential and perhaps most vital point on which "established reality" and "utopian reality" (if I may use these terms) differ, is upon the nature of happiness. For like Nietzsche's *Zarathustra*, the partisans of the New Left's ethos proclaim steadfastly:

> What good is my happiness! It is poverty and pollution and wretched self-complacency. But my happiness should justify existence itself.[17]

Notes to Chapter 11

1. Abbie Hoffman, "Freedom and License," in Peter and Deborah Babcox and Bob Abel, eds., *The Conspiracy* (New York, 1969), p. 44.

2. I highly recommend the works of historian William Irwin Thompson. See especially his imaginative and courageous books, *At the Edge of History* (New York, 1971), and *Passages About Earth* (New York, 1974).

3. Philip Kapleau, *The Three Pillars of Zen* (New York, 1965), p. 154.

4. Quoted in George B. Leonard, *Education and Ecstasy* (New York, 1968), p. 99.

5. Susanne K. Langer, *Philosophy in a New Key* (New York, 1951).

6. Langer, *Philosophy in a New Key,* p. 107.

7. That language is the particular tropism of mankind is generally agreed upon by most linguistic experts. Hence Chomsky has remarked that ". . . it is almost universally taken for granted that there exists a problem of explaining the evolution of human language from systems of animal communication . . . studies simply bring out even more clearly the extent to which human language appears to be a unique phenomenon, without significant analogue in the animal world. Noam Chomsky, *Language and Mind* (New York, 1968), p. 59.

8. Abbie Hoffman, *Revolution for the Hell of It* (New York, 1968), p. 27.

9. Ibid., p. 43.

10. The classic book describing the philosophy of play in action in the sixties is Tom Wolfe's *Electric Kool-Aid Acid Test.* This book describes the incredible, hilarious ruses of Ken Kesey and his Merry Pranksters as they drove all over the United States in a renovated van. See also Abbie Hoffman's *How to Steal This Book.*

11. Hoffman, *Revolution for the Hell of It,* p. 59.

12. Richard Neville, *Play Power* (New York, 1970), p. 19.

13. Herbert Marcuse, *One-Dimensional Man* (Boston, 1964), pp. 213-14.

14. Erich Heller, *The Disinherited Mind* (New York, 1967), p. 295.

15. From a paper by Steve Wood, June 1970. Washington State University.

16. Herbert Marcuse, *An Essay on Liberation* (New York, 1969), pp. 45-46. Reprinted by permission of Beacon Press.

17. Friedrich Nietzsche, *Thus Spake Zarathustra,* trans. Thomas Commons (New York, 1927), p. 7.

XII

Happiness is Being

... I claim my birthright!
      reborn forever as long as Man
          in Kansas or other universe—Joy
    reborn after vast sadness of War Gods!
A lone man talking to himself, no house in the brown vastness to hear,
      imagining the throng of Selves
          that make this nation one body of Prophecy
             languaged by Declaration as
                HAPPINESS*

Happiness as a value and as a goal is granted far greater status in the phi-losophy of the New Left than in "liberal capitalism." For if man is primarily a player and not a worker, he plays to be happy and to be joyous instead of working to achieve a high level of material existence. For the partisans of the New Left and the counterculture realize what Freud glumly concluded: happiness in the West has been so problematical in the last two centuries that it really "has no cultural value." Particularly since the First World War, it has become a kind of pessimistic hope for relief from pain, dutiful drudgery, and severe economic and social pressure. What has emerged is, as W. H. Auden and Christopher Isherwood remind us:

> Man divided always and restless always: afraid and unable
>   to forgive:
>
> . . . .
>
> Afraid of the clock, afraid of catching his neighbor's cold
>   afraid of his own body,
> Desperately anxious about his health and his position:

*"Wichita Vortex Sutra," © 1968 by Alen Ginsberg. Reprinted by permission of City Lights Books.

calling upon the universe to justify his existence,
Slovenly in posture and thinking: the greater part of
   the will devoted
To warding off pain from the water-logged areas,
. . . .
Examine his satisfactions:
Some turn to the time honoured solutions of sickness and
   crime: some to the latest model of aeroplane or the
   sport of the moment.
Some to good works, to a mechanical ritual of giving.
Some have adopted an irrefragible system of beliefs or a
   political programme, others have escaped to the
   ascetic mountains
Or taken refuge in the family circle, among the boys on
   the bar-stools, on the small uncritical islands.[1]

Like W. H. Auden, psychologist Karen Horney found that most people are so frightened to be happy and so trained to be serious, calculating, and so work- and survival-oriented, that they settle for a surrogate happiness. "Most patients have known merely the partial satisfaction attainable within the boundaries set by their anxieties; they have never experienced true happiness nor have they dared to reach out for it."[2] In the view of the New Left, this lamentable situation is primarily due to the fact that work as a cultural value has replaced virtually all traces of happiness as a cultural value. It is this state of affairs that was satirized in huge, bold headlines on the first page of the *Los Angeles Free Press* for October, 1967.

Why did you
Get up
This Morning

What
Are You
Afraid of

It seems to many that we live in a world of work which, while it may have an indirect relationship to happiness, ought better be described as tedium. For the contemporary work ethic creates cultural norms which so circumscribe happiness that it all but ceases to exist as a generative cultural value. "Happiness must be subordinated to the discipline of work as full-time occupation, to the discipline of monogamic reproduction, to the established system of law and order. The methodical sacrifice of libido, its rigidly enforced deflection to socially useful activities and expression *is* culture."[3]

What has become the "accepted" (normative) idea of happiness is clearly intended to perpetuate the profit motive—this results in exploitation, and thereby fosters the notion that consumption of material goods (which sustains profit) also results in happiness. Indeed, the tacit axiom might be "consumption is happiness." But today the radicals, the young, and the minorities are in revolt against the dearth of acceptable alternative ways for pursuing happiness or even of being allowed to explore the nature of happiness for themselves. In short, they are not happy with the pursuit of unmitigated materialism at the expense of community, creativity, self-determination, and play. In this sense journalist Irving Kristol was correct when he described the hippies as the only truly radical sect in America today because "they are dropouts from the revolution of rising expectations and reject the materialistic ethos that is the basis of the modern social order."[4] Happiness is the main concern, but not happiness achieved by the acquisition of this or that material object. Hence, the New Left rejects the ready-made blueprints for happiness peddled to the masses by capitalist advertising. Members of the New Left resent the value implied in the capitalist project that satisfactions leading to happiness are to be found primarily in the marketing and acquiring of material goods, and that somehow increased accumulation of material goods equals increased happiness.

> Advertising signs that con you
> Into thinking you're the one
> That can do what's never been done
> That can win, what's never been won
> Meantime life outside goes on
> All around you.[5]

The rejection of the materialistic idea of happiness is shared today by many more young people than those who constitute the political New Left, the hippies, and the freaks. In the motion picture *The Graduate,* well-to-do Dustin Hoffman (playing the title role) winced at the suggestion by his father's business colleague that he go into "plastics"; Hoffman was echoing the sentiments previously expressed by the Jefferson Airplane in their song, "Plastic Fantastic Lover." Plastic is the symbol of monied, phony happiness, phony love, and phony people. This message is also constantly expressed by Bob Dylan. Indeed, probably no other singer in the sixties and seventies has had such a powerful "antiplastic world" influence than has Bob Dylan. He has mercilessly pursued the lies, the deceit, and the cynical, pitiless half-truths espoused by the American materialistic ethos.

> Princess in the steeple
> And all the pretty people're drinkin', thinkin'
> That they got it made.
> Exchanging all kinds of precious gifts and things[5]

You used to ride on the chrome horse with your diplomat
Who carried on his shoulder a Siamese cat,
Ain't it hard when you discovered that
He really wasn't where it's at . . .[6]

Then where is *it*—happiness—to be found? Abbie Hoffman suggests it is "an experience so intense you actualize your full potential. You become LIFE. Life is fun."[7] The attitude of the counterculture is reflected in this answer. In this conception of happiness, there are traces of Aristotle as well as a mixture of eastern philosophies and the ideas of contemporary psychologists such as Gordon Allport, Frederick Perls, Abraham Maslow, Erik Erikson, and Erich Fromm. Fromm remains very popular among young people; his philosophy of self-realization comes about as close to the counterculture's general idea of happiness as one can get: "Happiness is an achievement brought by man's inner productiveness. . . . Happiness and joy are not relief from tension, but the accompaniment of all productive activity, in thought, feeling, and action."[8] The important words here are "inner productiveness." Happiness must come from the *intuitive* satisfaction an individual finds in knowing that he or she is engaging in pleasurable, natural, moral activity. No matter how many times and in how many ways a person might be *told* he or she is productive and therefore happy, only the individual can really tell for himself if his productivity is facilitating happiness or whether it is a fraud.

There are obvious deficiencies in such a crude formulation of a philosophy of self-realization. If self-realization is defined as just the realizing of the empirical "self," then obviously to exist is to be self-realized. This is not, of course, what Fromm meant, nor is it what the New Left meant. If self-realization is defined as becoming a self that one is not, then one is still faced with the problem of deciding what his "real" self is. Fromm's philosophy of realization of potential becomes ambiguous at this point. For potentiality is neutral—to realize potential is not necessarily good. The real issue is how and in what direction the potentiality is guided. Here, members of the New Left and the counterculture are careful to note that we cannot realize potentiatlities apart from our relation to other people and to nature. Thus, the notion of happiness which the New Left and the counterculture advocate is not the hackneyed self-realization philosophy of liberal individualism. Rather, as will be discussed later, it is a philosophy which disavows that sort of individualism and moves to a wider sense of consciousness.

In addition, the rational calculation of happiness (which is so often the concomitant of liberal individualism) is rejected; for how can man rationally control his relations with other people without controlling other people's relations to himself? In addition, a formal, structured approach to happiness via human relations almost always disintegrates into hostility and frustration.

No one can accurately predict that careful preparation for happiness will actually result in happiness. Accordingly, in the eyes of hundreds of thousands of young people, years of careful scheming to "have it made" sometime off in the future are often years misspent. Society's prerequisites for happiness—professional advanced degrees from prestigious schools, lavish houses, suburbs, marriage, neatly groomed opulent families, fashionable clothes, expensive automobiles, and summer places—these all become objects of ridicule. For to paraphrase John Dewey, the way to attain happiness is *not* to seek it.

What recourse do human beings have? The answer, which derives in part from Kant, is the creation of a world in which every human being is treated as an end in himself. This means creating a community where men live and pursue happiness in a "kingdom of ends," and where men are restrained from using each other purely as means. This would necessitate a radical alteration of the current structure of human relations, relations which emphasize functioning efficiently in an impersonal environment for ends only indirectly related to human happiness and almost always requiring exploitation of someone else. Furthermore, the particularity of the satisfactions a person chooses to make his own happiness is really the same as the autonomy of his will. And this freedom of the will is regarded as universal—the freedom of man and individual happiness are sought by all people. In freely choosing this or that satisfaction, the individual wills, first of all, his freedom to choose; and this freedom is shared with other persons. In striving for happiness, he seeks first of all happiness in general (a happiness of which the precise content is not completely specified), and this is also the primary goal of other persons. Happiness, then, is conceived of as an activity of relations—an open-ended process, a transcending of the so-called self, a bursting of the bonds of fear—rather than as a calculated appropriation, control, or possession of the outer world. The former concept opens man up and gives him to the world; the latter sees the world as man's possession.

The New Left and the counterculture point to the happiness of Being. In fact, the key to understanding the elusive but unifying ethos of the Movement lies in the idea of Being. Happiness is impossible without achieving Being. No honest member of the New Left or counterculture will compromise on this tenet—it is at the basis of what makes them radicals instead of liberals. Their idea of Being owes much to Eastern philosophies as well as to Marx, Marcuse, and the existentialist philosophers Nietzsche and Heidegger.

Contemporary western man simply fails to perceive the organic oneness of Being and reality. The famous existentialist philosopher Martin Heidegger (1889-1976) is of special significance at this point. (Indeed, much of what the counterculture inchoately decried, Heidegger had expressed philosophically forty years earlier.) The West, according to Heidegger, beginning with the last of the Greeks, started a kind of rationalism which destroyed Being. They detached things (particulars) from their general environmental background in order to get a better grasp of them. In short, they came to look upon the world as diversified as well as unified. But diversification required acts of intellectual judgment—one had to deliberately detach objects from the rest of reality. In doing so, the concept of truth became altered. No longer did truth reside in the totality, the perceptual unity of all; it existed in the intellect of the person making an intellectual judgment about the particular qualities of an object which he had "bracketed out of existence." This, of course, allowed the Greeks and later the West to develop science and technology, for it gave them particular skill at describing the behavior of objects differentiated from the larger reality. (Heidegger was not the first to posit this theory; it is also evident in Hegel and even more so in Nietzsche.)

Furthermore, as Watts, Snyder and others have pointed out, none of the Oriental civilizations insisted upon a similar detachment of "beings" from "Being." Nor did they claim that the truth was a form of intellectual judgment—that it existed in the human mind. Indeed, many Indian and Chinese thinkers argued that truth was attainable *only* when one curtailed human intellectual judgment, when one transcended the sensation of differentiation between subject and object, the ego from the rest of reality. For Heidegger and an increasing number of members of the counterculture, the essential distinction between Eastern and Western philosophy is that each has made a different decision as to what truth is and how to attain it. The vogue of Eastern mysticism among the hippies and freaks is testimony to their repudiation of Western post-Enlightenment rationalism. That is why I refer to them as "counter-Enlightenment."

It should be pointed out here, however, (as it has been by Nietzsche) that the Greeks were not rationalists in the sense that most modern Western men are. They still *knew* the larger unity of Being. And it was also Nietzsche who pointed out that it was the influence of Christianity, reaching philosophical culmination in René Descartes (1596-1650), which solidified the division between man and nature. The famed Cartesian dualism, which postulated an irremediable difference between man and nature, makes a unified Being impossible. The subject becomes cut off from the object even as his power to manipulate the object grows. Goethe warned that this would be the plight of the Enlightenment and modern science. Mankind would master beings, but Being—that perceptual, metaphysical state where there is no difference between object and subject, where truth is process as the totality of all things Being—that sort of truth, that notion of Being would be forgotten to the point of inaccessibility. Then, as Nietzsche foresaw, man would have so limited his reason that he would succumb to his Will to Power over objects. Man would then have so alienated his reason that he would be insane, suicidal, and self-destructive. And to a member of the New Left and the counterculture, that is precisely where we now are—a point reinforced by works of the popular culture, such as *A Clockwork Orange, One Flew Over the Cukoo's Nest, and 2001: A Space Odyssey.*

What the New Left and the counterculture attempt to do is to restore the older, prescientific concept of Being. They are thus often viscerally anti-rational, antitechnology, and antiscience—usually without knowing exactly why. To restore Being means to overcome alienation and to facilitate happiness. The first step, then, is obviously to overcome the Cartesian dualism—the separation of man from nature. While most members of the New Left look to Marx and Marcuse as guides for this task, and while most members of the counterculture think highly of Watts and Castaneda, the general philosophy of Being they both hold to is closer to Nietzsche and Heidegger: man overcomes his alienation from nature by realizing that what character-izes his humanness is his "Being-in-the-world." Man does not look out at an alien external world as an enclosed and isolated creature; he is, so to speak, "already out of doors." Man is Being-in-the-world because his existence sui generis totally involves him in the world. William Barrett, in his widely acclaimed book, *Irrational Man* (1962), has described this philosophical tenet. "Existence itself . . . means to stand outside oneself, to be beyond oneself. My Being is not something that takes place inside my skin (or inside an immaterial substance inside that skin); my Being, rather is spread over a field or region which is the world of its care and concern." [9]

This is a "field theory" of Being similar to Heidegger's. It is particularly relevant now, as the world becomes more technologically united and as it becomes a global, ecological field. In such a theory, the ego ceases to exist as historical reality. The unification of the globe technologically, hence visually and aurally, has produced a human being for which the older con-ceptions of ego, self, and "I" no longer seem accurate. "The mine-ness of my existence does not consist in the fact that there is an I-substance at the center of my field, but rather that this mine-ness permeates the whole field of my Being." [10] This means none of us has a private self which confronts a world of external objects. The concepts of "mine," "private," and "self," are totally different. We are One in the sense of the Beatles' song—"I am you, You are me. We are all together," and in the sense of Huey Newton's slogan, "I am we." The One is Being; it is impersonal and a field of Being which exists long before a person formulates an idea of his own oneness.

In an epistemological sense, Being is ascertained by the brain receiving messages from the external world every moment. Messages are received through the senses—patterned smell through the nose, patterned sight through the eyes, patterned sound through the ears, etc. But the awareness of these messages is of a single total experience—not a sight world, plus a hearing world and so on. The various sensory systems make a total immediate impression and result in instant, phenomenological distinction of what Being is. To disassociate the sensory systems is to interrupt Being, and attempts to enforce perception which divides reality, such as Western rationalism, produce discomfort and feelings of alienation. And so Marcuse remarked, "It blocks the erotic cathexis (the transformation) of his environment: it deprives man from finding himself in nature beyond and this side of aliena- tion; it also prevents him from recognizing nature as a *subject* in its own right—a subject with which to live in a common universe." [11] Because man is in nature, his domination and exploitation of nature affect man as well as nature. The despoliation of nature interferes with man's own Being; it hurts man not only ecologically but existentially.

In this philosophy of Being, the world *becomes*—it reveals itself to us in a phenomenological sense. That is, it reveals itself not merely in space and time, but also as a totality of qualities interacting with all the senses. This is the primordial stuff of reality, this is the truth, this is Being. *This dimension of totality is radical consciousness.* LSD can reveal it, although it is not neces- sary to drop acid to achieve it. The becoming, the unfolding, and the totality of process is experienced as *happiness*—a high, so high it is like being in love with the world. The way of knowing is experienced as love or as a profound aesthetic response.

What the New Left and the counterculture offer as an idea of happiness is a liberation from a truncated, one-dimensional reality and an entrance into totality, the world of Being. Their partisans *do* sense the world differently. The special importance of the cultural revolution is that it points to a new sensibility, the sensibility to Be, to be happy. The counterculture clearly negates the existing order with this philosophy and hence is regarded as subversive, although most people do not know exactly what the threat is. What they *do* know is that be-ins, love-ins, protests, drugs, and long hair all somehow go together in the lifestyle of a youth subculture. And indeed they do go together: the point of a be-in is quite simply to *Be*—happy— without working and without paying anything. The elusive Abbie Hoffman said more than the befuddled Establishment understood when he answered a question about the specific nature of his politics: "I believe in the politics of being, the politics of ecstasy." [12]

Happiness, then, is a universal ingredient of Being. So regarded, happiness is the *universal potential for interaction, for symbolization*—it is the joy which can accompany the process of playing with, transforming, and sym- bolizing the world. As a concept, it is the awareness of the process of ecstatic symbolization. So it is a process greater than any actual situation, just as hunger is a demand that cannot be satisfied simply by eating a meal. Man is happiest when his play satisfies his desire to transfigure the experiences that he encounters. And such transfiguration, such creation of symbols, is man's way of playing with the world. It is what makes man necessary in the world; it justifies his existence. Mankind was created to rescue the world; man enlivens the world by transforming it symbolically. And this is the same vision of Being that inspired Rilke when he declared:

> . . . These things that live on departure
> understand when you praise them: fleeting, they look for
> rescue through something in us, the most fleeting of all.
> Want us to change them entirely, within our invisible hearts,
> into—oh—endlessly—into ourselves! Whosoever we are.
>
> Earth, isn't this what you want: an invisible
> re-arising in us? Is it not your dream
> to be one day invisible? Earth! invisible!
> What is your urgent command, if not transformation?
> Earth, you darling, I will! . . .[13]

But as long as man does not realize that happiness is a universal, generic life process—not something to be acquired—man will not be happy. As the great Russian novelist Dostoyevsky wrote in *The Possessed:* "Man is unhappy because he doesn't know he's happy. It's only that. That's all, that's all. If anyone finds out he'll become happy at once, that minute. . . . That's the whole idea, the whole of it." [14] Let man play with the world and transfigure it symbolically and he will know happiness; he will be liberated. To know this is to know what the irrepressible Nietzsche meant when he wrote:

> One is necessary, one is a piece of fatefulness, one belongs to the whole, one is in the whole; there is nothing which could judge, measure, compare, or sentence our being, for that would mean judging, measuring, comparing, or sentencing the whole. But there is nothing besides the whole. That nobody is held responsible any longer, that the mode of being may not be traced back to a *causa prima,* that the world does not form a unity as a sensorium or as "spirit"—that alone is the great liberation: with this alone is the innocence of becoming restored.[15]

Prevent a person from symbolic interaction with the world and he will be unhappy, although he may not know why. But he *will* always sense that much of his activity is irrelevant and empty. And, if he is young and has spent most of his life in schools where he has participated in activities which have obstructed his Being, he will declare their product—knowledge, or discursive rationalism—to be irrelevant.

Notes to Chapter 12

1. W. H. Auden and Christopher Isherwood, *The Dog Beneath the Skin* (New York, 1936), pp. 97-98. Reprinted by permission of Random House, Inc.

2. Karen Horney, *New Ways in Psychoanalysis* (New York, 1938), p. 298.

3. Herbert Marcuse, *Eros and Civilization* (Boston, 1955), p. 3.

4. Irving Kristol, "The Old Politics, the New Politics, the New, New Politics," *New York Times Magazine* (November 24, 1968).

5. "It's Alright Ma, (I'm Only Bleeding)," words and music by Bob Dylan. © 1965 M. Witmark & Sons. All rights reserved. Used by permission of Warner Bros. Music.

6. "Like A Rolling Stone," words and music by Bob Dylan. © 1965 M. Witmark & Sons. All rights reserved. Used by permission of Warner Bros. Music.

7. Abbie Hoffman, *Revolution for the Hell of It* (New York, 1968), p. 62.

8. Erich Fromm, *Man for Himself.* (New York, 1967), p. 189.

9. William Barrett, *Irrational Man* (New York, 1962), p. 217.

10. Ibid., p. 219.

11. Herbert Marcuse, *Counter-Revolution and Revolt* (New York, 1972), p. 60. All references to this book are by permission of Beacon Press.

12. Abbie Hoffman, "Freedom and License," in Peter and Deborah Babcox and Bob Abel, eds., *The Conspiracy* (New York, 1969), p. 73.

13. Rainer Maria Rilke, *Duino Elegies*, trans. J. B. Leishman and Stephen Spender (New York, 1963), p. 77. Reprinted by permission of W. W. Norton, Inc.

14. Fyodor Dostoyevsky, *The Possessed*, trans. Constance Garnett (New York, 1961), p. 255.

15. Friedrich Nietzsche, *The Twilight of the Idols,* from *The Portable Nietzsche,* selected and translated by Walter Kaufmann (New York, 1954), pp. 500-501. Reprinted by permission of The Viking Press, Inc.

XIII

A Dearth of Meaningful Symbols:
The Irrelevance of Knowledge

During those long years in the Oakland public schools, I did not have one teacher who taught me anything relevant to my own life or experience. Not one instructor ever awoke in me a desire to learn more or question or explore the worlds of literature, science, and history.*

Huey Newton's statement, sweeping as it may seem, is crucial to an understanding of much of radical theory, especially when radicals proclaim high school and higher education irrelevant. For the complaint of the young that, as the Rolling Stones put it, "some useless information supposed to pry my imagination," is really the cry of people who can find no symbols and no modes of knowledge with which to make sense of the world. This has become apparent as the process of symbolization has virtually come to an end because scientific abstraction and rationalism (mathematical and word symbols) monopolize the forms of symbolization. To some extent, this accounts for the widespread criticism of science, technology, rationalism, and materialism. For we now confine our symbolization to the material world because we have taken the material to be the only "real" world, and therefore the only world to be symbolized. It should be clear then that the antirationalism and the anti-intellectualism of the radicals is not simply destructive negativism. It is a statement of the reality of postwar America, and, as Marshall McLuhan and others have pointed out, we now live in a "global village" of instant awareness and we can no longer symbolize or make sense of the global village using words and figures. It is not surprising, therefore, that Abbie Hoffman wrote: "Don't rely on words. Words are the absolute horseshit."[1] Allen Ginsberg expressed similar thoughts in his poem "Wichita Vortex Sutra."

*Huey P. Newton, *Revolutionary Suicide*. Reprinted by permission of Harcourt, Brace & Jovanovich, Inc.

> . . . The war is language,
> language abused
> for Advertisement,
> language used
> like magic for power on the planet:
>
> Black magic language,
> formulas for reality—
> Communism is a 9 letter word
> used by inferior magicians with
> the wrong alchemical formula for transforming earth into gold
> funky warlocks operating on guesswork,
> that never worked in 1956 . . .[2]

On the same subject of words, the Jefferson Airplane sang,

> Don't try to touch me with words[3]

Yet, at a time when there is such a need for the academic establishment (especially in history, psychology, communication, and the humanities) to experiment with new forms of symbolization, little experimentation is taking place. The situation is particularly acute in the humanities, which have a special responsibility to supply the techniques for making value judgments, to uphold the spiritual dimension of man, and to demonstrate its relevance in everyday life. Yet the humanities continue to imitate science in their approach, and they insist that they too can achieve "objectivity." But this means their judgments are in fact valueless, because the objectivity which science uses as a category is descriptive, not prescriptive. More and more, the humanities treat knowledge as if it is solely informational (objective descriptive statements). But in so doing, the humanities become irrelevant, for knowledge in the humanities is, as suggested earlier, not essentially informational, but normative, moral, and value laden. Although the classic article about the condition of the humanities was written several years ago by Professor William Arrowsmith, its conclusions are still valid. The "scientism" of humanist scholars, "and their uncritical commitment to bookish work have involved them in a vanity of business and productivity which has no longer any rhyme or reason, and which is as futile and compulsive as the arms race."[4]

Students and critics are correct when they place most of the responsibility for the irrelevance of current humanities and social science programs upon the government and certain businesses, such as General Dynamics, Boeing, General Electric, American Telephone and Telegraph, Weyerhauser, and Xerox. For it is now common knowledge that, since the Second World War, the government has helped business to subsidize a knowledge industry which uses the university faciltes for ends which consist primarily of profit and political imperialism. For example, in 1963 the production, distribution, and consumption of knowledge accounted for 29 percent of the gross national product and was growing twice as fast as the rest of the economy. In 1966, the president of IBM predicted that the nation was approaching a time in which more than half of the work force would be involved in processing and applying data.[5] This has come to mean that universities supply knowledge essentially of a political, military, technical, and profitable nature. This kind of knowledge is seldom relevant to or used for humanitarian values. Furthermore, universities are coming to have less and less control over the uses of their data. Instead of pioneering a morality of knowledge, instead of insisting upon the application of human values to the knowledge they produce, most universities and many academicians "sell out." In addition, increasing numbers of academicians no longer even teach; many of them do research and development work instead. In 1970, ten thousand faculty members had no teaching responsibilities; in 1975 the number increased to twenty thousand.[6] The knowledge they compile is often used for social manipulation, control, exploitation, and ecological despoliation. To a radical student or a radical teacher, therefore, the conversion of the universities into what amounts to vehicles of the state (an average of 40 percent of the total budgets for first-rate private universities comes from the federal government) and of the capitalist conglomerates is perhaps the most hated phenomenon of the American system.[7]

> Where Ma Raney and Beethoven once unwrapped their bed
> roll
> Tuba players now rehearse around the flagpole
> And the National Bank at a profit sells road maps for the soul
> To the old folks home and the college.[8]

The controversy over the relevance of education is not only a dispute over what will be taught and for whom research is done. In a broader context of western civilization, it is an epistemological crisis. That is, we need new ways of knowing and relating knowledge to cosmology (the totality of the causal sequence of phenomena) and to human action. We have *too much* information, and our experience is too variegated to make existential sense. In the jargon of the counterculture, it is extremely difficult to "get it all together." This is due in part to the gigantic knowledge explosion since World War II and to the immediacy of information. It is also attributable to the persistence of the conviction that all knowledge is worth having and that all knowledge by definition is relevant. By their continual production of knowledge, academicians perpetuate this obsolete notion while adding vast amounts of information to our already mammoth stockpile.

The epistemological crisis also comes from the peculiar historical circumstances following the Second World War, circumstances which are especially familiar to the postwar generations. Specifically, while logic and reason deliver reliable operational knowledge for science and technology, they do *not* or *have not* yet achieved such reliable operational knowledge about the most important part of postwar reality—namely, historical reality. The unprecedented technological changes since the war and the realization of the arbitrariness and the contingency of modern life is a reality which neither the logic of the sciences nor the categories of traditional history have assimilated into a system of personal or collective surety. As the vistas of man's knowledge have expanded, his ability to assimilate knowledge (that is, to make it practical and relevant) has not grown proportionally. Many people, especially students, are trying to integrate the disparate and arbitrary pieces of "knowledge" into an understanding which will make them comfortable in the world. But the traditional forms of knowledge—such as history, approached as a patterned linear record of political and social developments, or English, seen as the study of human nature and human relationships, or philosophy, appreciated as the study of metaphysics and cosmology—have faltered in their previous relevance: to make the world intelligible and to foster reasonably secure personal action. The techniques and the modes of knowledge are therefore being seriously challenged and, with them, the cultural value of rationalism upon which they are anchored. Rationalism simply does not offer a satisfactory orientation to the postwar world. This was brilliantly demonstrated in Mike Nichols's cinema production of Joseph Heller's novel *Catch-22*. The general attitude was also expressed by the incorrigible Bob Dylan.

> Now I wish I could write you a melody so plain
> That could hold you dear lady from going insane
> That could ease you and cool you and cease the pain
> Of your useless and pointless knowledge.[9]

What is the use of gaining knowledge if neither the society nor the individual is able to utilize that knowledge in ways which assist human happiness and bring man security? Are the postwar generations really supposed to believe that history will record that the application of our collective knowledge in Southeast Asia was, as ex-President Nixon said, "our finest hour"? If so, then life and history become, as Jean-Paul Sartre once described them, "the facticity of absurd existence." Philosophers and literary artists as well as rock stars such as Bob Dylan are insisting that this sort of approach to knowledge is spiritually irrelevant, burdensome to achieve, and ultimately empty.

Indeed, there is a profound feeling that our obsessive reliance upon rationalism and technology has, in large measure, *created* contemporary reality. Most persons in the counterculture agree with the conclusion reached by David Halberstam in his book *The Best and the Brightest* (1972). It was the super-rationalists of the Truman, Kennedy, Johnson, and Nixon administrations who made the colossal mistakes in Southeast Asia, in South America, and with the American economy. In this sense, the counterculture agrees with Daniel Ellsberg that the almost hysterical belief in the reports of the CIA and the military, combined with their scintillating presentation in perfectly logical arguments by Dean Rusk, Robert McNamara, and later Henry Kissinger, brought the United States government to ruin in Vietnam. Secretary of State Kissinger acknowledged this in May 1976. Consequently, many young people turn to the drug-induced perception of reality to offset the "rational" perception of reality. In the words of Timothy Leary: "Turn on, Tune in, Drop Out."

This is the situation which faces students in the humanities and social sciences in the 1970's. While the urgent need is to experiment with new forms, create new symbols, and use our technology to help make sense of existence, the dominant culture still insists that anything which cannot be symbolized mathematically or in words is not worthy of expression or study. To a student, this means that in high school and college he or she will find nothing which cannot be projected in a discursive form, and that he or she will not be asked to try to understand anything except known, demonstrable facts. And conversely, nothing is really known unless it is amenable to mathematical or linguistic organization. This leads a student to the conclusion that in the eyes of the professor, a student is not very successful unless he can use these forms to symbolize what he knows or has learned. So the system of written term papers, written examinations, and abstruse mathematical problems continues to determine the grade earned and the measurement awarded to a student's learning. This approach implies that the knowable is a clearly defined field, governed by the technical requirements of discursive symbolism. However, this places a vast amount of experience outside the realm of culturally acceptable knowledge. And it leads to the disenchantment so well expressed by Bob Dylan,

> To understand you know too soon
> There is no sense in trying.[10]

The realm of the ultimate or the desire to formulate a cosmology is a realm which was once the focus of philosophy and higher learning and is now, for all practical purposes, a defunct aspect of university training. As one disenchanted Harvard graduate described it: "The standing assumption is that ultimate questions are in principle unanswerable, and hence not worth asking seriously." For "the university on principle, concentrates on statistics, historical facts, historical intellectual positions, logic modeled on the discourse of the physical sciences, and ample documentation."[11]

And yet it is precisely for these reasons that students find college irrelevant: because their world transcends the world of rational discourse. What concerns students is not so much the world that we already can symbolize, but the world that they are growing up in and for which there seems to be no satisfactory form of discursive symbolism. This is the world in which there can no longer be intellectual compartmentalization. It is a televised "global village" in which we can simultaneously hear, see, and feel the people of the world. Such a world has made rational compartmentalization impossible as the means to explain reality. It has introduced experience which is not embodied in word symbols—instantaneous, unfiltered, raw experience. This kind of experience could be made meaningful by starting with a philosophy of Being, concentrating on experience rather than dead fact, and upon the way our cognitive faculties interact (eyes, ears, nose, etc.) with the given world. Then a person would make knowledge relevant, for he or she would be formulating answers to the most "relevant" questions of existence. Who am I? What are you? What is the rest of reality? What does this mean? These questions are neither new nor peculiar to the postwar epoch. Indeed, they received a brilliant and precise formulation over forty years ago by the spiritual physician of the 1930's, the late W. H. Auden.

> Here am I, Here are you
> But what does it mean
> And what are we going to do?[12]

Yet neither our politicians nor our institutions of higher learning seem to recognize that the situation is critical. Instead, they debunk the New Left and other critics of higher learning as being utopian and naively unrealistic. They argue that college education, though a growth industry, is also the practical tool for economic and social advancement—particularly for minorities. This view is widely held and utterly erroneous. College education has no direct discernible relationship to income, occupational status, or social mobility. This was made public as early as 1968 in the scrupulous work done by sociologists Christopher Jencks and David Riesman, entitled *The Academic Revolution*. A study by the Labor Department published in January 1973 corroborated the Jencks and Riesman conclusions except to point up a trend in the postwar epoch that is even more discouraging to minorities. The author of the study, Peter Henle, concluded that the trend toward a concentration of an increasingly larger share of wage and salary income among jobs and professions already enjoying higher pay is likely to continue for the predictable future. Inequality of income distribution was predicted to continue with the lowest fifth of male workers earning less while the highest fifth will earn more.[13]

Hence, with rising tuition and fee costs, many students have rightly concluded that there is no practical economic reason to believe higher education is the escalator to higher income and higher social status. Consequently, many argue that higher education is both practically and spiritually irrelevant to our existential condition. And what is our existential condition?

> Electric circuitry has overthrown the regime of "time" and "space" and pours upon us instantly and continuously the concerns of all other men. It has reconstituted dialog on a global scale. Its message is total change, ending psychic, social, economic, and political parochialism. The older civic, state and national groupings have become unworkable. Nothing can be further from the spirit of the new technology than a place for everything and everything in its place. You can't go home again.[14]

And this portentous statement by Marshall McLuhan is echoed by Bob Dylan in the title of one of his greatest songs: "The Times They Are A-Changin'." Thus the message of McLuhan permeates the counterculture and the New Left. Political, economic, and personal parochialisms are archaic; we are existentially and technologically unified. Hence, the message of "We Can Be Together," the title song from the Jefferson Airplane's highly political album *Volunteers,* is

> We can be together
> Ah, you and me
> We should be together
> . . . .
> We must begin here and now
> A new continent of earth and fire
> Tear down the walls . . .[15]

The meaning of the message is fundamentally the same, whether it is articulated by McLuhan, by Tom Hayden in the "Port Huron Statement," or by the various politically conscious rock groups. Much like the last days of Greek civilization, the West is fulfilling the ancient myth of the serpent biting its own tail. We have come full circle. Our supertechnological postwar society quickly demolishes the linear culture of the industrial age of literacy and forces man again to confront the universe with his body—his total sense, his Being. As predicted in science fiction novels like Robert Heinlein's *Stranger in a Strange Land,* Arthur Clarke's *The City and the Stars* and *2001: A Space Odyssey,* we have completed a wide historical cycle: we are back to the struggle of man against the mysterious, all-powerful, and undifferentiated reality of nature.

But it is not the same theme of man against nature as depicted in *Deliverance* by James Dickey; it is man against the artificial environment he has created through his own rationalism and spectacular application of technology. We are coming into a technological wilderness as fearsome and ominous as the untamed nature man faced when he first began to collectivize in order to survive. We are as strange to our own artifically controlled and modified external world as were the first civilizations to the natural world. Having tamed one, we have created another. The serpent bites his own tail. This is the sense of McLuhan's retribalization—the forces and operation of a technologically closed world and of a manmade, enshrouded planetary environment are so analogous to man battling nature in a tribal state that we can say the world is in effect retribalized. In both instances, the horror of the environment is so great as to *demand* collective organization in order to survive. But should this collective organization take a local, national, or generational form? Or should we all seek individual escape? These are the questions raised by those who share McLuhan's view of "where we are at." They are anchored in a common consensus of what our existential conditions are; and we must frankly acknowledge that, at present, it is primarily the postwar generations who see reality this way and see the historical cycle moving toward its completion. Both the counterculture and the New Left sense the danger. The New Left still sees politics as the chief vehicle to meet the crisis. The counterculture has at least two major apocalyptic visions of escape. One is that of Bob Dylan and Joni Mitchell: pastoral apocalypse; the other is that of the Jefferson Airplane, supertechnological apocalpyse. Both of these visions of escape will be examined in the next chapter.

The tragedy in this situation is that young people can make so few of the older people in power comprehend the existential situation as they see it. Nor can they convince the Establishment of the self-destructive path it is taking by maintaining its profit and expansionist ethos. What is taken for youthful ebullience and impatience by the Establishment is conversely regarded by young people as stupidity and as dangerous obstruction by the Establishment in the face of a critical situation. Listen to "Crown of Creation" by the Jefferson Airplane, as Grace Slick and Paul Kantner sing:

> In loyalty to their kind
> They cannot tolerate our minds
> And in loyalty to our kind
> We cannot tolerate their obstruction.[16]

The Establishment holds its breath until young people turn thirty and assumes they will then cease agitation. Yet every radical, every writer, and every rock performer quoted or mentioned in this book is thirty or over. And most of them have been trying to educate the Establishment for at least a decade, with negligible success—except for kidnapping.

Is it any wonder that on nearly every university campus many bewildered students are dropping out and living lives like those so brilliantly depicted in *Be Not Content* by the "freak" novelist, William Craddock. These are lives devoted to frantic attempts to create adequate symbolism in the plastic fantastic atomic age; symbols for luxury-induced fear, symbols for disappointed, drugged solipsism. And it is not just a few "freak" literati dropouts and rock performers who feel the present educational system is irrelevant; it is also educational experts such as George Leonard and Ivan Illich. These educators have labored for years to make education relevant. Like so many young people, Leonard has concluded that "the university is still a place where people are trained to split their world into separate systems. . . . Such 'education' . . . has made possible . . . space voyaging and the H-bomb. But it has not made people happy or whole, nor does it now offer them ways to change. . . ."[17]

If our culture and our educational institutions continue their present course, we shall soon achieve a total separation of thought and feeling, of discursive symbolization and free-floating imagination. We will have then further divided man from man and alienated man from himself. The word symbol (language) will then be the only vehicle of thought, and anything which cannot be put into language will be "relegated" to feeling, fantasy, or imagination. The fact that we commonly refer to the subjects taught in college as "disciplines" reinforces our assumptions regarding imagination. That is, we must discipline our imagination in order to learn and to organize reality into thought. But to discipline a person's imagination is really to anesthetize it. A disciplined imagination may indeed be a contradiction in terms, but whatever the conclusion, there is no question that the liberal arts are waging a war against feeling and imagination in the name of clarity of thought and exposition.

Furthermore, as long as we accept that only discursive symbolism can convey an idea, "thought" will remain our only intellectual activity. But thought is *not* the only intellectual activity of man; indeed, by such a notion, man is reduced to intellectual one-dimensionality. In addition, we must guard against the notion that thought is the highest mental activity and that it has reached its zenith in modern science and technology. Once again we are indebted to Levi-Strauss for pointing out that neolithic civilization as well as modern Christian civilizations had science and that in an anthropological sense there is no significant difference between modern and primitive civilizations. Levi-Strauss concluded in *The Savage Mind* (1962) that it is untenable to argue the superiority of modern science over primitive science. This has been reaffirmed by MIT historian William Irwin Thompson. "From the pyramids of Egypt to the megaliths of Newgrange, Stonehenge, Mexico, Peru, and Easter Island, ancient man and his Pythagorean science could do things we with our very different industrial science cannot understand."[18] This means we must acknowledge that our linear conception of history, which culminates in the "triumph" of the West and of industrial science, *is false.* (I realize that such a statement is unacceptable to most historians).

Linear history with its "progressive delineation" is, in the opinion of this historian, a fiction created to rationalize our present position of technological superiority on this planet. It is a form of intellectual imperialism as dangerous as its counterpart in politics; indeed, the two are probably inextricably linked.

Thus, there are so many dangers and limitations implicit in a rationalism which relies on discursive symbolism that continued uncritical acceptance of it is just plain stupid, and it is naive to consider it the keystone of happiness. Hence (although perhaps a bit prematurely), the counterculture and many young people declare knowledge and higher education irrelevant; the New Left is critical of education in general, yet remains unwilling to abandon discursive symbolism entirely. But it is difficult to separate, except arbitrarily, these two aspects of left wing radicalism, because both enjoy and practice aspects of life which are thoroughly nondiscursive—clothes, hair, music, magic, films, light shows, guerrilla theatre, and rock 'n' roll festivals such as Woodstock, 1969, the Isle of Wight, 1970, and Watkins Glen, 1973. Here, the intellectual activity of the participants is a purely sensory appreciation of experience. This sensory appreciation of experience is a way of living and perceiving a situation as a totality instead of dividing it into thoughts using word symbols or linear systems of organization. After all, our senses provide a better and more immediate guide to color, temperature, speed, texture, beauty—in a word, Being—than the abstractions of word or mathematical symbols. For the cohesiveness of the Movement is still the intuitive knowledge which inspired Spanish philosopher Miguel de Unamuno to write, ". . . living is one thing and knowing is another; and . . . perhaps there is such an opposition between the two that we may say that everything rational is antivital. And this is the basis of the tragic sense of life."[19]

Accordingly, much of the life of the counterculture (immortalized by Abbie Hoffman and Joni Mitchell as the Woodstock Nation) is simply gestalt life. Quite expectedly, therefore, the writings of psychologists Frederick Perls and the late Paul Goodman continue to be in vogue, as do the works of mystic anthropologist Carlos Castaneda. (Indeed, Castaneda's first book, *The Teachings of Don Juan: A Yaqui Way of Knowledge* (1968), was selling at the rate of 16,000 copies weekly in the first quarter of 1973). The hope is that the spontaneous ordering of experience in the act of perception itself is the principle of symbolization, and will yield the real phenomenological detritus of the universe. In short, this is an attempt to discover and/or create a prerational *Weltanschauung* like that of the Indians described by Castaneda, and akin to the epistemological revelations described by Bergson, Proust, and Rilke in the European tradition. This is why music, especially electronic rock 'n' roll music, is so vital to young people. For music is definitely a symbolization of a nondiscursive type, of "unspeakable things," as Wittgenstein once phrased it. And despite its increasing commercialization and cooptation by the Establishment, it remains perhaps the strongest pillar sustaining the counterculture.

Notes to Chapter 13

1. Abbie Hoffman, *Revolution for the Hell of It* (New York, 1968), p. 29.

2. Allen Ginsberg, "Wichita Vortex Sutra." Copyright 1968 by Allen Ginsberg. Reprinted by permission of City Lights Books.

3. "Young Girl Sunday Blues," words by Marty Balin, music by Marty Balin and Paul Kantner. © 1968, Icebag Corporation. All rights reserved. Used by permission.

4. William Arrowsmith, "The Shame of the Graduate Schools," *Harper's* (March, 1966), p. 53.

5. Michael Harrington, *Toward a Democratic Left* (Baltimore, 1969), p. 78.

6. Harold Hodgkinson, *Institutions in Transition* (New York, 1971), pp. 255-56.

7. William G. Bowen, *The Economics of Major Universities* (Berkeley, 1968).

8. "Tombstone Blues," words and music by Bob Dylan. © 1965, M. Witmark & Sons. All rights reserved. Used by permission of Warner Brothers Music.

9. Ibid.

10. "It's Alright Ma, (I'm Only Bleeding)," words and music by Bob Dylan. © 1965, M. Witmark & Sons. All rights reserved. Used by permission of Warner Brothers Music.

11. Michael Novak, "God in the Colleges," in Michell Cohen and Dennis Hale, eds., *The New Student Left* (New York, 1967), pp. 255-56.

12. W. H. Auden, *Poems* (London, 1933), p. 52. Reprinted by permission of Faber and Faber Ltd., publishers.

13. See *Monthly Labor Review* (U. S. Department of Labor), Dec., 1972, Jan., 1973.

14. Quoted in Harrington, *A Democratic Left*, p. 151.

15. "We Can Be Together," words and music by Paul Kantner. © 1969, Icebag Corporation. All rights reserved. Used by permission.

16. "Crown of Creation," words and music by Paul Kantner. © 1969 by Icebag Corporation. All rights reserved. Used by permission.

17. George B. Leonard, *Education and Ecstasy* (New York, 1971), p. 197.

18. William Irwin Thompson, *At the Edge of History* (New York, 1971), p. 197.

19. Miguel de Unamuno, *Del Sentimiento Tragico de la Vida,* trans. G. E. Crawford Flitch (London, 1926), p. 34.

XIV

Rock 'n' Roll and
Nondiscursive Symbolism

For the reality of what's happening today in America, we must go rock
'n' roll, to popular music.*

The German philosopher Arthur Schopenhauer is probably the best known
exponent of the idea that music is a symbolic language of an irrational aspect
of mental life, the Will. Schopenhauer suggested that music is a definite com-
municable symbolism with a content of ideas, and that fundamental laws of
life and of the world can be rediscovered through it even without any discursive relation between tonal events and concrete concepts. For music, to
paraphrase Schopenhauer, yields images not of a physical but of a metaphysical reality—not of appearance, but of essence.

Although perhaps few rock enthusiasts have thought of it in such lofty
terms, the music of rock 'n' roll is most certainly the single most powerful
"language" of youth. Rock music is not self-expression, but a formulation
and representation of emotions, moods, and mental tensions. It is universally
understood and appreciated by young people because it can incorporate and
communicate an unarticulated, inchoate impression of the contemporary
world. Hence, Marty Balin of the Jefferson Airplane said in 1966, "I never
have to explain my songs to my age group. There is instant communication
that goes on once you are familiar with Jefferson Airplane's language. It's
loud like the world we live in and it's strong too. . . . I feel like I'm talking.
It's the greatest way to communicate." Good rock music embodies an
intuitive insight, a certain metaphysical understanding of "what is really
happening." "Objects that embody such insights, and acts which express,
preserve and reiterate them are indeed more spontaneously interesting, more
serious than work."[1] And so, literally millions of young people all over the

*Ralph Gleason, The Age of Rock.

world will travel hundreds—sometimes thousands—of miles, to attend a rock festival. It comes as no surprise, therefore, that since 1970 rock in live performance has become the greatest audience gatherer in show business history. Indeed, Bob Dylan's return to a concert tour of twenty-one cities in January and February of 1974 resulted in the *turning away* of over two million persons who could not be accommodated. Rock 'n' roll magazines continue to top the sales of underground newspapers, with *Rolling Stone* selling over a quarter of a million copies biweekly. And other, more graphic rock newspapers like *Crawdaddy, Fusion, Zygote, Rock,* and *Creem* still have substantial appeal. Time-Life has recognized the market for rock and sold over one million reprints of their edition on Woodstock for $1.25 each. Rock 'n' roll music reaches people in virtually every city in the Western world, and in Japan and Southeast Asia. It is without class distinctions; it is international, primarily generational, and definitely alive. It has no progress and is ostensibly apolitical. But in actuality rock 'n' roll is the chief nonverbal source of the most political and cultural movement since Nazism: feeling. And its leaders—John Lennon, Bob Dylan, and Mick Jagger, to name only a few—are in their own way the moral and political prophets of a whole generation.

The message carried by rock music, personified by its heroes, and assisted by marijuana, is that there is no purpose to life; all the gods are dead. Rock says that there is nothing: no reason and no justification for any behavior in society or anywhere else. It says that the backbone of society, the ideals proffered to youth, are spurious; it is all a myth to facilitate social cohesion. But with drugs or alcohol and rock, it blends into an ironic, bittersweet, almost demonic joy. What was true in the "straight" world and exposed by Beckett, Sartre, and others—the total purposelessness of life—suddenly makes sense under the spell of rock. A euphoria builds—a hope that rises from the outward, social meaninglessness, veiled as the productive materialist ethic— that amidst all this obvious exploitive propaganda there is something that is real. And what is real is the body, the turned-on, sensuous, intuitive rocking and rolling body, mesmerized back into life by rock 'n' roll. The message is put succinctly in the title of a song The Who sang at Woodstock, "See me, Feel me, Touch me, Heal me."

On a different level, the message of rock is naked, defenseless realism. It is a realism misunderstood by even the most perspicacious of the liberal critics. They misunderstand the message because they still hope to construct some social or political-technical institutions to tap the potentialities of man. But what they refuse to acknowledge is that in the effort to help man to fulfill himself, they have generally made fulfillment more difficult. To continue to rely upon rational, technical answers to the human problem of happiness is foolish and unreal. Rock is a realistic, unabashed retreat from the rationally controlled, highly organized, unhappy technological world. Rock conjures up the primordial, the raw, the physical, the irrational, the mysterious, and the macabre, as touchstones to getting people back to themselves—back to inner sources of happiness and joy. The aim is the unexpected, unpremeditated joy of aesthetic, physical response. It is *play*—delight in the transformation of music, lyrics and color. And to the "hip," this is hope. This is a sort of Dionysian playing with the world, and it is uniquely human; perhaps it is the teleology of the species itself.

In rock music and its concomitant mind-blowing experiences, the Dionysian element reaches a current zenith. The emphasis on the visual and the ecstatic which is heightened by the volume of the music, the swirl of exploding lights and the distorted images—these, compounded with marijuana or psychedelic drugs and the dancing of groupies, consummate a collective tribal celebration of Dionysus. It is collective participation held up in contrast to the abstracted representative participation which characterizes modern bureaucratic democracy. And the Dionysian elements of nondiscursive culture are not confined to rock festivals or communal gatherings. They are present in living theater (in which the audience is invited to participate), and they are present in all happenings where freaks play games. But it is primarily in rock performance that the cult of Dionysus triumphs over the cult of Apollo. This is what Mick Jagger represents and what the late Jimi Hendrix and Janis Joplin represented. Against the dominant Apollonian rationalism of Plato, Aristotle, and their legacy in contemporary science—with its emphasis upon calculation, normalcy, individual self-sufficiency, and moderation—the rock star and the counterculture present the claims of the irrational, the intoxicated, the satanic, the abnormal, and the androgynous—or polymorphous perversity, as Norman O. Brown would say it. Everyone in the counterculture knows that he or she is involved in a cultural war against the dominant rationalist culture. Hence, the Jefferson Airplane brazenly proclaim:

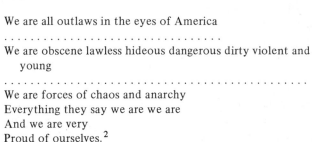

The ascendancy of the Dionysian means the overcoming or transcending of the purely rational. It points to the ineffectiveness of rationalism and to the "unreality of the world created by rational, technological differentiation. A writer for *Crawdaddy* summarized the appeal of rock:

> Bring along your liberal opinions. Your knowledge of atrocities committed by numberless power structures of the past. Your analyst's ideas about today's Oedipal hangup. Your own manipulative, categorizing, classifying S.A.T. braininess. You cannot only cross the rock threshold bearing this paraphernalia, you can retreat to it, any time you want—by tuning back into the lyrics. No obligation in this pop world to mindlessness. . . .
>
> But if you'd like something else—if you'd care to blow your mind, shed those opinions, plunge into selflessness, into a liberating perception of the uselessness, the unavailingness, the futility of the very notion of opinionated personhood, well, it so happens to happen there's something, dig, real helpful here. . . .[3]

When the "acid rock" group Iron Butterfly conclude a performance by igniting the entire front of the stage, separating themselves from the audience by a wall of fire, they are not just being theatrical. The fire symbolizes the apocalpyse, the end of the age of reason, and the birth of the Dionysus. This is precisely why Mick Jagger leaves the stage in a sheet of flames. Similarly, when Bob Dylan in "Desolation Row" sings:

> Now at midnight all the agents
> And the super human crew
> Come out and round up everyone
> That knows more than they do.[4]

he does *not* mean that "the agents" round up those better educated or better trained in logic. To the contrary, he means that "the agents" are the guardians of rationality who cannot tolerate persons who *know* intuitively. It is in fact "the agents" who *don't know*.

More effectively than any other singer of his generation, Dylan repeatedly silhouetted the dangers and the oppressiveness of rationalism. He depicted how rationalism can lead to a paranoid political madness (evident in 1973–74 with the Nixon administration's Watergate affair). His songs, "Subterranean Homesick Blues," "Desolation Row," "Tombstone Blues," "Ballad of a Thin Man," "It's All Over Now, Baby Blue," "Like a Rolling Stone," "Day of the Locusts," and "George Jackson Blues" are reminiscent of the 1930's plays of W. H. Auden and Christopher Isherwood. That is to say, they are full of invalids, neurotics, clowns, political pawns, and freaks of all sorts. His songs are strange, overflowing with disorder, chaos, and unexpected destruction. In "Ballad of a Thin Man," for example, Mr. Jones is the successful would-be hip intellectual who has "been through all of F. Scott Fitzgerald's books." He comes into the room secure in his rationalism, with a pencil in his hand to

record and analyze "what's happening." But suddenly he finds himself in
a vicious, insane, malicious world. He is utterly at a loss about what to do,
and he cries out: "Oh my God, am I here all alone?" The point here is that
rationalism can neither explain nor cope with this kind of reality. And Bob
Dylan's reality is still the reality of young people today.

Rationalism, as the means of relating *to* the world, is destroyed and
replaced by magic, as the means of relating *with* the world. Costumes are
magical; and, when one is stoned or far into a rock scene, all is magical.
Flowers have power, chants and hexes have power, love has power. The
Lovin' Spoonful sang "Believe in magic, it will set you free." And Bob
Dylan asks his famous Mr. Tambourine Man to:

> Take me on a trip upon your magic swirl 'n ship
> My senses have been stripped, my hands can't feel to grip
> My toes too numb to step, wait only for my boot heels
> To be wanderin'
> I'm ready to go anywhere, I'm ready for to fade
> Into my own parade, cast your dancin' spell my way
> I promise to go under it.
>
> Then take me disappearin' through the smoke rings of my
>   mind
> Down the foggy ruins of time, far past the frozen leaves
> The haunted, frightened trees out to the windy beach
> Far from the twisted reach of crazy sorrow
> Yes, to dance beneath the diamond sky with one hand wavin'
> free
> Silhouetted by the sea, circled by the circus sands
> With all the memory and fate driven deep beneath the waves
> Let me forget about today until tomorrow.[5]

Temporarily, at least, the world is transformed through man. Both participate
in magical ecstasy—play—which relates to Nietzsche's philosophy. Indeed, it
was Nietzsche who described it exactly: "Man now expresses himself through
song and dance as the member of a higher community; he has forgotten how
to walk, how to speak and is on the brink of taking wing as he dances . . .
no longer the artist, he has himself become a work of art."[6]

And so the first postwar generation made the start of a new culture, using
a new form and using electronic equipment. Many partisans of the counterculture believe it will alter the values of society. They can cite at least one
venerable authority (Plato) supporting their capacity to achieve substantial
change. "The new style quietly insinuates itself into manner and customs and
from there it issues a greater force . . . goes on to attack laws and constitu-
tions . . . until it ends by overthrowing everything, both in public and in
private."[7] And of course partisans of the counterculture and especially of

rock music still avidly sing along with that famous pioneer of rock, Chuck Berry: "Hail Hail rock 'n' roll/Deliver me from the days of old."

But while the obvious significance of rock 'n' roll music is cultural (it is a new medium, a new form, and primarily electronic), its pioneers continue to use it to convey visions of life which have revolutionary political implications. It is impossible here to deal with the development of even one great rock artist or group. But it is possible to deal briefly with the apocalyptic visions which are best typified in the work of Bob Dylan and the Jefferson Airplane. (Here, *apocalyptic* is used in the sense of "any remarkable revelation.")

Certainly, even the critics of the counterculture would admit that the poets and prophets understand or think they understand a new order. And, of course, the poets and prophets express the new order through apocalyptic music. This is not unusual, since apocalyptic myths and works of art are part of a deeply rooted tradition in both the Judeo-Christian and Indo-European cultures. Anthropologists and mythologists have categorized apocalyptic visions into at least three broad areas: the black or cataclysmic; the red or revolutionary; and the green or pastoral. (Charles Reich gave his book on the counterculture the title *The Greening of America* essentially because he interpreted the whole movement as pastoral apocalypse.)

The black, or cataclysmic tradition is evident in the works of such Old Testament prophets as Isaiah, Jeremiah, and Ezekiel. The black cataclysm is also to be found in the New Testament, in the "Revelation of St. John the Divine." Certainly the black mass and witchcraft cults of the Middle Ages were enshrouded in the myth of the black apocalypse. Currently the tradition is evident in the clothing and life style of the Hell's Angels and the exorcism frenzy exploited by the motion picture production of William Peter Blatty's book *The Exorcist* in 1974. In rock music it is evident in the neosatanism of Mick Jagger and the Rolling Stones. The symbolism in their song "Paint it Black" is obvious, as is the name of another popular rock group, Black Sabbath.

The green, or pastoral apocalpytic tradition first appears in Judeo-Christian culture in the myth of the Garden of Eden (Genesis), where God and man are said to have walked and talked with one "voice." The pastoral apocalypse is present in the poetry of Virgil and Homer, in primitive Christianity, and in the monasticism of the Middle Ages. In modern times, the pastoral vision is particularly evident as a reaction to urbanism and industrialism—for example, the Levellers and Diggers of mid-seventeenth-century England, the utopian communes of early nineteenth-century America, and the Populist party platform of 1892. In music it is expressed in much of what the Beatles did, as well as in the music of Joni Mitchell and Bob Dylan. Until Dylan's return to concert touring, it looked as though the pastoral apocalypse had culminated in the Woodstock Festival of Life held in the summer of 1969 in upstate New York. Listen to Joni Mitchell's celebrated "Woodstock."

> I came upon a child of God
> He was walking along the road
> And I asked him, where are you going?
> And this he told me
> I'm going on down to Yasgur's farm
> I'm going to join in a rock 'n' roll band
> I'm going to camp out on the land
> And try an' get my soul free
>> We are stardust
>> We are golden
>> And we've got to get ourselves
>> Back to the garden
>
> . . . .
> By the time we got to Woodstock
> We were half million strong
> And everywhere there was song and celebration.[8]

In modern Western history, the red, or revolutionary apocalyptic tradition appears clearly in Marx and essentially becomes an attempt to give direction to the black and green apocalyptic traditions. Like them, its impulse is somewhat religious, promising vindication and salvation to the oppressed. Its major spokesmen since Marx include Lenin, Trotsky, Ho Chi Minh, and Mao Tse Tung. While there are many musicians of our time who have employed the myth of revolutionary apocalpyse, none have been as consistent, militant, or futuristic as the Jefferson Airplane. Accordingly, their revolutionary fervor in "Volunteers,"

> Look what's happening out in the streets
>> Got a revolution   Got to revolution
> . . . .
> One generation got old
> One generation got soul
> This generation got no destination to hold
>> Pick up the cry
> Hey now it's time for you and me
>> Got a revolution   Got to revolution
> Come on now we're marching to the sea
>> Got a revolution   Got to revolution[9]

Within the counterculture, it has been the revolutionary and the pastoral traditions which have been most drawn upon. The pastoral apocalyptic tradition is one of innocence—hence the poses of flower children, children of God, etc. It is also the tradition of those who have never had power; hence the cry "power to the people"—that mystical body politic which has never really employed political power. And of course it is the Edenic, populist tradition which Bob Dylan, the poet, composer, and musician, did the most to revitalize for the first postwar generation.[10]

With the release of the album *Bringing It All Back Home* in the spring of 1965, Dylan transformed the music of black and country western rock 'n' roll into a new art form. Riding the crest of a folk-protest movement, by 1966 Dylan began to reshape the cultural and political imagination of a new generation of Western European youth. The album's lead song, "Subterranean Homesick Blues," with its use of intense and strident tones, knifed through the conformity, hypocrisy, hostility, and fear which was the binding force of America's advanced technocratic society. In "Subterranean Homesick Blues," Dylan insists that young people will not go to school for twenty years and will not work as automatons in capitalism's conglomerates.

> Ah get born, keep warm
> Short pants, romance, learn to dance
> Get dressed, get blessed
> Try to be a success
> Please her, please him, buy gifts
> Don't steal, don't lift
> Twenty years of schoolin'
> And they put you on the day shift
> Look out kid they keep it all hid
> Better jump down a manhole
> Light yourself a candle, don't wear sandals
> Try to avoid the scandals[11]

And of course it was also from the "Subterranean Homesick Blues" that the Weatherman faction of the SDS derived its name:

> Keep a clean nose
> Watch the plain clothes
> You don't need a weather man
> To know which way the wind blows.[12]

But perhaps of even more significance in the album *Bringing It All Back Home* was Dylan's first and most coherent introduction to his vision of the pastoral apocalypse, "The Gates of Eden."

> ... There are no kings inside the Gates of Eden.
> . . . .
> And there are no sins inside the Gates of Eden.
> . . . .
> And the princess and the prince
> . . . .
> Discuss what's real and what is not

> It doesn't matter inside the Gates of Eden
>
> . . . .
>
> And there are no trials inside the Gates of Eden
>
> . . . .
>
> And there are no truths *outside* the Gates of Eden.[13]

Late in 1965, Dylan released his "monster" album, which was a devastating critique of American liberal capitalism in juxtaposition with his Edenic vision. In *Highway 61 Revisited* Dylan casts his piercing eye on an upper-middle-class, would-be-hip college girl, "Miss Lonely." In what is probably Dylan's most famous song, "Like a Rolling Stone," he describes Miss Lonely as,

> Once upon a time you dressed so fine
> You threw the bums a dime in your prime,
> Didn't you?
>
> . . . .
>
> You've gone to the finest school all right Miss Lonely,
> But you know you only used to get
> Juiced in it.
>
> . . . .
>
> You never turned around to see the frowns on the jugglers and
>   the clowns
> When they all come down
> And did tricks for you.
> You never understood that it ain't no good
> You shouldn't let other people
> Get your kicks for you.[14]

Then he asks a question of all upper-middle-class students who fit the above general type:

> How does it feel,
> How does it feel,
> To be without a home,
> Like a complete unknown,
> Like a rolling stone?[15]

There is no institutional answer to Dylan's questions, and he knew it. The most brilliant person will eventually have to come to grips with the exploitation, hypocrisy, and pretentiousness of opulent American life. Thus, Dylan's viciously antirational, antiliberal "Ballad of a Thin Man," ends by exposing every guise, every pretense, and every excuse for perpetuating the established culture of rationalist oligarchy.

> You walk into the room with your pencil in your hand;
> You see somebody naked and you say, "Who is that man?"
> You try so hard, but you just don't understand

Just what you will say when you get home,
Because something is happening here,
But you don't know what it is.
Do you, Mr. Jones?[16]

Highway 61 is an actual highway in America that begins near the Canadian border and runs down through Hibbing, Minnesota, where Dylan was reared. It runs through St. Paul, where F. Scott Fitzgerald grew up. Then it moves on through Hannibal, Missouri and East St. Louis, homes of Mark Twain and Chuck Berry, past Dyass, Arkansas, home of Johnny Cash, past Memphis, home of Riley B. King and Elvis Presley, past Meridian and Oxford, Mississippi, homes of Jimmy Rodgers and William Faulkner. It ends at the mouth of the Mississippi River in New Orleans, which is for Dylan "Desolation Row." Accordingly, the album *Highway 61 Revisited* concludes with the song "Desolation Row." On Desolation Row freaks of all kinds abound. It is an orgy of chaos enacted by America's itinerants, pariahs, and deracinated youth.

Yes I received your letter yesterday
About the time the door knob broke
When you asked how I was doing
Was that some kind of joke
All these people that you mentioned
Yes I know them they're quite lame
I had to rearrange their faces
And give them all another name

. . . .
Don't send me no more letters no
Not unless you mail them from
Desolation Row.[17]

But while "Desolation Row" might be the counterculture's twisted Eden, it was too toxic to support life in the mid-sixties. The pastoral bliss pioneered by Dylan and others could never be achieved in the cities of New York, London, Los Angeles, or New Orleans. (This is also what Captain America, in the motion picture *Easy Rider,* finds when he and his sidekick finally reach New Orleans.) And this was the message of some of Dylan's later albums, especially *John Wesley Harding* (1968), *Nashville Skyline* (1969), *Self Portrait* (1970), and *New Morning* (1971). In *Planet Waves* (1974), Dylan says "goodbye to the haunted rooms and faces in the street." For by 1971, Dylan and many in the counterculture had learned from black blues and country western singers to accept the mysterious and tragical in life and to be less concerned with politics as a vehicle of millenarian/utopian possibilities. In the tradition of Huck Finn and Ishmael, Langston Hughes and William Faulkner, they accept death and suffering of the spirit as an *essential* characteristic of existence. Dylan and the majority of people in the counterculture had turned at once cynical and compassionate. Accepting progress as a deleterious myth (in the song "Dirge," from the album *Planet Waves,* Dylan refers to progress as the "doom machine"), technological domination and imperialism as evil, success as a sham and largely, as Dylan put it, "a failure," they proclaimed their willingness to accept a flawed life—a life where persons exist in their own right, making mistakes, but communicating and sharing communion with each other. This is the vision put forth in "Father of Night" from *New Morning.* One accepts with reverence one's position vis-à-vis a hostile but ordained natural world. And so, for the most part, Dylan's songs in the early 1970's were bucolic, personal, and pastoral.

Yet Dylan cannot be dismissed so easily. He proved that with another powerful album, *Desire,* recorded in November 1975 and released in January 1976. By February 1976 it had become the best selling album in the United States. Dylan again stepped forth like a voice from the past, combining highly critical political songs of reawakening with rhythmic concatenations of African and Latin American derivation. Both the mass media and the underground media were stunned. Dylan, the recluse, had produced an album comparable to *Highway 61 Revisited.*

With the assistance of a new compatriot, Jacques Levi, Dylan again turned his indignant eyes on American social inequities and American pretentiousness. Side one opened with a lengthy, bitter defense of Rubin Carter, contender for the middleweight boxing crown, who had been imprisoned for murder. Dylan, with help from playwright Arthur Miller, prize fighter Muhammad Ali, and others, subsequently secured the release of Carter in the spring of 1976. Dylan's song "Hurricane" depicted Carter as having been framed.[18] "Hurricane" alone made the album. Other songs, such as "Joey," continued a relentless attack on the mentality that had produced Watergate. These were songs, as Dylan put it, of "American redemption." The album was a shrill cry of danger, a cry of pain, and an indication that the "people" demanded change, at least in Dylan's eyes. The album further indicated that Dylan was serious in his song, "Idiot Wind," from *Blood on the Tracks* (1974). The "wind" must change direction. In this album, Dylan again announced: "O Generation, keep on working." It remains for the future to show the influence of this great poet-musician.

But certainly not all partisans of the counterculture (despite Charles Reich's contention) look to a nostalgic, Edenic past. Indeed, many look to the fantastic hopes (and horrors) of a technology which took its initial form as science fiction. When we look to rock 'n' roll, the future-oriented, revolutionary, apocalyptic end and new beginning are best exemplified in the work of the Jefferson Airplane.

The music of the Jefferson remains deeply embedded in the radicalism which came out of the Berkeley Free Speech Movement, flower power, and the radical élan which has characterized the San Francisco Bay area since the beatnik era. Singer Marty Balin put the Airplane together in the summer of 1965. They opened at what was then Balin's small club in San Francisco, the Matrix. By 1966 they were playing at the Fillmore West—one evening they even performed behind the poetry reading of famed Russian poet Andrei Voznesenski. Before 1967, the talented, comely Grace Slick was not with the group; instead, their female vocalist was folk singer Signe Toly Anderson. Although the group gained notoriety because of its increasing political radicalism, inspired in part by Grace Slick, from the beginning it sought to create the impression of being highly technological, futuristic, and revolutionary. In short, the Jefferson Airplane's music did not come from the folk music tradition that spawned Bob Dylan. Even the name *Jefferson Airplane* has technological overtones—after all, the airplane is a recent technological development. Their first notable album, *Jefferson Airplane Takes Off* (1966), so impressed music critic Ralph Gleason that in 1969 he devoted the major portion of a book to their history, music, and message.[19]

The story of the Jefferson Airplane is in large measure the story of the recent San Francisco–Berkeley cultural and political radicalism. It meshes with the rise of other great rock groups, like the Grateful Dead and Big Brother and the Holding Company, and with the vicissitudes of the great rock meccas—the Fillmore West, the Family Dog, and Winterland. It figures prominently in the Kool-Aid Acid Tests sponsored by Ken Kesey and the Merry Pranksters. And, of course, the be-ins, starting with the one at Golden Gate Park on January 14, 1967, owed considerable inspiration to the Jefferson Airplane (although I believe they were originally conceived by Allen Ginsberg). It is clearly impossible here to trace the development of the group. But we can outline their persistent revolutionary apocalyptic vision—especially after Grace Slick left The Great Society to join the Jefferson Airplane in 1967.

When Grace Slick came to the Jefferson Airplane she brought with her two songs which have since become the most famous of the group, "Somebody to Love" and "White Rabbit." The former was written by Darby Slick, Grace's brother-in-law, and the latter by Grace herself. Though The Great Society had performed these songs, they failed to catch on until they were released by the Airplane on their best-known album, *Surrealistic Pillow* (1967). Both "Somebody to Love" and "White Rabbit" carry imagery which is destructive, antirational, and revolutionary red. Listen to what Grace Slick does with Lewis Carroll's *Alice in Wonderland.*

> Go ask Alice I think she'll know
> When logic and proportion
> Have fallen so I'll be dead
> And the white knight is talking backwards
> And the red queens are ahead

> Remember what the doormouse said;
> "Feed your head Feed your head." [20]

The point is, of course, that you cannot possibly "Feed your head," because the world is dead as a rational entity, everything is backwards and "the red queens *are* ahead." Similarly, in "Somebody to Love," there is destruction by fiery apocalypse which brings liberation.

> When the dawn is rose they are dead,
> Yes, and you're mine, you're so full of red. [21]

It is the rising sun that kills "them" and gives "you" life. Red is the color of destruction, but also the color of liberation.

It was not until 1967, however, that the Jefferson Airplane became totally revolutionary, both in the use of their equipment and in their lyrics. Ironically, their now famous album *After Bathing at Baxter's* was too radical for their audience. The album did not sell and was severely criticized. Grace Slick made some public statements about the lack of appreciation of the critics, but the group suffered visibly. By 1971, the album was reissued and demand was great for it. It contains essentially electronic street music laced with drug-induced tribal fantasies. "Streetmasse" and "How Suite It is" have become classics. "Saturday Afternoon" was inspired by their participation in the January 14, 1967 Golden Gate Be-In. Grace Slick's resolute antiwar sentiments are aired with supreme irony in her song "Rejoyce."

> War's good business, so give your son
> And I'd rather have my country die for me
> Sell your mother for a Hershey bar
> Grow up looking like a car. [22]

Though *After Bathing at Baxter's* met with a dull reception, a second album released some months later was more successful. With the release of *Crown of Creation* in 1968, it was clear that the Jefferson Airplane had committed themselves to a particular style of rock 'n' roll music. It can be described, but not characterized. Bass guitar by Jack Casady was prominent and powerful, electrified variations and flirtations of incredible complexity reverberated from the lead guitar of Jorma Kaukonen and the rhythm guitar of Paul Kantner. The lyrics were virtually incomprehensible without extreme concentration upon the pieces themselves. The album concludes with what might be construed as an electronic Third World War, the famous "House at Pooneil Corners." Tremendous volume and intensity accompany the portentous concluding verses:

> Everything someday will be gone
>   except silence
> Earth will be quiet again

Seas from clouds will wash off the
    ashes of violence
Left as the memory of men
There will be no survivor my
    friend
Suddenly everyone will look
    surprised
Stars spinning wheels in the skies
Sun is scrambling in their eyes
While the moon circles like a
    vulture

. . . .
EPITAPH
The cows are almost cooing
Turtle doves are mooing
Which is why a poo is pooing
In the sun
SUN[23]

Again it is the red or revolutionary apocalypse symbolized in the cosmic power of the sun.

Since *Crown of Creation,* the Jefferson Airplane has further explored the imaginary cosmic apocalypse. Perhaps this is why they left RCA in the early 1970's and created their own recording company, Grunt Records (the group has never lacked humor). *Volunteers* (1969) rocked with the revolutionary fervor of the times, as students and youth and thousands of others protested the war in Vietnam. The album, of course, was a call for volunteers for the "revolution"—which at the time was manifest politically in SDS, the Black Panther party, and The Resistance.

Following upon the heels of *Volunteers,* which was so obviously political, came their incredible *Blows Against the Empire* (1970). This was an album of pure "acid" science fiction, yet it still used the revolutionary apocalypse as its motif. The album told a story; its plot was to skyjack a starship and escape from the irremediably polluted and corrupted earth; through his "civilization," man had ruined himself, and his collapse was imminent. What was necessary was to move back through time into the future and rediscover Atlantis. Hence the album insert concludes: "Search out Atlantis. It lives and breathes inside of you." In this album the Jefferson Airplane explicitly reject the pastoral apocalypse. In their song "Hijack" they say,

Genesis is not the answer to what we had before
. . . .
You know—A starship circlin' in the sky—it ought to be ready
    by 1990
They'll be buildin' it up in the air. Ever since 1980

> People with a clever plan can assume the role of the mighty
> Hijack the starship[24]

And with starship,

> We gotta get out and down
> Back into the future
> Beyond our own time again
> Reachin' for tomorrow[25]

And what is the purpose of the skyjacking, the goal of the revolutionary apocalypse? It is Being—the same vision of Being which was described in the chapter on happiness. This is made clear in the opening song, "Mau Mau (Amerikon)"

> I AM ALIVE
> I AM HUMAN
> I WILL BE ALIVE AGAIN
> So drop your fuckin' bombs
> Burn your demon babies
> I WILL BE AGAIN[26]

In the 1970's the Jefferson Airplane have continued their basic radical tenor, although by 1973 they were often recording with many other artists— Papa John Creach, David Crosby, Jerry Garcia, Graham Nash, Jack Traylor, David Freiberg, and even the Edwin Hawkins Singers. The album *Sunfighter* (1971) carried the obvious symbolism of cosmic apocalypse in its title, and the familiar theme was reiterated in the title song.

> And there ain't no more room here no more room here
> No more room on this planet to grow
> . . . .
> Sunfighter—Gunfighter[27]

The imagery of red is continued. Grace Slick and Paul Kantner renamed their daughter China—and they did not mean Taiwan. They meant what was then still referred to as Red China. As might be expected, they cut a song with the same title. Similarly, the album *Bark* (1971) bore the stamp of Paul Kantner's futuristic mind. His song "When the Earth Moves Again" is reminiscent of the science fiction vision on *Blows Against the Empire.*

> if you've lived on earth you've never seen the sun
> or the promise of a thousand other suns
>   that glow beyond here
> and if you care to see the future look into the eyes of your
> young dancing children don't be afraid of our ways
> . . . .
> Moses Moses the red sea closes

over you when you least expect it to
when the earth moves again
when the earth moves again[28]

Probably the most pronounced change recently evident in the music of the Jefferson Airplane has been their increasing anticlericalism. It is as if they came to the same conclusion as Nietzsche: Christianity is inhibiting, and it militates against the Dionysian element, which must be freed in order to liberate man. Accordingly, both *Long John Silver* (1972) and *Baron von Tollbooth and the Chrome Nun* (1973) are laden with criticism of the cultural influences of Christianity. Nevertheless, Paul Kantner continued his pioneering of the supertechnological apocalypse in his song "Have You Seen the Saucers," recorded live on the album *Thirty Seconds Over Winterland* (1973). The song is highly electronic, using Papa John Creach. Kantner transforms Joni Mitchell's children of Woodstock nation into "star children," whose salvation is not the Garden but a starship to escape to the "other side of the sun." Hence, when Kantner and Slick play without Jorma Kaukonen and Jack Casady, they refer to themselves as the Jefferson Starship.

Indeed, when Kantner and Slick released *Dragon Fly* in 1974, they billed themselves as the *Jefferson Starship*. Again, consistent with their political bent, the songs on *Dragon Fly* are for the most part indictments of the Establishment and carry red imagery. "Devils Den," written by Grace Slick and Papa John Creach, is an obvious reference to the Watergate affair, with "King Richard" symbolizing ex-President Nixon. But more important, it is criticism of the fear-obsessed conduct of Nixon's subordinates as well as the American people for having been so gullible and so frightened themselves. And, as might be expected, the imagery and lyrics of the two longest songs, "All Fly Away" and "Hyperdrive," continues to stress the red or revolutionary apocalypse whose dynamic is still presumed to be supertechnology.

After rejoining forces with Marty Balin in 1975, Kantner and Slick recorded the album *Red Octopus*, which was released in 1976. Balin's voice and lyrics carried their single, "Miracles," to the number one position on the popularity charts, thus greatly assisting the sale of the album itself. But Kantner and Slick still insisted on being called the Jefferson Starship, and that is how the group's name appeared on the album. Using drummer John Barbata, whom they borrowed from folk-rock group Crosby, Stills, Nash, and Young, they combined politics with love songs to step again into a rock renaissance. This happened simultaneously with the release of Bob Dylan's *Desire* and indicated that the big names of the 1960's were still alive and concerned.

Significantly, almost ten years after they had become internationally famous with their album *Surrealistic Pillow*, Kantner and Slick concluded their album with the words, "All I see is you," the verse they used so well in their much neglected album *After Bathing At Baxter's.* It was their way of saying, "listen again" to the first song on *After Bathing at Baxter's,* which is entitled "How Suite It Is." And finally, the first song on side two of the *Red Octopus* echoed the theme of the decade 1966–76, "Play On Love." The album and its success completed their dream as well as that of the San Francisco sound—a dream of love revolved. Just as with Bob Dylan, their influence upon the late 1970's remains to be seen. (It is impossible at this stage of printing to include a discussion of either Bob Dylan's album, *Hard Rain* or that of the Jefferson Starship, *Spitfire,* both released in October 1976.)

Notes to Chapter 14

1. Susanne K. Langer, *Philosophy in a New Key* (New York, 1951), p. 138.

2. "We Can Be Together," words and music by Paul Kantner. © 1969, Icebag Corporation. All rights reserved. Used by permission.

3. Quoted in Benjamin DeMott, "Rock as Salvation," *New York Times Magazine* (August 25, 1968).

4. "Desolation Row," words and music by Bob Dylan. © 1965, M. Witmark & Sons. All rights reserved. Used by permission of Warner Brothers Music.

5. "Mr. Tambourine Man," words and music by Bob Dylan. © 1964, M. Witmark & Sons. All rights reserved. Used by permission of Warner Brothers Music.

6. Quoted by Ralph Gleason, "Like a Rolling Stone," in Jonathan Eisen, ed., *The Age of Rock* (New York, 1969), p. 76.

7. Ibid., pp. 64-65.

8. "Woodstock," words and music by Joni Mitchell. © 1969, Siquomb Publishing Corporation. All rights reserved. Used by permission.

9. "Volunteers," words by Marty Balin, music by Marty Balin and Paul Kantner. © 1969, Icebag Corporation. All rights reserved. Used by permission.

10. I am in debt to Professor Gregg M. Campbell for much of the information presented here on Bob Dylan. Professor Campbell's paper "Bob Dylan and the Pastoral Apocalypse," presented at the University of Southern California in August 1971, supplied me with insights into Bob Dylan's music. See also Dylan's biography by Anthony Scaduto, *Bob Dylan: An Intimate Biography* (New York, 1971), and *Writings and Drawings by Bob Dylan* (New York, 1973).

11. "Subterranean Homesick Blues," words and music by Bob Dylan. © 1965, M. Witmark & Sons. All rights reserved. Used by permission of Warner Brothers Music.

12. Ibid.

13. "Gates of Eden," words and music by Bob Dylan. © 1965, M. Witmark & Sons. All rights reserved. Used by permission of Warner Brothers Music.

14. "Like a Rolling Stone," words and music by Bob Dylan. © 1965, M. Witmark & Sons. All rights reserved. Used by permission of Warner Bros. Music.

15. Ibid.

16. "Ballad of a Thin Man," words and music by Bob Dylan. © 1965, M. Witmark & Sons. Used by permission of Warner Brothers Music.

17. "Desolation Row," words and music by Bob Dylan. © 1965, M. Witmak & Sons. Used by permission of Warner Brothers Music.

18. For an enlightening account of the Rubin Carter affair, see the interview with Carter published in *Penthouse* magazine, September 1975, pp. 68-70, 100-102, 115-16, and Rubin Carter, *The Sixteenth Round* (New York, 1975).

19. See Ralph Gleason, *The Jefferson Airplane and the San Francisco Sound* (New York, 1969).

20. "White Rabbit," words and music by Grace Slick. © 1967, Irving Music, Inc. (BMI). All rights reserved. Used by permission.

21. "Somebody to Love," words and music by Darby Slick. © 1967, Irving Music, Inc. (BMI). All rights reserved. Used by permission.

22. "Rejoyce," words and music by Grace Slick. © 1967, Icebag Corporation. All rights reserved. Used by permission.

23. "House at Pooneil Corners," words and music by Marty Balin and Paul Kantner. © 1969, Icebag Corporation. All rights reserved. Used by permission.

24. "Hijack," words and music by Paul Kantner, words by Marty Balin, Grace Slick, and Gary Blackman. © 1971 by god tunes. All rights reserved. Used by permission.

25. "Starship," words and music by Paul Kantner, words by Marty Balin, Grace Slick, and Gary Blackman. © 1970 by god tunes. All rights reserved. Used by permission.

26. "Mau Mau (Amerikon)," words and music by Paul Kantner, words by Grace Slick and Joey Covington. © 1971 by god tunes. All rights reserved. Used by permission.

27. "Sunfighter," words and music by Paul Kantner. © 1971 by god tunes. All rights reserved. Used by permission.

28. "When the Earth Moves Again," words and music by Paul Kantner. © 1971 by Dump Music, Inc. All rights reserved. Used by permission.

XV

Coda: The Disinherited Children

Show me the way
Search for the way
    out
    into. . . .

And something was dying
And something was changing
And something else was on the way.*

In most eras a dissenting philosophy emerges to jar the prevalent philosophy. Such is the impulse of the Movement, the New Left, and the counterculture: these are three aspects of the same dissent. Their existence as a philosophical concatenation calls into question what seems most unshakable, points up contradictions in what is generally considered axiomatic, and derides the popular common sense by reading meaning into what seems to be absurd. Of course such movements and their adherents run the inevitable risk of seeming ridiculous. And in any era the conflict between the philosophers of play and the philosophers of work looks something like the spirited argument between the adolescent and the senile. This certainly appears to be the case in the postwar era. To a person who matured after World War II, the existing political, social, and economic arrangement—call it corporate socialism, government corporatism, or liberalism in its widest operation—looks like the survival of the past intact in the present. For the reality of repressive liberalism is not only a certain intellectual attitude toward the world, it is *the form* of the world's existence, to those who believe it. Or, put another way, it is the factual continuation of a reality which no longer exists except in the mind of the beholder. But in large measure the same thing can be said

*William Craddock, *Be Not Content.*

about the New Left and the counterculture. A possibility may materialize and become real to the player before it exists in fact. In both cases, our thoughts about reality are also part of, if not the entire structure of, reality.

The dissenting philosophy which has erupted in the postwar epoch, however, although obviously cast in generational terms, really signifies that in the history of Western civilization, an older age, utilizing a symbolism of human interrelations which began with the Greeks and reached its peak in the high Middle Ages, has now ended. Its demise was foreseen in the Enlightenment and the coming of the modern industrial age, whose symbolism came more and more to deal with and explain the functional relations of the material universe while tending less and less to explain man's place or purpose in the world. While our ability to symbolize the workings of the material world has flowered since the time of Sir Isaac Newton (1642–1727), our ability to symbolize the historical world—the everyday world of relations between men and between man and nature—has greatly diminished. Because of the enormously accelerated pace of history and communications, which is ten million times faster today than in 1900, we need symbols for a general orientation in nature, in society, and in world history—symbols of our *Lebensanschauung*. We must recognize that since World War II the changes in the world have been so vast that virtually everyone is disoriented. Technique has made men so mobile that many have never known a home as a symbol of the roots of their childhood and adolescence; many have no mother tongue. We no longer have rituals to communicate cosmology or community dances and festivals to strengthen personal ties to a group identity. Nor do we have widely recognized religious rites to give orientation to our private and public lives. We have only a painfully isolated individualism, a mystique of private life, and this no longer offers secure orientation, especially to young people.

> No longer can we learn our good
> From chances of a neighborhood
> Or class or party, or refuse
> As individuals to choose
> Our loves, authorities, and friends
> To judge our means and plan our ends;
> For the machine has cried aloud
> And publicized among the crowd
> The secret that was always true
> But known once only to the few,
> Compelling all to the admission,
> Aloneness is man's real condition.[1]

Seen in this light, the New Left and the counterculture are manifestations of a counter-Enlightenment; they are attempts to escape the philosophical and historical suicide that the Enlightenment has been effecting through technological development since World War II. They are protests against the dangerous one-dimensionality which the Enlightenment has bequeathed to us as a materialist conception of reality. And more than anything else, the New Left and the counterculture are statements that we have perverted the faculty of reason, that we have alienated ourselves from reason. We have alienated ourselves from reason by the way we *use* it. That is, increasingly we have circumscribed reason in order to provide a particular, presupposed meaning about the Being of the world. And in so doing we have not satisfied the biological demands of reason itself, for we have assigned reason to discover Being without allowing it to do so; thus, we have alienated reason. For reason as a faculty will not lie to itself; it will not be satisfied until it knows Being, indeed, it cannot *be* healthy unless it participates in Being. The point of a be-in is Being.

Because we have alienated ourselves from reason and from Being, we have the impression of living in a period of chaos and fear. And, unfortunately, at the present time we seem to have little material to make the symbols which might serve to stem the tide of chaos and provide us with a comfortable orientation to life in a technological age. As philosopher-biologist René Dubos has indicated, living in such a fast-moving age with such a paucity of symbols and an absence of a metaphysics (a philosophy of Being) is a profoundly unnatural situation for man. And this situation in its *generality* seems to many—the young, particularly—to result in a stultification of freedom. The crucial question in everyday life then becomes "freedom." And it should not be reduced to the two most popular working definitions: one epitomized by Kant, the other by Skinner. For Kant, freedom exists a priori synthetically, absolutely, as a static characteristic of the human mind. For Skinner, freedom is a culturally induced epiphenomenon, and therefore most certainly not an absolute. Yet certainly there is another possibility: that freedom is Being, the process of the human organism simultaneously decoding the world through all the senses. Freedom is the process of phenomenology, the organism making or allowing things to reveal their essence to man, allowing things *to be.* This, then, is not an intellectual fact, it is a biological process from which man cannot escape short of cognitive emasculation, which is really a form of suicide—though limited in that the organism does not physically perish. *Reason is therefore also crucial, for it is a primary faculty in the realization of freedom; its free expansiveness is vital to the achievement of Being.*

Put another way, freedom means the opportunity to engage in symbolic transformation of the world, to interrelate in a public, secure, playful way, to participate in Being. This is the telos of man and this is what T. S. Eliot meant in "Little Gidding," the last of his great *Four Quartets.*

> . . . See, now they vanish
> The faces and places, with the self which, as it could, loved them
> To become renewed, transfigured, in another pattern.[2]

The prevention or frustration of this activity, often mistakenly blamed entirely upon a political system, becomes therefore a violation of the instinctual need to be free. This is what Alfred North Whitehead was trying to make people understand over forty years ago. "The essence of freedom is the practicability of purpose. Mankind has chiefly suffered from the frustration of its prevalent purposes, even such as belong to the very definition of its species."[3] One of the purposes of man is his orientation in the world and his enjoyment of the world through symbols. As rational symbolism no longer supplies a secure orientation and does not facilitate pleasureful aesthetic response, *it appears to be an infringement upon human freedom.* And it results in an instinctual impulse toward radicalism—personal, cultural, and political.

The present situation is critical because we do not allow the creation of life-symbols to replace the dying symbols of rationalism. A society which is so functional, so efficient, and so rationalistic that it discourages any attempts to devise new symbols—such as long hair, carnival dress, or community happenings like Woodstock—just exacerbates the crisis and increases the disorientation of its people. In addition, if our universities teach that the only path to personal and social orientation is the rational, they are bound to continue to alienate thousands of students. And furthermore, a political system whose leaders ridicule and disparage everything irrational and emotional, calling it neoprimitivism or neo-Fascism, cannot hope to offer equilibrium or incentive to those attempting a nonrational approach to personal security.

It would be well advised for the critics of the New Left, be they politicians or educators, to remember that the battles between the exponents of rationalism and mysticism, between self-conscious thought and mindless reverie, goes at least as far as the rift between Greco-Roman rationalism and Christian mysticism. It was revived by the Romantics, especially Schelling, who believed that self-conscious thought stands between man and his desire for the spontaneity of innocence which he must have in order to feel whole. As Professor Erich Heller has indicated, Schiller, Kleist, and Hegel believed that a paradisiacal, harmonious relation of man with the world, once lost, could only be regained by rational symbolization (thought) reaching new heights of consciousness. But others, such as Nietzsche, Lawrence, and Yeats argued that the path of irrationalism and mysticism was the correct one.[4] This is why Nietzsche enthroned Dionysus, the god of intoxication and ecstasy, a god who today might find his henchmen in rock 'n' roll bands. The point is that man is possessed by feeling (call it fear if you like) that he must connect himself, orient himself, and move with his environment. Western rationalism is only one possible means of achieving an agreeable relationship with the world, and it has failed to do so.

Indeed, perhaps as Nietzsche and Lawrence implied, the direction of civilization or of man himself may *not* be from natural, instinctual functioning evolving toward consciousness, organized and culminating in materialism and rationalism. Possibly the opposite is true: that rational, reflective consciousness may be the primitive beginning, and unreflective intuitive consciousness, the end. Perhaps novelists Joseph Heller and Ken Kesey are correct: the irrational, so-called insane *is* really the sane, while the so-called rational, or sane, is no longer sane. Then the rise of the irrationalism of the New Left is a prescient rather than an anomalous trend. Possibly the technologically advanced countries are moving into an aesthetic historical epoch where rationalism will fade and creativity, the language of the intuitive consciousness or unconscious, will flower. Then we might see ourselves entering a period in which a generation sensing the contours of the future is straining to inaugurate it by consciously induced spontaneities, without realizing, however, that ultimately there is not salvation through drugs or consciously stimulated ecstasy—that consciousness must dim first before the future will inaugurate the reign of the instinct, of the unself-conscious consciousness. Perhaps then we might begin to see that the postwar generations are part of a transitional period and remember with Rilke that:

> Each torpid turn of the world has such disinherited
>   children,
> To whom no longer what's been, and not yet what's coming,
>   belongs.[5]

This is, of course, historical speculation, for we cannot know the future, but only predict its faint outline. So the philosophical problem remains acute and is deeply felt by the postwar generations. This problem is that despite the obvious triumph of materialism and rationalism which have "killed God," there persists the faith that a supranatural order exists (Being), is knowable, and that knowledge of it implies ethics, teleology, and a happiness that will end alienation. But the realization of that faith (which is metaphysical) is peculiarly difficult in this age because traditional philosophical approaches to it have so dissected it that it no longer seems to offer substantial hope of reaching a supranatural order. Metaphysics, which should be on the rise in the United States, is all but dead in academic circles. Pascal's and James's "reasons of the heart" (intuition) has deteriorated into solipsism which many young people mistake for spirituality. The reasons of understanding, so strong in Plato and Kant, are now relegated to a crude empiricism. Even in the nineteenth and twentieth centuries when the imagination and when art itself endeavored to blunt the antivital implications of rationalism, it failed miserably. Realism, naturalism, psychology and even Dadaism, all of which attempted the cooptation of Enlightenment rationalism, scarcely affected it. The imagination was unprotected from the voracity of rationalism.

Nevertheless, the real essence of the radical impulse of the youth movement of the 1960's and early 1970's was, and still is, an attempt to discover or to create a metaphysical order which might supply a moral, safe, and happy orientation to reality. This is why irrationalism, intuitiveness, aesthetics, drugs, and slogans such as "make love not war," all go together. They blend together in the metaphysical conviction that Being, "what really is, is not a dream or shadow, not the meaningless agony of the Will, nor the abstractions of Reason, but the living revelation of the unfathomable. Yet why should the unfathomable be beautiful? Because it can only be comprehended by the unfathomable, and the only truly unfathomable faculty of man is love." [6] Hence the world which is sought is not the one of reason, or material goods, or predictable, controlled social and personal relations. Rather, it is the world of love—intelligible only through love, meaningful only to love, and capable of being lived only in love.

It should be clear, then, that the New Left and the counterculture are serious when they insist they are fighting for survival—the survival of the spiritual faculty of love. And joy for its youthful partisans can come only through the magical transformation of the world through love. As John Lennon and Paul McCartney indicated in their Beatles' song "Tomorrow Never Knows," love is a way of knowing, a way of knowing the meaning of within and without.

> Turn off your mind relax and float downstream,
> it is not dying, it is not dying,
> lay down all thought surrender to the void,
> it is shining, it is shining.
> That you may see the meaning of within,
> it is speaking, it is speaking,
> that love is all and love is ev'ryone,
> it is knowing it is knowing. [7]

In this vision, the Being of the world is perceived as infinite life, and love is the consciousness of the unity, the continuum of life, and of the unity with other people through life. Liberation means having seen this infinite principle of life and falling in love with it as the highest absolute known to man. It means realizing that the infinite potentiality which seems to be negated by finite actuality need not be so negated, that Being is not a mirage, but rather demands transformation of the actual world guided by the light of love. This then becomes a global awareness, fed by the utopian possibilities of modern technology. This awareness sustained and continues to sustain both the cultural and political aspects of the youth movement. Its dynamic is the conviction so eloquently described by Aldous Huxley that "we can never know completely what we do not love. Love is a mode of knowledge, and when the love is sufficiently disinterested and sufficiently intense, the knowledge becomes unitive knowledge."[8] The organ of mediation between the finite and the infinite is love, not Enlightenment rationalism. And since man is aware of the infinite as somehow the highest absolute, his best means of knowing it and keeping it before him becomes love. Therein lies the optimism and the resilience of the committed New Leftists and counter-culturists. It is the ethos which has been immortalized in Edwin Markham's poem "Outwitted":

> He drew a circle that shut me out—
> Heretic, rebel, a thing to flout.
> But Love and I had the wit to win:
> We drew a circle that took him in!

Notes to Chapter 15

1. W. H. Auden, *Collected Longer Poems* (New York, 1969), pp. 125-26. Reprinted by permission of Random House, Inc.

2. T. S. Eliot, "Little Gidding," *Four Quartets.* Reprinted by permission of Harcourt, Brace, Jovanovich, Inc.

3. Alfred North Whitehead, *Adventures in Ideas* (New York, 1933), p. 84.

4. Erich Heller, "Yeats and Nietzsche," *Encounter* (December, 1969), p. 71.

5. Rainer Maria Rilke, *Duino Elegies,* trans. J. B. Leishman and Stephen Spender (New York, 1963), p. 63. Reprinted by permission of W. W. Norton & Company, Inc.

6. Erich Heller, *The Disinherited Mind* (New York, 1959), p. 108. Reprinted by arrangement with Bowes & Bowes, Ltd., London.

7. "Tomorrow Never Knows," by John Lennon and Paul McCartney. Copyright 1966, Northern Songs, Ltd. All rights for the USA and Canada controlled by Maclen Music, Inc. c/o ATV Music Group. Used by permission. All rights reserved.

8. Aldous Huxley, *The Perennial Philosophy* (Cleveland, 1962), p. 81.

Index of Names